CATHERINE GILLING

CORINNA

Will a daring bid to save a beloved
brother lead to romance – or disaster?

CATHERINE GILLING

CORINNA

Will a daring bid to save a beloved
brother lead to romance – or disaster?

MEREO
Cirencester

Mereo Books

1A The Wool Market Dyer Street Cirencester Gloucestershire GL7 2PR
An imprint of Memoirs Publishing www.mereobooks.com

Corinna: 978-1-86151-286-4

First published in Great Britain in 2014
by Mereo Books, an imprint of Memoirs Publishing

The address for Memoirs Publishing Group Limited can be found at
www.memoirspublishing.com

The Memoirs Publishing Group Ltd Reg. No. 7834348

The Memoirs Publishing Group supports both The Forest Stewardship Council® (FSC®) and
the PEFC® leading international forest-certification organisations. Our books carrying both the
FSC label and the PEFC® and are printed on FSC®-certified paper. FSC® is the only
forest-certification scheme supported by the leading environmental organisations including
Greenpeace. Our paper procurement policy can be found at
www.memoirspublishing.com/environment

Typeset in 10.5/15pt Bembo
by Wiltshire Associates Publisher Services Ltd. Printed and bound in Great Britain by
Printondemand-Worldwide, Peterborough PE2 6XD

For Patricia Agnes, my dear mother

Austria, 1860. Franz Josef had been Emperor for twelve years and the country was at peace. The whole of Austria had settled back into its old comfortable existence once more, and nowhere more than in the regional provinces.

Outside the town of Gmunden, a sprawling period residence continued its dominance over the surrounding landscape. The solid stone-built mansion, with its iron entrance gates, sweeping driveway and extensive outbuildings, stood as a timeless example of continuity and calm. Yet within its walls, all was not quite so tranquil.

CHAPTER ONE

Corinna and her brother Maximillian raced, pushed and tugged at each other to reach the long gallery first, their shrieking and squealing shattering the temporary calm of the upper floors. There they fell down giggling and breathless into the window seat, their faces beaming with satisfaction that such exciting reckless behaviour had not reached the hallowed silence of the world below.

Maximillian let out a deep sigh of pure contentment and Corinna smiled back at him, wishing their lives could always be this carefree. Then, distracted by movement in the courtyard below, Corinna pressed her nose against the window to peer at the carriages waiting there.

"I see some of our fine respectable brothers and sisters are here" she remarked, not showing any great enthusiasm for their arrival.

"And no doubt including Beatrice," Max yawned, wishing he could dismiss the prospect of their combined appearance here.

"You don't think…"

"What?" Max queried.

"Well – just as long as – they might have found out?" she replied with some slight concern.

"Found out about what in particular?" he laughed in mock innocence.

"Max, you know full well. How can you pretend otherwise?"

"Oh Corinna, don't nag. Why should they suddenly be interested in us? Besides, there would have been repercussions before now, if they had found out anything. Wouldn't there?"

"I suppose."

Corinna certainly hoped he was right as she leaned forward thoughtfully to rest her elbows on her knees and cup her chin in her hands, trying to push aside the spark of unease she felt. She could not help it; Beatrice's presence always filled her with trepidation, because her whole manner was so like their father's imposing attitude towards them.

"Don't look so glum. You enjoyed yourself last time, didn't you?" Max asked, with a warmth in his voice, trying to lighten her thoughts.

Of course she had, although she knew that eventually their recent escapades would come to light. It could not be avoided. That they had got away with anything outside the strict routine which governed their lives even once had been a miracle, but to continue the deception undiscovered would be too much to expect. Corinna did not believe in luck, at least not in their case.

"Then it was worth it," Max concluded.

They had been both naughty and strangely rather brave, they knew that. Max, being a year older, of course should have known better, but typically he refused to show any regret for their few hours of freedom. Indeed why should he, when they agreed their snatched hours had been such a delight?

Then her thoughts were interrupted.

"Why Corinna, you have no idea how to behave like a

lady!" came her brother's voice, mischievously mimicking their older sister, Edith-Louisa.

"Sssh, Max! If she heard you!"

Corinna lunged at him in retaliation, always delighted at his talent to cheer her up within minutes, and their spontaneous laughter rang out again as she enthusiastically chased him along the gallery once more. Their scuffing, sliding feet resounding on the polished floorboards, these youngest members of the Schopenhauer family revelled in this rare opportunity to exhibit their youthful pleasure without hindrance and the usual disapproval.

Max dodged and ducked to avoid her, only to find himself suddenly slipping on the polished floor and vainly struggling for balance. He grabbed at the curtains, which simply ripped in his hands. Corinna, unable to avoid him, crashed into him in a flurry of arms and legs, sending him, part of the curtain still in his hand, disastrously towards the far wall. There he hit the fine, ornate table with a loud thump and a groan, causing the furniture to scrape against the wall and the display of delicate china proudly set there to waver ominously.

"Max!" Corinna screamed. The table rocked back and forth, balancing tantalizingly while they both held their breath, then, terrifyingly, the whole display of china finally toppled, breaking into hundreds of shattered pieces. The noise was deafening. An awful explosive crash resounded through the whole house, even echoing down to the distant sanctum of their father's domain. It was followed by a long, frozen silence.

Both of them were too stunned to move as they sat engulfed by the evidence of the dreadful destruction, Max holding his leg where he had hit the furniture and Corinna with her hands still over her ears to shut out the sound, both staring at the chaotic debris. Exchanging a desolate glance with Max, he asked if she was all right, to which she nodded, unable to speak, before automatically starting to pick all the broken pieces off her skirt.

With the temporary quiet over it seemed that almost every door shot open and a deluge of hurried footsteps swept upstairs to discover what had happened. The imposing faces of older brothers and sisters loomed around them, shouting at them both, the combination of harsh voices almost as loud as the terrible noise the china had made. Then, equally deafening, came an angry shout from below, the voice they dreaded, their father summoning them. Corinna's little face crumbled instantly into the timid child she felt she was, her lip trembling, knowing they were going to be in such desperate trouble. All her energy had deserted her. She felt weak at the knees and faintly sick as she was hauled to her feet by Beatrice. Pale as a ghost and silent, she allowed herself to be propelled downstairs with Max.

"Don't you dare cry!" Max hissed in a whisper to her amidst the surrounding shaking heads and sombre faces. It was not that easy. She dreaded the inevitable impending scene and she was terrified of her father, unlike Max, who had long since learned to be oblivious to the endless torrents of words raged at him when he was in trouble.

She had no choice except to somehow make herself meekly follow her brother to the study where side by side they stood, their eyes dutifully cast down to the floor, to face their father's wrath.

"So what have you got to say for yourselves?" demanded their father.

"It was an accident" declared Max.

"Accident! Do you realise the amount of damage you have caused, yet again!" he bellowed.

"We were only playing," Corinna managed to whisper, not daring to look up.

"Playing! You are not young children any more." the severity of his tongue made her flinch.

"There is no need to shout at Corinna. It was totally my fault," said Max.

"That comes as no surprise!" their father snapped harshly back at his son.

Corinna's heart pounded. She took a quick glance at her brother, but he gave no sign of buckling under the onslaught. He continued to present his normal easy-going facade.

Their father drummed his fingers on the desk top while the rest of the room fell quiet, but their ordeal was far from over as Beatrice decided this was by far the best time to add her own contribution to add to their condemnation. Their eldest sister took great pleasure in informing all in the room that she had seen the pair of them loitering in the town square last week, when Corinna should have been at her music lessons. Trust Beatrice! Corinna's heart sank. Despite their best efforts that day to elude her notice, it seemed that their sister had unfortunately spotted them. Her sudden appearance in Gmunden had been an unwelcome surprise, forcing them to hurriedly retreat under the shaded colonnade, shifting their positions in the shadows to avoid her as they waited for her to leave.

"We arrived too early for Corinna's piano lessons, so we wandered about for a while. It was a nice afternoon," Max replied casually, hopefully bluffing it out, without sounding the least defensive.

It was half the truth and certainly plausible, for Corinna had been only too glad of any excuse to avoid those horrible, tedious piano lessons. The slight pause in the proceedings allowed

Corinna to think that they might get away with it, that they were safe, although the purposeful stare from Beatrice was not a good sign.

"Nice enough for you to be wasting time gazing in shop windows, I noticed." Beatrice challenged them.

Corinna gave a little gulp, her own guilty conscious making her not quite sure if she had imagined the way Beatrice stressed 'shop windows'. Did she know anything more?

"Why shouldn't we be allowed a little innocent freedom, a little fun for a change? In this strict household, neither of us have had any semblance of consideration," Max retaliated boldly.

Corinna was horrified at his outburst. Max had gone too far this time and with it went any chance of forgiveness. Didn't he know better than to provoke their father? How could she help? There was nothing she could do. She slid her hand into his as they stood close together and he squeezed her hand in response, each drawing comfort from the other.

"How dare you speak to me in such a disgraceful manner. Get out of my sight!" their father exploded, his words ringing in their ears and echoing about the room. Meanwhile Beatrice, Leopold, Basil and Edith-Louisa eagerly continued their criticism as the pair of them made for the door. Corinna marched out beside her brother, determined to be as brave as he. Besides, it was not as if they had not endured it all before, and the constant wagging fingers which accompanied it.

"I had to say something. I had to put them off the track somehow," Max explained swiftly to her under his breath as they escaped.

Once outside, the pair of them rushed up the stairs, Max ahead, almost dragging her to keep up with his great athletic strides to the safety of their rooms. There he threw himself on the sofa and she fell down next to him, almost out of breath.

"It needed saying Corinna, even though it may have made matters worse," he admitted. She smiled weakly. She understood, even agreed, although it banished any hope for leniency from their father. As it was, they could only wait and contemplate the outcome. It was not their fault that she and Maximillian were at odds with the rest of the family, just as it was not their fault that there was a large age gap between them and their older brothers and sisters. Her eyes flashed for a second to their mother's portrait, regretting she was not here to protect them against the harsh Habsburg autocracy their father enforced over their lives.

Nevertheless there was only one thing important to Corinna: that whatever the outcome, whatever the consequences, Max was always there to keep her cheerful and make her smile. Max at his best, entertaining, gallant, and attentive, the instigator of most of their snatched little moments of happiness, moments she treasured. Dear, incorrigible Max.

Only recently had the few opportunities arisen to allow them to play truant from their normal abominable strict routine. There was the time they had spent a beautiful afternoon in a hired rowing skiff on the Traunsee, one of the most beautiful lakes in Austria, the sun's reflection dancing brightly on the lazy, rippling water when Max put the oars up to let the boat drift. There, with enormous pleasure, she had tugged off her horrid hat and pulled her hair loose as they splashed the water at each other. Both were thrilled to be totally free and without a care for a while.

Then there had been the afternoon tea on the hotel terrace in Gmunden where Max had teased her for staring at a handsome stranger with such obvious admiration, and how she had blushed and diverted her gaze to the ground to hide her embarrassment. That had been followed by a visit to the bandstand in the gardens along the promenade from the hotel, to listen to the music and revel in the whole atmosphere. She had enjoyed every minute of it, to say nothing of the other forbidden activities Max had encouraged her to try, letting her drive the carriage and learning to ride his horse astride, all so very unladylike! Oh, Max. Dear Max, boys were supposed to be naughty and get into trouble, but what excuse did she have?

The sound of the logs shifting in the grate and the hiss of the embers caught her attention, bringing her back to reality, to her brother's voice.

"We could always sneak back down and listen outside the door," Max proposed tentatively.

"Don't you dare!" Corinna warned him. They were safe enough where they were for the present; she did not want to think about what was happening below. She wanted to keep the hope for their future outings intact, she wanted something to look forward to, such as the promised carriage ride to Traunkirchen next week. Impossible dreams maybe, but her dreams.

It took two days before the summons from their father came, two days which had given them a false sense of their own invulnerability as the apparent indifference and lack of reference to their accident or behaviour made them feel safe. They had begun to think of their plans ahead, when their father's voice once more bellowed throughout the house, making servants glance apprehensively at each other and then slip discreetly away.

"Have you nothing else you wish to tell me, either of you?" began their father.

Neither of them answered, unwilling to volunteer any information to him. They were not that stupid. As it was their father did not expect or wait for a reply, declaring he found the number of recent accidents were beyond Max's usual carelessness and more like a deliberate act of vandalism.

"W-What?" stuttered Max, shocked at the accusation.

Their father continued to state that he found it very suspicious that the choice of items broken by Max were of some value, as if they had been picked out on purpose. Corinna felt annoyed at his gross exaggeration. Although she was not about to voice her views, she knew they were not that valuable because she had been so careful in her research. She had made sure of that when they chose them for their scheme.

"They were accidents! The rest is just an unfortunate coincidence," Max protested.

"Then why have these accidents coincided with Corinna's devoted interest in books on china antiques in the library?"

Corinna shuddered nervously. She had not realised that Edith-Louisa had taken much notice of what she had been reading and her mind turned to finding a plausible excuse in preparation for the questions which were bound to be directed at her soon. If only she could think fast enough. But she could not, she was not good at any game of wits.

Luckily for her Max kept control of the conversation by arguing that there was no logic in breaking any selective expensive item, as there was nothing to be gained by such action. Max made perfect sense, yet their father pursed his lips and shook his head with disbelief.

"Indeed it was not until recently that the significance of such events were brought to my attention," he said.

"They were accidents," Max insisted.

"Then explain to me why Beatrice found the very same items you had supposedly broken previously for sale in a small back street shop in Gmunden?"

He paused deliberately and leaned forward to glare at them, his eyes like marbles, piercing and cold, waiting for their confession.

Corinna felt suddenly very sick and faint. Beatrice's subtle remark about the shop window during their previous scolding should have been a warning, and now their father knew about the shop as well, their guilty game would be exposed.

Max had persuaded her that no one would miss a few small pieces, and despite all her misgivings there had been no alternative to his astonishingly foolish scheme. By pretending to break some of the china figures, which were in reality pieces of similarly-coloured china lying scattered on the floor, Max willingly endured the inconvenience of an uncomfortable scene with his father to obtain his objective.

Only Corinna's total loyalty to Max had outweighed the fear she had felt as she accompanied him on his errand to dispose of the china items. She remembered only too well the sharp noise of doorbell of the shop startling her as they entered, and how she had held her breath as Max engaged the proprietor in quiet conversation, nervously watched the man dither, then give a small flicker of a raised eyebrow and a doubtful frown. Somehow, unbelievably, in the next moment the transaction had been completed. Except that then Corinna had to run like mad down the street so as not to be late for her dreaded piano lesson, in order to avoid suspicion and any awkward questions. Of course the lesson itself had been unbearable and, unable to concentrate at all, she had made more mistakes than normal. Not that it had mattered; she had never wanted to play the piano anyway.

"A fine pair of conspirators you are. Do you suppose I have not made enquiries? You have been using the sale of items to finance some private excursions of your own, I believe."

He knew it all! Corinna's little frame slumped. What was done was done now, there were no miracles to put it right. Her only concern was to protect Max. For his sake she must not let anything slip, not be bullied into making a mistake. She screwed her lips together tightly and focused on the floor, trying to concentrate her mind, to shut the present scene out. How would this end?

She was soon brought back to the present as Max's voice filtered through the confusion in her mind. He was still arguing. Corinna could not believe her ears. Silently she pleaded for him to stop, knowing he would suffer the more for this outburst, but he ignored her and stood his ground, so composed, so defiant. Why did he pretend to be so brave, when it only made their father more angry?

"According to you I am a constant disappointment, so why should I try to live up to your impossible standards? What do you expect from me?" Max declared.

"Maximillian, this amounts to criminal behaviour! Yes, criminal! You are out of control. Your wild youthful spirits need to be curbed."

Her brother's further attempt to answer was swiftly drowned by the volume of the contemptuous onslaught against him. The relentless hostility, ridicule and bullying continued unabated; there was no sign of compassion. Corinna did not understand, for guilty as they were, there was no reason for her father to be so particularly cruel to Max. The resentment was evident in his contorted face muscles, his narrowed eyes and his tight mouth.

She flashed a glance at her brother. Normally he would have reverted to his usual defence of blocking out their father's words by pretending not to care, but she knew from the tense atmosphere that this time was different. Corinna could only witness his silence with apprehension. His knuckles had gone white on his clenched fists and there was an odd starkness on his face which she feared. About to abandon common sense, he was near to irretrievable retaliation. It was her turn to save him.

"Stop it, Stop it! Stop picking on Max, it is not fair!" she screamed, stamping the floor.

Their father turned his head, staring at her, stunned into momentary silence by her impertinent interruption. Corinna hesitated, daunted by the unusual experience of having his full attention for once. With a heavy bang on the desk from his fist, he immediately took back his command of the proceedings. Drained of energy, Corinna's courage deserted her now and she stepped quickly to her brother's side, grabbing his hand tightly in hers and holding onto him.

"How dare you criticize me, Miss!"

"Did I?" she whispered to Max.

"Corinna, I find your part in this outrage totally incomprehensible. I had expected better of you. Maximillian is obviously a bad influence on you. To avoid any further attempts on your part to follow his example I am going to send you to live with my sister, your Aunt Theodora in Innsbrück, as soon as it can be arranged."

Corinna stood dumbfounded, clutching at her brother for support. Then it was his turn.

"As for you Maximillian, your recent actions condemn you. You disgrace our family, but you can think yourself lucky that Leopold has intervened on your behalf. Nevertheless, at seventeen you are eligible as a cadet for the Military Academy in Vienna. Maybe they can deal with your excessive irresponsibility and reform your ways."

A cadet! Vienna! Military Academy! he could not mean it.

Max was speechless and Corinna horrified. Both of them were utterly stunned and shocked. They stood rooted to the spot, unable to offer any cries of protest.

"Consider yourself fortunate we are no longer at war. This time last year you would have been sent to the front line," Leopold went on. If their eldest brother had wanted to scare them further, he had succeeded. The recent war against Italy and France had resulted in the worse casualties in history. The rest of their father's announcement outlining the details of their future passed over their heads unheard, until they found themselves dismissed.

Like two lost souls, they silently retreated to their rooms to come to terms with their respective sentences. For Corinna this was a worse catastrophe than she could ever have imagined, and as the full meaning sank in, the turmoil of tumbled thoughts made her head spin, she would not, could not accept the idea of being separated from her dearest brother. Never that. Dear darling troublesome Max, who seemed bent on self-destruction at times, yet she had not known a day without him. They had been bound together since they were infants; they were part of each other's lives. She needed him. Oh Max, Max! How could she believe this was happening? To be parted!

"No!" Corinna pleaded aloud. The thought was too painful to bear. Max was her only friend in the world, the only one she could talk to and confide in. He was the only one she cared about, and likewise he was the only one who cared about her.

Max sat down heavily, burying his head in his hands, still unable to speak, while Corinna, equally miserable, stoked up the dying fire and, pulling her shawl closer around her, stood staring into space. Her mind racing, her stomach churning, she wished this was some simple nightmare she could ignore by waking up, but it was not.

"I am sorry Corinna. This is all my fault. Although something was bound to happen eventually to give him the perfect excuse he needed to be rid of us. We did not stand a chance, he never really wanted us here," Max growled, finally lifting his head.

She did not want to think that Max was necessarily right, yet Max, convinced of his own desperate theory for their predicament, paced the floor, his eyes wild and his head shaking.

"Well – I shall be glad to be free of him."

She saw his eyes flash for a second to their mother's portrait and then lower, touched by an instant of desperate sadness. The times they had both wished she had been here, a protective mother who would have prevented this happening to her children. But she had died so long ago that neither of them remembered her.

Thus unable to think of a way out of this awful situation, they found themselves offering hopelessly inept suggestions, then falling silent at the ridiculous futility of their plans and holding each other's hand, for no other reason than they needed to. What was to become of them, she questioned feebly, to be cast to opposite sides of the country? Were they never to see each other again?

Corinna lay in bed in the darkness, the day's events churning over and over in her head. There was no point in even trying to sleep as she restlessly tossed and turned. The chiming mantel clock told her how the hours dragged by, but there was no reprieve to her unquiet mind. She tugged at the pillow and hit it again. How had matters become this serious? She did not understand. Was there no way to prevent this happening?

By the look of Max the next morning, he had suffered the

same problem. The pair of them spent the following days making empty, difficult promises which both knew neither could keep, until eventually they were exhausted by the effort of containing their own fears. They read everything in each other's searching faces and tried to convince themselves there was hope, when in their hearts they accepted there was none.

The next morning Maximillian was gone. Corinna had watched him leave; he had walked straight down the stairs, out of the front door and into the closed coach without a word to anyone. He did not even turn to wave or cast her a last farewell look, and his thoughtlessness hurt her deeply. Her hand slid down the window pane, fresh tears trickling down her crumpled face. Her eyes, head and heart ached with the pain of this moment and the sight of the carriage eventually disappearing made her shudder. She felt empty and alone. She had lost him and nothing would ever be the same. It was too real, too real for her to cope with. Unable to pretend any longer, she sank in overwhelming misery, exhausted to the floor.

Unlike Max, who had left without a fuss, Corinna meant to mark her departure by being stubbornly as awkward as possible, even though she was usually as timid as a mouse. This would be her one attempt, a final protest of defiance to show them how she felt about their plans for her future. As far as she was concerned, she had no future. She being abandoned, without a second thought on their part.

When the actual day came, she refused to finish dressing in her travelling clothes and sat motionless, resisting all the bullying and threatening efforts to force her obedience. Her only voluntary movement was to flinch from the blow she saw coming as Beatrice, towering over her, lost her temper.

All too soon the supervised packing of her remaining clothes was finished and the closed trunks were taken away. Her belongings gone, Corinna looked around her room. Now sadly empty of her personal possessions, it no longer held the familiar comfort of old and her resolve faded. Her last useless gesture had naturally failed to make any difference; they did not care. Well, she sniffed, neither did she! She could manage without them around continuing to ruin her life. How could it be much worse in Innsbrück?

Suddenly she understood the reasoning behind the manner of Max's departure. Like him she should be glad to leave this place, her father and the rest of them. She would only be miserable if she stayed in this intolerable house without Max here. They were welcome to this horrid place. Yes they were!

Corinna stood up smartly, put on her travelling jacket and marched head high past her surprised sisters to the stairs, to copy the very pattern of Max's leaving. She did not look back to either side or acknowledge anyone;, she left without a word.

During the long journey in the company of her other sister, Edith-Louisa, Corinna's proud bravado slowly ebbed under the persistent scolding she received. She shrank a little more with every complaint aimed at her, staring forlornly at the passing scenery and becoming more subdued as they travelled on. When the coach eventually rumbled into the city outskirts and finally halted in front of a very impressive large house, Corinna had an awful feeling in the pit of her stomach. She was here to live with a relation she had never heard of, one she knew absolutely nothing about, and she dreaded what might be in store for her.

Whilst her sister ushered herself into the private sitting room to await their aunt, Corinna was left standing forlornly in the vast entrance hall, once more alone and unwanted. The hushed atmosphere of her new surroundings, almost identical to those she had just left, gave little indication that she would fare any better here.

The gentle sound of rustling silk made her turn, and her attention was instantly drawn to a most magnificently dressed older lady sedately descended the main staircase towards her. Corinna stared and her mouth dropped open. She had never seen such wonderful, beautiful, elegant clothes in her life. They were – well she could not even try to fathom the detail she saw.

The woman stopped on the bottom step to eye Corinna intensely, and with a stern frown, proceeded to study her up and down before shaking her head slightly.

"What on earth has my brother sent me?" she exclaimed aloud.

Overawed and tongue-tied, Corinna was unsure whether an answer was expected or not. Theodora however immediately gave a sudden sharp clap of her hands together, the signal bringing staff from nowhere to expertly fulfil the unspoken tasks of swiftly dispatching Corinna's meagre belongings left in the entrance, to be taken upstairs out of the way. Then, just as quickly, the servants vanished, to leave the hall empty again except for her aunt and herself.

Startled by this unexpected burst of activity, she had not recovered before Theodora ushered her through to where Edith waited. The formal greetings were exchanged and the obligatory tray of refreshments appeared, to be set next to her aunt. The servants appeared and disappeared like magic, just as before.

"Sit, sit, sit girl!" instructed her aunt impatiently, waving to a chair near her. "I do not expect to have to tell you your every move."

Corinna sat obediently, taking the plate with a piece of cake which was handed to her, but somehow she found it difficult to eat. It went round and round in her mouth, despite every effort to swallow. Even the liquid she supped to help wash it down made no difference. Struggling under the steely gaze of her aunt, Corinna reverted to viewing the floor wishing it would swallow her up or at least if not her, then this horrid dry cake. For such a small amount, it took forever for her to finish eating it.

"Hmm," murmured Theodora, "this will not do at all."

Nothing more was said to her, whilst the two older women politely exchanged conversation and Corinna idly traced the pattern of the carpet with the toe of her shoe for the lack of anything else to do. Thus Corinna remained silently seated, not moving an inch for another whole tedious hour, before her older sister eventually made her farewell.

Aunt Theodora returned from seeing Edith-Louisa to the door and checked her appearance in the mirror, gently fussing with her lace edging and twisting her head sideways to see if her hair was still perfectly in place. Satisfied, she turned back to her niece.

"Heavens Corinna, you are a timid creature. I can see there is a lot to improve on. I am shocked at your lack of social graces and your provincial clothes. Of course I blame your father, he should never have had you two youngsters so much later than the others, if he was not prepared to take better care of your upbringing."

Corinna was astonished. This was not quite what she was expecting from her aunt, having assumed she and her father were both from the same mould.

"You will find I believe in speaking my mind, especially when there is good reason to do so. I am no fool, you forget I put up with my brother's ways long enough. Thank goodness my late husband was nothing like him." Theodora gave Corinna a gentle smile, a smile which seemed to grow so bright that her eyes twinkled.

"I doubt he gave either of you any thought at all. Girls are supposed to have pretty dresses and go to parties, I don't expect you have experienced either. Have you?" she asked gently.

Corinna shook her head, unable to answer.

"It will be a delight to have you in my home Corinna. You have nothing to be frightened about and I mean to rectify all the neglect they showed you."

Corinna could not believe the kindness and understanding now offered to her. It was all too much, and she burst into tears. Huge great sobs shook her body, great gulping sobs she could not easily stop, as the pent-up strain of hiding all her emotions broke free.

"There, there, my dear, you might as well let it out," Theodora comforted soothingly, giving her a handkerchief.

"It was only a torn curtain - and." Corinna gulped, "and some china - and an antique table, all smashed to bits," she gushed rapidly, the tears still trickling down her unhappy face.

Having started the tale of woe, Corinna found she could not stop; her aunt deserved the whole truth, the accumulation of their misdemeanors and everything, her muddled mumbled words running into each other until she did not know what she said or if she made sense and her voice finally faded away completely. Her aunt took hold of Corinna's hand and pulled her towards her, then lifted her lowered head between her hands to look her into the face. Her own features were less stern than expected after such a confession.

"My dear poor Corinna, there is no need to cry any more.

You are in my charge now and my responsibility. I am going to do my best for you. I do not believe there is a jot of harm in you and I intend to turn you into a very fine and proper young lady. I may appear to be an ogre to those who cross me, but I am determined you are going to be the best of that family, despite any opposition from certain other quarters," she confided softly.

In the weeks and months that followed, Corinna could not believe the kindness her aunt showered upon her; she had never experienced so much gentle affection and attention. She was allowed to express opinions, laugh and chose things for herself. Similarly she had never had, or indeed seen, so many lovely clothes; hats, jackets and shoes and a complete new wardrobe began to fill her room. Her life was so different that even for ages afterwards Corinna would still wake up every morning, wondering briefly if this was really happening or it was just some dream.

Although she had been nervous at the onset of this whole venture, as time passed Corinna began to feel a contentment she had never experienced before. Now a willing pupil, she was keen to learn everything she could. As she was instructed and fussed over, her manner, posture and the social etiquette of society was absorbed. There were books to read and discussions on a wide variety of topics, all to further her education and broaden her interests. Her mind was in a whirl, as she relished everything her aunt had proposed for her.

From then on, swept along by her determined relative, Corinna found herself on carriage rides, shopping expeditions and accompanying her aunt to selected social gatherings amongst her own circle of influential friends, her confidence growing with every venture. Soon she was going to galleries, attending musical recitals, galas and receptions, all under her aunt's firm guidance.

Then, as if this were not enough, Corinna could not believe her good fortune when her aunt decided to engaged a tutor for dancing lessons, considering it as one of the most important accomplishments that every young lady should have. Dancing lessons! Such an indulgence and one she had certainly been denied at home. Corinna could hardly wait. Indeed she discovered it was a talent she excelled in. Every step felt like magic as she glided effortlessly around the floor, and the whole enjoyment of it filled her fit to burst. Oh, she had never been so wondrously happy or exhilarated. She was sure her father had never intended her life to improve to such an extent.

The sheer delight in her wonderful new life was exceeded only by her anticipation for her very first ball. She was going to a real society ball, who would have imagined it? Never in her wildest fantasy had she ever contemplated such a thing. Like a fairytale come true, dressed in the finest gown she had ever seen and with her hair elegantly arranged, pinned and decorated, Corinna stared at her reflection in the mirror. She had never felt so very, very special, a sensation which remained with her for the whole of the evening. Not for one second did she notice the other young ladies or their gowns, if they were prettier or finer, because she was lost in the whole euphoric atmosphere of the dazzling ballroom. Her dance card carefully arranged with selected partners by her chaperoning aunt, she floated in another world. The rest of the illustrious assembly, the finest of fashionable, distinguished Innsbrück society, remained a haze as she danced on and on. Swept off her feet by polite young men, the sensation of utter contentment filled her whole being from head to toe.

The hours flew, until her aunt gently tapped her new protégée on the arm to convey that it was time to leave. The night had been perfect. As Corinna rode home, she sat snug in the corner of the coach. The memory of the last few glorious hours could not remove the smile which seemed to have become fixed on her face. She felt so exhilarated and suddenly tired, not that she would admit it to the last, although the gentle rocking of the carriage made it harder and harder to keep her eyes open.

She gazed with affection at her aunt who sat opposite, Dear Aunt Theodora, who, faintly amused by her niece's reaction, also allowed herself the luxury of leaning back into the soft upholstery, warmed by the satisfaction that the event had been a success.

Corinna floated through the following days smiling at every attempt to bring her back down to earth. She moved in a trance, her head full of music, of handsome, dashing men and romantic notions. The memory of a stranger she had seen once on the hotel terrace in Gmunden returned, and her mind wistfully tried to remember every detail of the handsome stranger. Not that he was difficult to forget; she had been struck by his quiet ease of manner, his relaxed frame, his features, his especially dark eyes and the equally dark hair which curled at the nape of his neck. She had studied him intensely. And how Max would have teased her.

Thus Max invaded her daydreams. Dear Max! She sighed. Life had been so exciting and the months had passed with amazing swiftness, with the result that Corinna had only once or twice guiltily spared a thought for her errant brother in Vienna. She should have written to him, but then he had not written to her either. It seemed that they were as bad as each other at keeping in touch, after all their promises. Had he changed at all? She hoped that he had also benefitted in some way from having left home, and was happy. He was safe in Vienna, what could possibly go wrong there? Yes, she would write to him tomorrow, she promised herself. She had so much to tell him.

At the approach of summer Aunt Theodora removed them all to her summer home in the green slopes of the Tyrol, as was her custom, and Corinna found herself suddenly missing the many exciting events, interesting visitors and enthralling entertainment she had become used to. The days here were quieter and the odd informal social gathering of other local gentry reflected the less demanding acceptance of this period spent away from the city. Corinna read and sewed, walked with her aunt, took the occasional carriage ride with her to local villages, or was allowed to ride out across the countryside with a groom as an escort. At times the quiet days dragged by, and Corinna found her pent-up energy hard to contain; she longed to explore those tantalising wide open spaces surrounding the house and gardens. So when her aunt became indisposed for a few days and took to remaining in bed, Corinna decided to make the most of this opportunity.

She woke to a beautiful morning, the sun drifting in soft rays into her room, illuminating the particles of dust in the air. She sat watching them, hugging her knees to her chest, then stretched out and lay back again, but try as she might she could not remain still. Kicking her feet impatiently against the bedclothes, she threw them back and ran barefoot across the floor to the window, promising herself that today was hers and she was determined to make the most of as many hours of freedom as she could get away with. Outside the clear blue sky beckoned, the sun shone and in places the hills were decked with colourful wild flowers. Everything was so inviting. She smiled mischievously as she crept along the landing past her aunt's room and then leapt down the stairs in twos and threes in childlike glee. She could hardly wait for breakfast to be over, to escape.

As Corinna paused later at the open door of her aunt's room, instead of the familiar voice complaining about her wretched condition to her maid, her aunt's comments were solely directed at a letter she had received.

"What can my brother be thinking of? Ridiculous man!" she moaned.

Another letter from her father. Corinna pulled a face; she did not want to know its contents and was determined to avoid any shadow on her day. She hurried back downstairs and out of the back of the house, increasing her strides towards the outbuildings and stables. Did she want one of the ponies saddled for her, she was asked as she crossed through the yard? She shook her head and replied that she was merely taking a stroll, besides they could see she was not dressed for riding.

"Be careful Miss," the coachman warned, as she left the yard. "Don't stray too far on your own."

She nodded her promise, smiled to herself and carried on, casually making her way past the paddock to reach this far corner of the grounds. Here she briefly checked to see if she was being observed before slipping through the gate to explore those wide and empty green slopes ahead. Onwards she went, brushing happily through the long grasses and wild flowers, across the fields, further and further from the main building, without a backward glance. Eventually, satisfied with her progress, she threw herself on the ground under the dappled shade of the trees, to relax with her mind full of mellow dreams and nothing else to disturb her on this beautiful day.

Much later Corinna roused herself as a cool breeze suddenly reminded her that the hours were passing, reluctantly admitting she would have to return and probably face a scolding. As she dusted down her skirts, she caught sight of a figure below, walking slowly yet steadily and purposefully in her direction. Expecting it to be one of the servants sent to find her, she pulled a face and begrudgingly kicked the ground, waiting for a voice to call out for her, but none came.

Curiously she peered down the hill again, searching for the person she had seen earlier, but she was unable to locate him. She was just about to dismiss the whole matter from her mind when a movement in the further clump of woodland caught her eye. The shadow of a man ducked through the saplings on the slope below her and disappeared into the dark line of trees. The stranger kept to the gullies and secluded cover, stopped, looked around, vanished briefly, reappeared and paused again, apparently checking to see if he had been observed.

Corinna began to feel a little uneasy, the man's furtive actions making her nervous. She realised that she really should not have come so far on her own. She had naturally thought this wonderful scenery would be perfectly safe; never in her wildest dreams could she have imagined there would be any sort of danger in such a beautiful setting. She should have had more sense. So much for her lame attempt at a little private exploration. Whoever the man was, she was glad she had not waved or called out earlier when she had thought him to be someone from the house. He was still coming her way and this worried her. She was nervous; more than nervous, she was actually becoming quite scared, there was no denying it. Instinctively she edged backwards under the trees, to hide amongst them.

As Corinna stood in the unusual chill of the afternoon waiting for what seemed like ages with no further development, she tried to convince herself her imagination must be playing tricks. Surely the man must have gone by now. She hesitantly snatched a quick glimpse around, only to duck back immediately, because the distant looming figure, no longer that distant, seemed to be coming almost straight towards her. Did he know she was there? If only she had the sense to go back when she had first seen him; now he was between her and the house and too near for her to now make a dash for safety. Huddled there against the tree to make herself as invisible as possible, with her heart beating faster than ever, she held her breath, listening for his steps, quietly hoping the man who ever he was had not seen her and would soon pass by.

Who was this man? Why had he waited so silently? Not that she wanted to find out and as he stopped once more, she heard the swish of his cloak all too close. Then her position betrayed by her flapping skirt caught by the sudden gusting breeze, gave her no choice, fear stirred her into life and she ran, ran for all she was worth, blindly and desperately. There was no reason for the man to chase after her, but he did. Hampered by her skirt she stumbled on, sliding and tripping on the uneven ground, frightened as she heard his steps not far behind her. Changing direction, she ducked sideways, anticipating the grabbing hand which brushed past her. A low curse followed as the man crashed into the branches, the brief halt in the pursuit allowing Corinna the opportunity to drive herself on and on again, panting and short of breath, her vision blurred, unaware of exactly where she ran.

A shout sounded behind her, warning her that it had taken no effort for him to catch her up again. Her legs were aching and heavy, her starved lungs fit to burst, gulping for air. She desperately pushed through bushes and ferns, the stones hurting her feet. She had tried to head for the house, but she seemed to be forced the wrong way and knew in that second she could not escape. A dirty hand came in front of her and a strong arm caught her about the waist to swing her unexpectedly off her feet, leaving her too breathless to scream her protest. Struggling and twisting, she unbalanced her attacker, with the result that she found herself falling to the ground, trapped in his arms.

Dazed and bruised, with his breath on her face and his panting in her ears echoing her own, she refused to give in easily, although his grip on her remained just as tight. She lashed out wildly in an effort to be free, beating her fists into his chest and kicking out, her hair in disarray, the loose strands on her little face obscuring her aim. However feeble she was against his strength, she meant to fight.

"Corinna, will you stop it before you hurt yourself or me." the voice snapped, shaking her fiercely.

She stopped struggling instantly. Max!

CHAPTER TWO

Max! But how? It was impossible. She could hardly believe her eyes as he pushed her hair from her face. Exhausted, hot, and dusty, her heart still thumping in her ears, Corinna threw herself at him, so pleased to see him. She was delighted he was here, for he would soon liven up the dull atmosphere which had settled on the house. She had missed him, his reckless manner, his charming ways, in fact everything about him. Oh, she was so glad he had come. Then she slapped him hard for scaring her like that, she had not liked his stupid game.

Without demanding to know why he had acted so strangely, Corinna happily babbled on, insisting he would like their aunt. She had no regrets about coming to live with her. Her life had changed so much. Could he see the change in her, she asked, although her bright eyes and smile really required no answer. No of course he couldn't, he had just made a complete mess of her and her dress! She had learnt all about their mother Theresa and her brother, an uncle Michael whom their father refused to communicate with. Wasn't it intriguing? They had so much to tell each other and so many plans to make while he was here. How long was he staying? She was relieved to see him unharmed.

Corinna could not stop talking, so distracted that she did not notice his reluctance to interrupt her or indeed to speak at all.

Gradually Corinna realised that something was not quite right. Max's unusual silence was accompanied by a worried expression, and she began to study him properly for the first time and noted the way his eyes constantly darted about the place. He looked worried and was strangely quiet as if he was struggling within himself. There were scratches and bruises, weary lines on his grubby face, the unkempt hair, his uniform dirty, untidy and well worn, indicated he had travelled fast and obviously without rest. His tired eyes surveyed her face, silently pleading. He did not need to tell her. She knew he was in trouble.

"Oh, Max. What is wrong? What has happened? Let's go back to the house and tidy you up."

"No, Corinna, I cannot come to the house. No one must find out I am here."

All her initial joy at Max's arrival vanished as he explained that he had been in hiding there for several days, anxiously watching the place and waiting for the chance to speak to her alone. He visibly shook as he confessed how his stomach had been in knots. He had felt almost physically sick; he had never been so wretched or so afraid. He had pleaded with every god there was for the chance to see her in secret.

"Poor Corinna. I thought you knew – but you could not, being so remote out here in the country. At least I knew where to find you from your last letter. There was no way I could have dared gone to Innsbrück. I would easily have been spotted in a city. Maybe I should not have come, yet I had to, because there is only you who might help me. I am sorry." he gripped her hand in his.

She had never seen him like this, never heard him talk like this before. What had put him in this state? She could feel his heart thudding nervously as she drew him closer and she was startled as he held on to her desperately.

"I am a fugitive, a deserter. I am wanted by the military authorities. I am on the run. I had to run. No one must find out I am here. Please don't let them catch me!" He searched her face, which stared back into his.

Corinna's head was spinning as the enormity of his words echoed in her brain, her heart sinking as she tried to absorb the perilous fix he was in. Her skin went cold.

"But why Max? What has happened?" she heard herself whisper.

"Oh Corinna, I was continually taunted, picked on and bullied at every opportunity, it was awful. I took it for as long as I could. If I had stayed I might have ended up killing one cadet in particular, or he me. I had to get away."

"Was there no other solution?"

Max shook his head, his anxiety still pained on his face. "God, what a state of affairs, how can I expect my little sister to help me against the army? I must be mad! I need you to listen. I'm hiding at the derelict mausoleum in the woods. Come tonight if you can. I need a change of clothing and some food. Can you manage any of that? Please try, please. I know it's a lot to ask."

Corinna nodded, fingering the grubby uniform Max wore beneath the cloak, still unable to think clearly enough to work out how exactly she was supposed to do any of what he expected of her, but knowing she had to try.

"And – I need a fresh horse. It's been a long journey coming here. I have risked leaving mine in the woods at the back of the mausoleum for now," he whispered, clutching her hand tight.

She pictured the horses in the paddock and the few which were returned to the stable block at night, all of them fine animals, but to take one - that was different! She remembered the fuss her aunt had made about bringing them from Innsbrück, especially the best matched pair of carriage horses. Her mouth was still open when Max pressed her again.

"I must have a fresh horse. I could use the one you ride when you bring those things to me. I am desperate."

"No Max. I can't! It's impossible. You're not thinking straight. The food and clothes might be plausible, any vagabond might have dared to steal those. Aunt Theodora would certainly be more than disgruntled by anyone having the nerve to break into her house, but to take one of her horses, never! She will have every neighbour within miles helping to search the whole countryside immediately. She has influential friends, she would make a fuss. That would certainly draw the attention of the authorities. You will have to manage with the animal you have."

He nodded, reluctantly seeing the sense in her argument. He could not risk them coming here yet, he need more time to escape.

"I can't stay any longer. I had better leave you now. For all I know time is running out even as we speak." Max told her, gently pushing her away.

"No!" she protested. "Wait!"

"Corinna, Corinna please, I must go," he pleaded earnestly, and within an instant he had disappeared.

She stared after him, a lump in her throat and catch in her breath. Max! There was nothing else to do but slowly retrace her steps, collect herself together enough to hide her anxiety and to pretend everything was the same, that she was the same on her return to the house.

Preoccupied by her brother's plight, her silence was luckily mistaken for repentance during the severe scolding for her earlier truancy and Corinna was relived to be dismissed from her aunt's room without any further inquisition. Afterwards she made her way to the dining room, sadly aware that despite loving her aunt as much as she did, she was prepared to lie to her to protect Max. Nothing was as important as saving Max. He would always come before anything else.

Corinna sat nervously through the evening meal, impatient to be done with this increasingly awful ritual. She picked at the food in front of her, finding it hard to swallow even the smallest morsel. She was glad to be alone, thus avoiding her aunt's observant glances, although she worried that the servants could tell the state she was in. She did not dare look up at them, just in case. She tapped and fidgeted with her feet under the table and pretended boredom as the different courses came and went. Then at last the meal was finished and she escaped to follow the routine of adjourning into the small sitting room to apparently while away the rest of the evening reading.

How many times did she look at the clock and pace the floor? Why did the hands move so slowly? Only a few hours had passed, but it seemed days. She did try to read, but the book remained open at the same page for the whole of the evening as she stared blankly at the words. She could only concentrate on Max. A deserter! She was frightened for him; with the rumours of war which had circulated in Innsbrück before they had left, this would surely now be seen as cowardice as well. He could be shot! She shuddered; he was in mortal danger. Although the rumours had not persisted and the Emperor might never send cadets to fight, the whole prospect put Max in the worst of situations.

Had her aunt been right in her assessment concerning the unlikely prospect of their young Emperor Franz Joseph being drawn into another war? Corinna hoped so, but it had not stopped her aunt bringing all the livestock with her to the Tyrol, to prevent any compulsory purchase of her horses.

Corinna wished she could shake off these terrible doubts. Retiring as normal, she tried to stay calm as gradually the house became dark and the sounds died away to silence. She peered out into the darkness, knowing Max was out there, far from safe and waiting for her help. She had promised she would be there for him, and despite any obstacle she must be, or she would never see him again. How long should she wait for everyone to be asleep, she wondered, as she sat by the cold air of the open window in an effort to stay awake herself.

She allowed an hour to pass before she felt safe to tiptoe along the landing and venture below. She had to find a change of clothes first. She turned the laundry baskets upside down, pulling out one item after another to hold it up for size, then pausing to listen before discarding it by throwing it back into the great tangled muddle she had created. Hurry, she kept telling herself. I must hurry. What did she need, a shirt, trousers or breeches, a jacket? Where to find outdoor clothing! Impatiently she searched the downstairs recesses until she found a coat. Thank goodness! She gathered the rest of the chosen garments into a bundle to wrap them in the coat and then pushed the other clothes back into their various baskets, trying to make it look less as if anyone had been through it. There was such a lot to remember.

What next? Food. That was easy, some meat, bread and cheese, wrapped in a napkin. Was there anything she had overlooked? She shook her head and made for the door, knowing time was of the essence, but as she slipped the bolts on the door and turned the lock, they creaked noisily and she forced herself to wait. Did anyone stir, she wondered as she listened intently, her heart pounding in her ears as the precious minutes ticked by. When would they notice? How soon before they realised what was missing, and what questions would they ask? Who would they ask? All these niggling thoughts clouded her actions. It was hard to believe her luck was holding this far, but since there were no telltale sounds from above and she was desperate to be on her way, she gently eased the rear door open.

It had barely moved when she stopped suddenly and leaned against the door in frustration. She had not thought this through. He would need money, and she had only a few coins in her purse! She ran upstairs and back to her room before she could change her mind, her hand trembling as she tipped her treasured trinkets from the carved wooden box out onto the bed. Although a great personal sacrifice, it was the only solution. She had offered a few of them to him last year in an effort to stop him embarking on that stupid scheme with the china to fund their secret excursions, but he had refused. Well, he was in no position to argue this time.

Would they be enough? None of them looked of any great value. Her eyes blurred emotionally as she picked over her mother's few pieces of jewellery. What was more important, her few sentimental items or Max? In the end she grabbed two items and, leaving everything else scattered where they were, she hurried back downstairs again. She hoped he was still waiting where he said; she prayed he was.

What about the repercussions tomorrow morning? A great number of questions would be asked, but then she had a brainwave. The coachman had mentioned seeing a vagrant in the area a few days ago. What would be more natural than for a vagabond to steal whatever he could? They certainly would not look too far afield before accepting the loss as inevitable. At least they would never find the stranger and Max would be long gone by then. If she opened one of the pantry windows wide enough, to make it look as if someone could have got in, that would provide perfectly plausible evidence. Then she would leave unlocked the outside door which he would have used for his escape. Yes! That should satisfy any investigation. At last she had it all worked out.

She closed the heavy outside door and took a deep breath as she made her way across the yard. Slowly her eyes adjusted to the dark and the brief snatches of moonlight allowed her to see what she was doing. She found an empty sack in the feed store, packed in the food and clothes, tied the top with a knot and dragged it along to the stables. It was a long way to the derelict mausoleum. She had not thought much about it earlier, but now she did not feel so confident. She shuddered. The mausoleum was a dark, horrid creepy place; everyone knew where it was, but no one ever went near it, and no one liked the place even in daylight. But much as she didn't want to do this, she had to. For Max. That was all she kept reminding herself.

She knew this final part of the task would be the most difficult, because horses were unreliable animals at the best of times. Most of them were in the paddock, which limited her choice to those few kept in the stables, and since the large chestnut was the only one in a loose halter, her decision was made for her. Fitting the bridle, she tied the reins to the iron ring, to enable her to deal with the saddle. The side-saddle she would normally have used obviously would not fit this larger animal, which forced her to use the other heavier saddle nearby. Although this meant she would have to ride astride, she considered that was no problem given her past lessons from Max.

It was the actual saddling itself which proved the problem, as dragging the saddle down from the rack, it fell onto the straw, blowing dust in her eyes, causing both her and the horse to jump. This made it almost impossible to throw the cumbersome saddle on to the unsettled animal. Her arms ached as she coaxed him, following him from side to side about the stall until she finally succeeded in getting it on his back, before tightening and checking the girth. She felt exhausted and took a deep breath, knowing she could not afford time to rest.

Trying to balance the sack over the saddle, she had her hands full as she led the chestnut hunter out of the yard, trying to avoid the gravel walk. The horse, excited by the night air and the springy grass, pranced, fidgeted and threw his head in the air, jangling the reins and jerking her arms. She glanced towards the house, praying that no one would wake. She somehow managed to keep hold of the precious bundle across the saddle as she scrambled on to him.

She had hardly settled into the saddle before he was off, skittishly cavorting about, dancing all over the place, before she could gather him into the right direction, setting off into a wild gallop towards the woods and onward down the twisting track. Relieved to put distance between herself and the house, she let the horse have its head for a while. No one could have followed them at that speed. The twigs, branches and dark shapes rushed past, brushed against them, spurring them onward until they arrived at the mausoleum, where thankfully she managed to persuade the troublesome beast to halt in the small clearing.

Still in one piece and breathless from that breakneck ride, she urged the horse closer to the old stone burial chamber, slowly circling the derelict ruin to wait for Max to appear. She whispered his name nervously, but there was no movement in the black recess, no reply to her soft repeated calls and no sounds other than the stirring of the trees. Surely she hadn't missed him?

In panic she nudged the horse nearer, slowly circling the derelict ruin and fearing the worst with every second which passed. The place filled her with a terrible trepidation. Then, as she was about to turn away, Max finally showed himself from the depths of the darkness.

Corinna jumped from the horse and ran to him, to hug him desperately while Max stared straight ahead, unable to bear the sadness in her lovely dark eyes. He held her briefly, until his own fear made him push her away.

"I am sorry I had to involve you. I know I have let you down."

He removed the clothes bundle from the sack and went to change in the dark interior.

"All I ask is for you to deny you have seen me, to anyone who may come after me. Lie, Corinna, lie! My life depends upon it. It won't be easy. It won't be just the military and civil authorities with a warrant for my arrest. Others ask questions."

"Oh Max!" she knew exactly what he meant – their father! As if things were not bad enough, she did not want to think about that possibility.

"What will you tell them when they discover these things are missing?"

"Nothing. A vagabond was reported in the area not long ago, so they will not be too surprised at things being stolen. I doubt they will look too far afield."

A vagabond – he would normally have joked at the

subterfuge, but jokes were the last thing on his mind. All he felt was anxiety gnawing away at him.

"You must get rid of my uniform, I have left it in the sack beneath some broken masonry inside, but it may not be hidden well enough. I can' tell in the dark. Try to come back sometime in daylight, to make sure."

Fetching his horse from behind the building, Corinna watched him tighten the girth, check the leathers and adjust the well-worn saddle bag, ram the food into them, buckle down the flaps and turn. The closeness of his departure instinctively made Corinna chew her lip unhappily, an old habit of hers.

"Where will you go?" was all she could think to ask.

"Somewhere where I will be just another stranger amongst many others. Germany. I am not sure. Heidelberg – I might go there. I will find some work. I can turn my hand to most things. It won't be so bad," he added, somewhat unconvincingly.

An agonising silence hung between them, as they both realised there would be little chance of their ever seeing each other again, nor could they even risk any communication.

"Take me with you." Corinna suddenly pleaded, for how else would she know he was safe.

"I can't. I will barely be able to take care of myself. How could I provide for both of us? Please understand."

She did not want to understand or accept his logical reasoning, as he also pointed out that her disappearance would instantly alert the authorities to the fact he had certainly been here. If she wanted him to be safe, she had to let him go.

"Wait!" she said. She grabbed his sleeve, fumbled in her pocket and then thrust her present into his hand and closing his fingers around it, she momentarily wrapped both her hands own over his.

"Take them," she urged.

Max recognised the jewellery immediately and shook his head, a lump in his throat. He could not take much more of this unselfish devotion. The gold and emerald brooch in particular was probably quite valuable. How could he accept? His tired eyes misted; this act tormented his soul.

"I never wear them. They live in the carved box," she whispered, guiding his hand to his pocket.

"No, Corinna," he choked. "I can't - Mother left them to you."

"And you have nothing!" she uttered angrily, grabbing his wrist. Max winced at his ever-loyal sister's outburst and lowered his head, reluctantly accepting them and wishing none of this had happened. There were no promises he could make to her. Then he leapt upon the horse. This was it then, the moment they both dreaded. They had no words left; they had to let each other go. He gave her the best smile he could manage and spurred the horse forward and out of her life.

Rooted to the spot, she heard a cry escape her throat, one she could not control. Her eyes fixed on those last few seconds' view of him, to lock his image within her forever, determined to hold on to him. Then there was only the darkness. She sank to the ground, cold and heavy-hearted, struck by the dreadful reality of her loss. Distraught, she wept bitterly for him and herself, the sobs echoing in the night, with no one else to hear them.

Eventually she pulled herself together, remembering she still had to complete the last part of his request. Max was depending on her, she could not let him down. She rode back to the house, this time at a much slower pace, unsaddled the horse, rebolted the stable door, crept into the house and finally sank into her bed. She had done all she could.

In what seemed moments later, she found herself being woken for breakfast. She was too tired to move after the night's activities. She threw her head back on the pillow and mumbled incoherently that she wanted to be left alone. She had no intention of getting up today. Assuming her to be coming down with the same complaint as her aunt, the maid duly left without any fuss, allowing Corinna to snatch a few hours' extra sleep.

When she eventually stirred to rejoin the daily routine, she discovered that the connection between the stranger seen previously and the missing items had already been made, and it was the subject of gossip throughout the household. The clothing was of little value and would be easily replaced, but her aunt was absolutely furious that property had been stolen from her home and ordered that from then on all the doors and windows were to be checked every night. With the culprit obviously well out of the area by now, no attempt was made to search the countryside for him.

This meant that the uniform was in no danger of being discovered for the moment, and that Corinna felt perfectly safe to let the dust settle for a few days before returning to the mausoleum.

Safe in her room, pretending to be still a little under the weather, she waited and began to mull over the situation. How soon would it be before the news about Max reached here? Once Aunt Theodora learnt the rumours about him, she would guess the truth about the servants' clothing; her aunt knew her too well. Therefore she dare not wait too long to bury the uniform.

That night she tossed and turned, fighting the tumbled nightmares which plagued her mind. The horror of the men chasing her brother, their large faces cruel, ugly and twisted, their laughter and whispers, filled the room. The scene was so vivid that she woke in a panic. Her heart was racing, sounding like a hammer in her chest and in her brain. She could not shut out the alarm which now filled her. It meant prison or worse if they caught Max. It was hard not to cry, and she stifled her sobs deep into the bedding, frightened to let anyone hear her.

How long before the military themselves came, she wondered, imagining the degree of questioning from those faces she had just pictured. Yet they would not be the only ones demanding answers; her bullying father would arrive to hound the truth from her. Did she have the strength to lie constantly and convincingly enough?

Corinna began to work out her next course of action. It was a long way to the mausoleum, although in daylight the ride would not be so frightening. But she knew she would have difficulty getting away during the day, let alone being allowed to go riding alone, which meant she would have to leave before the servants were up and about. Of course her disappearance and the missing animal would be noticed almost immediately the household stirred, but by using her normal mount and riding side-saddle, she would avoid any suspicion concerning her actions. Luckily, since the vagrant incident, most of the other horses were being brought into the sables overnight, including her favourite pony which made it the whole prospect much easier.

Which was all well and good, but how was she to stop them coming after her too soon? She would write a note to her aunt, explaining that she had gone riding early, to avoid having an escort hampering her taste of freedom, and that she would probably be back late afternoon. Then no one would start worrying too much, she hoped. With any luck her behaviour would be put down to a girlish whim and it would not be so necessary for anyone to be sent after her immediately. She did not mind a severe scolding for being irresponsible on return; it would be worth the trouble.

As for the uniform, left lying under bits of masonry, it did not seem that safe from discovery. In fact the mausoleum seemed an obvious place for the authorities to search first, and likewise the surrounding woods. She would have to bury it somewhere completely out of the way, where it would not be noticed. If she could hide it even in the next valley, that would be better. Better there, than on her aunt's estate. Then, if it was ever found, being so well away from here, they might assume that Max had never been heading in this direction.

Could she get that far and back, before late afternoon? It would still be early when she reached the mausoleum. She could safely reach the next valley by noon, hide the uniform and come back. How would she know when it was noon? If she turned back as soon as she reached the next valley, surely that would be all right. It could not be that far, over a few hills was nothing; she was sure she could manage.

Then a wild burst of ingenuity hit her. If she wore Max's uniform and rode astride, she would not be recognised. Besides, no one would be near enough to see it was actually a uniform she was wearing. At a distance anyone would assume it was a man. If she was dressed as a man, no one would take much notice. Any sighting for anyone other than a girl would be dismissed as unimportant. She could remain incognito until she was ready to come home. Yes! Her face lit up. She beamed. Why not? Dare she? It made perfect sense.

Corinna lifted the candle to cast a quick glance about the room;

she was already in riding clothes. She hesitated, then gently fingered the top of her precious carved wooden box. "Wish me luck" she whispered, before putting it back in the drawer. Then, candle extinguished, she crept along the corridor to her aunt's door. Her dear aunt, this was no way to show her gratitude.

She tapped the letter in her hand. If she left it under the door, it could so easily be brushed aside and missed altogether. There was no alternative but to put it on the bedside table, propped up where she would see it instantly. With the satisfying sound of Theodora's heavy slumber in her ears, Corinna felt encouraged as she gently placed the envelope on the wooden surface and made her way back to the hallway.

Slipping out through the kitchen scullery, she made her way out to the stables, comforted by the knowledge that having managed to borrow a horse once, this time should not be so difficult. But she had not considered the problem sufficiently. If she was going to pretend she had just gone riding, she would have ridden side-saddle, but she would have to ride astride in the uniform, which would be awkward with no stirrup or saddle flap on the other side. Think, think she told herself. She glanced around for inspiration, aware that these delays were wasting time. Come on, come on… Yes - a long piece of rope. She searched the tack room and found several discarded pieces which she could knot together. If she made a long loop, she could fix the rope around the leg rest and let it down the other side, then knot the end into another smaller loop to form a stirrup. This would be really uncomfortable, but she had to arrive home in the same manner she had left, to avoid instant suspicion. Gathering the rope pieces together she hurriedly completed the alterations.

Having survived the journey back to the awful gloomy mausoleum, she surveyed the sack on the ground in front of her.

Max's uniform! Fully aware that everything of his would be too large, she tried it on over her blouse and breeches. The jacket sleeves hung over her hands and the trousers were too long over her boots, so they would both have to be rolled up. The battered squashed cap fell over her face until she fixed it by stuffing her hair up into the crown. Obviously the ill-fitting uniform would not stand much scrutiny, but it would be sufficient at a distance to achieve this vital deception, she convinced herself.

The rope worked as the other stirrup and disguising the leg rest with the sack carrying her other clothes to change back into later, then she rearranged herself on the saddle. She had a whole day in front of her. Her main aim was to put as much distance between her and the house as possible, as quickly as possible. She did not want any sightings near her aunt's home. It was a brilliant idea, and it would make all the difference to Max's chances.

Corinna rode on, allowing the horse to go at its own pace, gently guiding it towards the next valley, content for a while and smiling cheerfully at the easy pace they were setting on the unknown track. She followed the dips and hollows, and with the sun on her back and the countryside changing at every bend, she felt quite pleased with herself.

After a few hours she rested the horse, pleased that the morning had gone well, because she had already crossed the next valley. Ahead lay a scattering of larger buildings and a better road, both of which she wanted to avoid, which would require her to make a wider diversion around the outskirts of the village. She crossed another ridge. Riding astride had become easier, but her legs had begun to ache and the make-do rope stirrup was making her other leg sore. Added to which she realised how hungry she felt. That was one thing she had forgotten - food! But with a shrug she managed to help fight off the niggles of her journey for a while.

It would soon be time to find somewhere suitable to change back into her own clothes, bury the uniform and start for home. Home - what a lovely thought. Her stomach rumbled and she was ravenously hungry; she could not wait to get back. And she would easily be back tonight, of course she would!

From her new vantage point, she spotted an isolated farm house, with a selection of outbuildings, which looked a promising place for her transformation. Eagerly she made her way down the slope, intending to make sure it was perfectly safe, before approaching too close. But as she turned the corner, she was horrified to find it alarmingly busy. Men with pitchforks and long staffs were searching the place, beating the bushes, poking in the corners and recesses of the wooden outbuildings. Whatever they were after, this was no place for her.

She had to hide. As carefully and as quietly as she could, she turned the animal away, gently edging it out of sight, off the track, to retreat slowly back to the thickest copse, listening for any sounds behind her. She stopped when she heard men's voices unexpectedly nearby and soothing the horse, she held her breath as they passed within inches of her, making their way to join the others. Suddenly a wild pig burst out from the bracken, snorting and grunting loudly. Birds screeched skywards, startling both her and the horse. The horse reared, and it took all of her strength to regain control of the agitated animal. Meanwhile she heard the shouts from below which indicated that the encounter with the pig had been heard. With the animal's four feet back on the ground, Corinna did not wait around. She urged the horse forward, kicking and kicking for all she was worth to get away from here. A shot rang out behind her, coming dangerously close, the bullet hitting and splitting the tree bark near her head. Her face went white with fear, and with the animal now out of control, all she could do was lean close over his neck to let it run and run. Dizzy and sick, her stomach churning violently, she desperately clung on as the horse careered at great speed on its own course. The blurred ground rushed by, on and on. It seemed like some endless tunnel, until the pounding gallop eventually giving way to a rhythmic canter a good time later, then, a few steps on stopped completely. They were both trembling and breathless.

The actual danger of being shot at came as a tremendous shock, and the taste of real fear made her cry. She could have died out here, all alone. She did not want to die! She just wanted to be safe. She wanted to be safely back enjoying the comfort and kindness of her aunt. Dear Aunt Theodora!

Corinna sat there for ages, not daring to dismount from her only means of escape from danger. Thoroughly depressed, starving, aching and very, very sore, she had had enough of this adventure. It had seemed so simple and straightforward in the beginning. Now Corinna did not feel quite so pleased with this impulsive plan

After a while she mustered the energy to nudge the horse forward again, desperate to find somewhere soon to get out of this uniform, because now she had no idea of where she was; she was lost and would need to find some friendly rural community for guidance. Oblivious to all else except this objective, she let the horse plod along, but she failed to notice an overhanging branch. Corinna found herself knocked off the horse and rolling head first down the bank.

Confused and disorientated, Corinna lifted her head to see her horse, free of its rider, deciding to continue without her, leaving her to stare up at the now empty track. No, no, no! The horse, and more importantly her clothes, were gone.

"Stupid animal. Come back!" she yelled, as if it would obey.

What was she to do? She had no choice except to trudge after it, hoping it would stop to graze a little further on. Goodness, she mumbled to herself, all these stupid incidents were not helping. She wanted to be on her way home.

Emerging from the ditch to dust herself down, the first thing which became apparent was the difference the oversized uniform made to her progress on foot. The rolled-up trouser legs, no longer held back by the stirrups, now fell over her toes, so that she had to keep bending down every so often to roll them up again, as they refused to stay in place. Tired of bending in a fruitless quest, her only option meant was to haul them up at the knees and permanently hold them in that position to avoid tripping, which of course made her arms ache. So with the sleeves now hanging down over her hands as well, Corinna pushed herself on, up and down the endless slopes, dragging her tired limbs, until, feeling a little wobbly she took a rest. Where was this confounded beast? How much further was she going to have to go? What if someone else found it?

It was already late in the day, and it was becoming obvious that she could not possibly reach home before dark. Unsure of which direction to go in, she could only hope she would be lucky enough to find a village soon. Even then, how was she to explain her appearance? She would have to get rid of the uniform before she could persuade someone to take her back to her aunt.

Disgusted with herself at this turn of events, she tugged off the damn cap and threw it furiously out of sight. She had thought of discarding the rest of the uniform right now, but she needed the extra layers as it had started to turned cold. She would wait; there would be plenty of time once she reached civilisation. Meanwhile she pulled her tangled hair straight back into the nape of her neck, to make herself look more presentable to anyone she approached for help. The rapidly failing light made the unknown track difficult to see. It would soon be night. A little longer, she promised herself, the next shelter. Corinna was frightened, very frightened - what if she did not find help or get back? Poor Aunt Theodora would be frantic and the household would be in turmoil by now. She hoped they would start looking for her tomorrow. She could still successfully explain this prolonged absence to her aunt by saying the horse had bolted, she had fallen off and become lost. Which was completely true! She could still retain the credibility of her original story. It could still work. Besides, her grubby clothes would substantiate her excuse, although the missing riding jacket and skirt-mantel might be difficult to explain.

She could hardly keep her eyes open any longer. She had to rest, somewhere safe. She could not risk being found sleeping in the open countryside, for she did not know who might find her or what might happen to her. Stumbling off the track, she avoided the nearest clump of trees and instead found an outcrop of rock further up with a partially-collapsed weatherbeaten old tree lying over it. It provided a sheltered hollow to one side. Thank goodness. Pulling aside some of the dead branches which littered the ground, she crept inside, pulled the branches back over her and let her weary body sink to the ground.

When Corinna woke, her starving stomach immediately complained of hunger, but that was soon forgotten the instant she tried to get up. The hard ground had prodded and dug into her bones. She was painfully stiff, every single muscle hurt and it was agony to walk. She hoped it would wear off, but with every jolted step it seemed worse and the weather conspired to add to her discomfort, as it was now becoming hot, sticky and oppressive. Her head ached and the unbearable stifling and prickly uniform left her drained of any energy. Lethargy took its toll. Soon Corinna no longer cared which trail she followed, for every view looked the same.

Inevitably a dreadful storm engulfed her, circling round and round overhead, and the deluge of torrential rain soon soaked her. Dishevelled, stiff and cold, and feeling decidedly sorry for herself, Corinna cursed the whole miserable experience. She had had enough! This pathetic foolish ruse to help Max had cost her dear. Alone, unprotected and easy prey, lost and without money, it could not be much worse. What was to become of her? She had certainly achieved her own ruination, for how could she retain any respectability in these new circumstances? She was so angry with herself. Even her dear aunt, if she ever saw her again, would have no reason to forgive this behaviour, and she couldn't blame her. Disowned, she would probably be sent back to her father, and that thought was too awful to contemplate.

On the horizon the last efforts of the storm reflected in the dark clouds, the bursts of light and distant rumble of thunder, making their last attempts to shatter the tranquil valleys as Corinna trod another steep uneven path. Cursing her heavy, wet clothes, particularly the trouser bottoms which dragged in the puddles, she tripped on the loose stones and fell again, her hands wildly snatching at the rough ground in an effort to break her fall. Down, down and down she slid and tumbled over and over, the world propelled past at an increasing rate, until, her head spinning, she crashed to a stop on a bed of rocks. Dizzy and sick, her stomach churning violently, she was left battered and bruised. Vague shades of grey replaced her vision and the whirling in her ears drowned all else other than her own rapid panting. Her face pale, her body limp and her other senses strangely sluggish to respond, she was convinced it was best just to lie there.

Slowly she began to regain some composure, calmly accepting the fact that unless she found help, she would lie here forever. She had to make the effort, but as she did, a crippling, piercing pain shot through her leg, agonising every nerve. She quickly lay back, waiting for the pain to ease, but it did not. At first glance she saw a very blood-soaked knee poking through both the uniform trousers and her fine linen breeches, before the shock of the blood made her head swim as nausea swept over her. She closed her eyes to stop herself thinking about it; to keep breathing steadily, in and out, was all she concentrated on, and that helped. Corinna tried to control her fear, but she knew she could die out here, all alone. She did not want to die!

"Oh, Aunt Theodora. I am sorry," she wept. This was not supposed to happen. The shivers were shaking her from head to toe as she feebly pulled the torn pieces of the uniform trousers away from the breeches, which were stuck together around the wound. The trousers were in shreds now anyway and deciding to abandon them right here, she struggled to remove this extra outer garment completely. She hoped to make a makeshift bandage from the strips, except that despite the rips in the material, it refused to tear any more. She did not have the strength, however hard she tried, it was so stubborn. Everything was against her. Reluctantly she sacrificed the sleeve of her blouse, which was much easier to tear. She gritted her jaw in determination, to bind the wound tight and ignore the sticky blood squeezing out between her fingers. She had done the best she could and swiftly put the uniform jacket back on over her bare arms to protect her from the cold.

She felt so cold and so helpless. There was nothing around to help her walk, no broken fence and no piece of wood within sight to lean on for support. Clutching her throbbing leg, she pulled herself up to sit on the rocks. She could barely put any weight on that leg, the pain was too much and she wanted to cry out, but her choked sounds were lost in the air. Her damp clothes were clinging to her skin and her mouth was dry, but ahead she was sure she could hear voices, horses, and maybe the creak of wheels. Whoever they were, she hoped they would not harm a girl, whatever condition she was in. She could only crawl forward, dragging her injured leg, another few feet and then another few more; she must reach them, she pleaded to the sky. They seemed a little nearer – or was she dreaming? – when she sank to the ground unable to move any more, the pain in her leg too much to endure.

Hallucinations played tricks in her mind, and she could not distinguish the confused, fuzzy shapes which appeared and then just faded away. At some point she was aware of being in a bumpy cart surrounded by straw, the cart probably taking her even further away from Aunt Theodora, she concluded. Then she stirred once more, and this time she imagined herself wrapped in a thick blanket in a comfortable padded carriage. Real or not, nothing mattered any more. She did not want to think. If she just closed her eyes, all the hallucinations and pain would end.

CHAPTER THREE

Corinna floated gently on a wonderful soft world of clouds supporting her body. A warm calmness spread through her, and she felt relaxed and at peace. Maybe she was heaven, in which case she decided she quite liked it; it was pleasant, she was safe here. But then a sharp pain interrupted this tranquil repose, convincing her otherwise. The pain began to return in irregular spasms, together with a blurring light which drifted back and forth.

The disjointed and confused moments continued as she slowly became aware of other sensations; the gentle touch of a hand on her skin, the tending to her wounds, the sound of a voice, kind and soothing, and the consuming softness of a bed which comfortably cradled her injured frame. These combined to bring about a gradual focusing until Corinna eventually woke.

It seemed like that she really was in heaven, as she stared at the subtle decoration of this quiet, beautiful sunlit room, softer and less cluttered, with dazzling pale silk furnishings, indicating the understated, simpler quality of the house. She did not understand what miracle had brought her here, when she could have been taken anywhere, left at some institution or workhouse, destitute and abandoned. Instead fate had been kind, and for the moment these surroundings gave her comfort enough to let her sleep again.

As for the passing days, they could only be measured by the conversations which passed her room.

"Why has he sent this baggage here to be looked after? What has got into him, I do not know! Has the army addled his brain? No good will come of this kindness," a woman complained.

"Now mother, Etienne has every right to put what demands he likes on his own household. It is his house after all," a male voice answered.

"Then why doesn't he spend more time here?"

A discreet clearance of the throat was followed by a laugh.

"His career. Too many females. And maybe he can't stand the fuss you make of him?"

"Let alone the continual bickering between you and your sister," the woman grumbled back.

The other voice laughed again and the pair of them walked away, leaving Corinna to once more savour the magical environment she found herself in. She had almost dropped off to sleep again, for rest was her only way to recover, when fresh voices sounded from beyond the door. At which she lay still and closed her eyes, as had become her habit.

"No, Etienne. No!" she recognised the woman's voice from earlier.

"Now aunt, I haven't much time. I must join Lietner. How is she progressing?"

"Tolerably slow. Really Etienne, what possessed you to have her sent here? Why bring her halfway across Austria? You are irresponsible!"

"Why aunt, I knew you would be compassionate enough to look after her. Besides we made enquiries, no one in the area knew her. She was obviously lost. Would you prefer I left her in the road to die?" he teased.

"What about the inconvenience?" she complained.

"I could not just abandon her. Now let me in, or I will think you have done away with her."

The door opened and Corinna half opened her eyes, curious to see this man who had saved her, but a quite roundly-built older woman stood in the doorway with her back to her, blocking the view. All she could see was the top of his very dark hair.

"This is a respectable household and I will not have you gad about here in your army ways" she was telling him. "You placed her in my charge, she is my responsibility and I will not have you swanning in and out of there just as you please." Her hand was firmly on the doorknob, refusing to give way.

"Aunt, you forget whose home this is. I will not be kept from anywhere in it I choose to go." The man's tone had hardened.

"You may be master here, Etienne Metzger, but there will be no hint of impropriety by this mad deed of yours! Go back and play soldiers and save us from your further acts of charity" the woman declared, as she straightened herself in defiance.

The man gave an exasperated sigh and turned on his heel, leaving his aunt to close the door and follow his departure.

Etienne! So this was the name of the man who had saved her, who had been so kind. The very sound of it purred in her head, but – it turned out that he was in the army! Had he recognised the uniform? Her hero could yet prove to be her enemy. Corinna panicked and closed her eyes tight, the safest recourse for the moment being to pretend sleep.

All Corinna could think of was that her host, however kind, was a threat. As a soldier there was every possibility he might recognise the cadet jacket she had been wearing. And if not now, he might later. Although not incriminating enough on its own, if the jacket became linked to Max's desertion, it would inevitably mean questions. The uniform had been in a terrible condition. Maybe it would not have been recognisable, maybe it had been destroyed. Maybe she was worrying about nothing. How would she know?

Nevertheless she was taking no chances, preferring to remained mute, her dull expressionless eyes conveying a solemn blankness in response to their encouraging gestures. In fact her limp, unreceptive response was barely a sham. She was weak and her leg ached and throbbed nearly the whole time. She preferred to be left alone. Even the doctor conveniently assumed it was best left to nature to take its course, and the household staff merely whispered or cast a pitiful glance in the direction of their invalid guest.

Her safety relied on her silence, and with this firmly fixed in her mind, she concentrated upon the snippets of overheard conversation, to find out more about these people. So far Corinna had learnt that the Metzger family consisted of Sophie, her two children, Frederick and Charlotte, and Etienne, the owner of the property, who apparently would soon be away again.

Later, after her tray had been removed and the door absently left ajar, the first serious after-dinner conversation drifted upwards as two people crossed the hallway below.

"The girl cannot even walk yet. Is she to stay up there indefinitely?" Sophie complained.

There was a long pause as Corinna listened intently. She

could not hear any reply, so she assumed thankfully that no plans had been made on her behalf as yet.

"She is free to leave when she is better. Then she can go back to where ever she belongs," the man replied.

"If she wants to go back! You said yourself she could have run away from anywhere. She has not spoken a word to anyone yet. If you cannot trace where she came from, then what will you do?"

Again there was no answer, although Corinna naturally worried about what he had in mind.

"We are not a charity for waifs and strays, Etienne. Goodness, you will have the house turned into a hospital for the rest of your men at this rate."

"Do whatever you think best, aunt, I don't care," he snapped.

"You are the limit! You never think of the consequences to your kindness!" Sophie's voice exploded. The doors below slammed shut and the debate concerning Corinna's welfare came to an abrupt end.

Corinna lay there thinking. So far there had been no indications that this man or the family had shown any immediate concern about finding anything out about her, but how long would that last? Somehow she must get out of here before they started to make serious enquiries about her, for while Etienne, with his military background, remained in residence, she felt at risk. Therefore the announcement of his return to army headquarters a short time later, came as a very welcome relief to her. At least she had a little more time.

The solution to leave was obvious, for every day, little by little she was improving and every day it became more difficult to hold her tongue. Yet she had no idea of her location or how long she had been there and she could not very well ask.

This house was in the countryside and the gentle green slopes from the window gave no indication of anything else. 'Half way across the country' Sophie had said. Corinna tried to remember the map of Austria; her geography lessons had never been so important as now. Innsbrück and the Tyrol were to the west, Vienna was on the furthest eastern side of the country. Yes she had that right. The middle was all mountains, with the gentler slopes to the northern or to the southern parts; that was all she knew. She shivered slightly, as the one awful possibility filled her with horror, that this house was close to Salzburg, because Salzburg was too near Gmunden and her awful father. Please no!

What was she to do? If she didn't know where she was, how would she know which direction she should take? And who would help her once she had left? She had no one to turn to. She sighed, desperate for Aunt Theodora herself. She missed her, but having behaved so badly Corinna knew she could not go back, however much she wanted to. If only she had simply done as Max had asked and nothing more, it would have been all right. She had been so stupid. She even wondered if she had helped Max at all. He might have avoided being seen altogether on his journey to her, yet by wearing his uniform she could have inadvertently placed him in that area after all. She could have made it worse, although whatever they suspected, it was surely too late to make a difference. No, it didn't matter, they would not catch him. He would have reached Germany by now, Corinna comforted herself.

In accordance with the latest routine, Corinna sat by the window, settled comfortably with a mass of cushions plumped around her and a rug over her lap.

"If she is to sit out of bed, then she should be properly dressed," she heard Sophie instruct.

"Mother! That doesn't meant she has to have some of my things. Why can't she have some of the servant's clothes to wear?" came a young girl's raised voice beyond the door.

"Charlotte, she is more of your size. Don't be so selfish, the poor girl has nothing. You have plenty of clothes you do not wear any more."

"Well she can't have anything too pretty!"

A male laughed, before interrupting, "Everything you have is pretty! Even your old cast-offs."

"Go away, Frederick. This has nothing to do with you!" the girl snapped as all of them retreated along the landing.

Corinna could hardly believe she was being given good, serviceable clothes, ideal for her purpose, even shoes, comfortable shoes which would help in her departure. While she continued her deception during the day, at night she secretly prepared for her intended journey. Each night she walked further and further, across the room, the corridors and then the stairs. Up and down, and round and round the various hallways she went, as many times as she could, occasionally peeking into the rooms, until she practically knew the layout of the house by heart.

Impatiently she waited for the prearranged outing to the village festival which had been widely announced throughout the house for some time. The day duly came when most of the occupants, both family members and the staff, were absent from the house, allowing her to limp her way undetected through the building.

She hesitated as she opened the front door. The space beyond looked deserted, almost too deserted, and everywhere suspiciously quiet. Don't stop, she told herself. She had to do this, right now, and she carefully pulled the door closed behind her. Now what? She still had no idea where to go or what she would do. Just follow the road and see what happened. She had to! She could not stay where the owner's military connections were a possible danger to her and Max.

Her footsteps echoed on the stone steps from the front door, and the gravel on the drive crunched noisily despite her extra care to walk as softly as she could.

"You are surely not running away from us, are you?" came a mocking voice.

Corinna spun around at the sound, at first seeing nothing in the shadows of the porch from where the voice came. Then she saw a figure leaning casually against one of the columns and making no move towards her.

"Well, well, you are a surprise package. After all that has been done for you, I would have expected something better from you. This is certainly no sign of gratitude for my kindness."

She was caught. Corinna found herself frozen to the spot, aware that she now found herself facing an indignant host who sounded as if he had every cause to detain her. She chewed her lip and looked to the ground; she could not answer, dare not speak, even now.

"No explanation, no denial? You still will not speak, will you?" he prompted.

His natural movement forward made her back away sharply and then stop just as suddenly when the sunlight revealed the full features of the man. Her eyes flashed wide and her mouth dropped open, for this was the last person on earth she expected to come face to face with. She recognised him. This was the man she remembered from the hotel terrace, the same handsome stranger she had admired so long ago in Gmunden. The one she had worshipped that day, with those striking features and the thick dark hair which curled at the neck. Now close up she saw his haunting beautiful eyes and his subtle smile. It was not fair, he was too handsome for words. How had this happened?

"Tell me your name at least," he asked kindly.

She only stared. There was no mistake. It was really him, she remembered every detail, but worse now were her new fears. How often had he been to Gmunden? Did he know people there, and more importantly, was he acquainted with her father? He was too close. And why did he still smile?

"I wondered how long it would be before you made your move. Your nightly excursions and performance have been a revelation. It was a pleasant diversion to my sleepless hours, watching your secret activity." He was grinning. "You obviously have plans of your own. Where are you going?"

How could he have guessed her intentions, when she had not been aware he was even in residence? She clenched her fingers tighter and tighter, while her eyes searched for escape. Her plans were in jeopardy. She had stood too long, the world was greying around her, and she felt herself beginning to sway. The instant he moved to help her, she recovered herself and instinctively reeled back from him.

"Why do you cower from me? That is not the usual reaction I receive from the other ladies of my acquaintance" he remarked, smiling again.

In any other circumstances Corinna would have liked to speak, but it was too late as he gathered her into his arms and carried her back inside the house, up the stairs and into her room.

"You are not strong enough to go off gallivanting just yet" he commanded flatly, before sitting her down at the little desk by the window. "Now wait there a minute."

She could not imagine what he was going to do. He disappeared briefly and then returned with a writing slope. He sat it in front of her, placed paper on top and dipped a pen in the ink, offering it to her.

"Is there anyone you would like to write to? You must have family who are worried about you."

She shook her head.

"Your name then," he asked, still holding the pen out to her. She shook her head again.

He put the pen down and stood back.

"Still afraid. I wish I knew what of. No one here will hurt you."

She looked at the floor, rather than at him, and all she could hear was his breathing as he waited, and waited, until he gave up and took the slope away and left the room. He did not return.

Strangely there were no repercussions from her attempt to run away. No one mentioned it, and everything carried on exactly as before. No one seemed to know about their short encounter. She did not understand. So for the time being she remained in her room, not even daring to continue her nightly exercise. She could only imagine he was waiting to see what she would do next, until she discovered that the next day he had gone again.

A few days later, there were the sounds of unusual disturbance at the front door, and Sophie hurried downstairs to find the cause. The exchange of voices became more exaggerated and flustered at the moments passed.

"Is she here?" came the sound of a man's voice.

Corinna's heart sank. Her father? No, it wasn't his voice. She feared the worst; she had been found out, the military authorities had arrived to question her. There was a flurrying of light steps, and the sound of a man's heavy boots rushing up the stairs. She was trapped. She was in no fit state to run anywhere and she had nowhere to hide.

The door flew open and an elderly, well-built man with a thick grey and white curly beard appeared, his jolly face beaming as he rushed forward to sweep her into his enormous chest to hug her affectionately. At which Corinna stiffened, instinctively defensive of this display of affection from a complete stranger.

"Oh my dear, I am sorry," he sighed, taking a step back, "I did not mean to startle you. I forgot, you have no idea who I am. I am your Uncle Michael, your mother Theresa's brother. We have never met before, but that is your father's fault, a long story for another time. Oh Corinna. My dear. You are safe, thank goodness! We have been searching everywhere."

We? Who was 'we'? she wondered silently. Her answer came in the next breath.

"Theodora, not one to flap in a crisis, has been frantically organising everyone to search for you and she began to think the worst had happened to you. It was only through a casual remark in the village near to where your horse was found that we learned of your injuries and subsequent rescue. Theodora wrote to me immediately once she had found out where you had been taken. In the whole of Austria, it is hard to believe that you have landed right on my doorstep."

The rush of words had swept over her, without her being able to take them all in.

"I must send word instantly to Theodora. She will be so relieved. She blames herself for your disappearance, convinced that your father's letter demanding you return to Gmunden made you run away."

Corinna remembered her aunt raging about the latest letter from her father, prior to her departure, but she had not known the contents. At least this reason for running away seemed an easier story to admit to, rather than divulge the truth.

"Theodora would never have let you go back to your father, whatever you may have thought."

Corinna nodded, of course not. She was such a wonderful person. She found she was crying. "She will never forgive me!" she whispered.

"Nonsense, my dear. The world is not as black as you think." he chuckled at this last phrase.

"Now enough of my chatter, we shall have plenty of time to talk later. Oh Corinna, Corinna! I am so pleased to have found you. I would have recognised you anywhere, you are so like your mother. The same small features, those pretty eyes. As soon as you are able to travel, you shall come to stay with me. I assure you I have Theodora's consent to look after you."

His deep, warm voice felt like a comfortable blanket being wrapped around her, dispersing any worries she had, and when he spontaneously bent down to kiss the top of her head, she felt her heart would burst. What had she done to deserve such a dramatic reversal of fortune, once again? It could not be real. It was hard to comprehend that the endless unconditional affection she had received from her aunt was about to be repeated by another relation. Dare she hope everything was going to be all right?

"But how did you find me?" she whispered.

"Etienne, soldier or not, would not be callous enough to bring you here without leaving word as to where exactly you could be located. An army unit, always on the move, did not have time to find out where you belonged. I am so grateful that he found you and arranged to send you to Sophie."

Her uncle was astonished that she had been so close during all these weeks of uncertainty, but declared he was immensely pleased that she owed her recovery to his old family friends the Metzgers. Suddenly Corinna realised that this could be an awkward situation.

"Uncle, I did not know where I was. I refused to tell them who I was, in case they sent me back to Gmunden. They will be angry at my lack of manners."

"You were frightened. There is no disgrace in making a mistake, I shall explain."

He made it sound such a simple matter to excuse, and somehow she trusted him to manage anything.

Sophie had understood instantly and forgave Corinna's behaviour easily, being so pleased to find that she was a relation to Michael, one of her oldest friends. Indeed from then on, Sophie would often pop into her room to chat away about just anything, in an effort to make Corinna feel relaxed and secure in her surroundings. She also looked forward to having Corinna as a neighbour and insisted she should come to visit them as soon as she wanted, once she was settled with her uncle.

Thus, barely a week later Corinna was snugly installed into her uncle's lodge, where the charm of this sturdy, comfortable masculine domain far exceeded her every expectation. Although small, it was ideal for a well-travelled bachelor and all his belongings, and it had enough rooms to house them both. As for her uncle, she never felt so at ease or relaxed as she did in his company. Day by day she was getting stronger; the fresh air, the wholesome food and the walks with her uncle to lean on were exactly what she needed. The idyllic rural atmosphere and much less formal country ways were a whole new experience, to which she easily adapted. With only a part-time housekeeper to help around the lodge house, she looked forward to her errands into the village, the friendly familiarity of the locals and the normal chores expected of her.

The correspondence between Uncle Michael and Aunt Theodora resulted in a mutual agreement for her to stay snugly cocooned there for the present. Theodora saw no disgrace in Corinna's previous actions; in fact it gave the girl more character, in her opinion, and she welcomed the prospect of her eventual return to show the rest of Innsbrück society precisely how proud she was of her protégée. Life was suddenly wonderful once more.

Returning from the village after being delayed as usual by her talking, Corinna headed the pony and trap up the last turn in the lane and was surprised to see a horse tethered beneath the front steps of the lodge. Inquisitive, she burst into the hallway to listen for voices, only to be disappointed to hear only muffled sounds from behind the study door. Undeterred, she ran to the kitchen to interrupt Martha, who was in the middle of preparing the vegetables.

"Who is in with my uncle?" she asked tugging at her sleeve.

"I thought you were going to be back in time to help me. Now move that basket off the table, Corinna. I don't have enough room as it is."

Corinna removed the offending basket, to Martha's nodding approval.

"Who is with my uncle?" she repeated.

"Gracious, child! The neighbour, Metzger," Martha mumbled.

Etienne Metzger, Etienne! Heavens, why had he called?

Now he knew about her, what would he think of her? With her uncle as an old family friend, there was every possibility he would not think that badly of her at all and she hoped he would be gracious enough to forgive her previous conduct without too much animosity. Goodness, they might even become well acquainted. Wouldn't that be wonderful, to have such a handsome neighbour coming to call!

But first, convention demanded that she should personally thank this man for saving her, and it was important to give a good impression. Her heart leapt, she was all of a dither. She rushed into the hall, Martha's voice trailing off behind her. She glanced at her clothes and ran upstairs to change into her prettiest blouse and tidy her hair, and then ran back in case Etienne left too soon. At the foot of the stairs she checked her appearance in the mirror again. She did not look her best in borrowed clothes, but collecting her composure, she took a deep breath and walked slowly down the hall.

"What are you hanging around there for?" Martha asked from the kitchen.

Corinna merely shrugged and continued her nervous pacing near the door, eventually sitting down to wait in the hallway. Steps sounded near the door and she jumped up, brushing and straightening her skirt, fingering the stray wisps of hair back from her face. She stood squarely facing the door for full affect, erect and far from brave, hoping he would be as handsome as she remembered. Then at the very moment the door opened, she found she dare not look him in the face and quickly she diverted her eyes to the floor.

"Ah, Corinna. Good. I was about to come in search of you," her uncle began, tucking his arm around her shoulders and cuddling her again, as was one of his habits whenever she returned. Corinna saw the shining boots and slowly lifted her head to look at the thickest mop of blond hair and the clearest of blue eyes she had ever seen. Open-mouthed she stared, struck dumb like some idiot. This was not the dark-headed Etienne she expected to see; it was not the right person at all who stood there.

"I see I had better introduce you both properly to each other. Frederick, this is my niece Corinna. Corinna, this is Frederick Metzger."

She bobbed a polite curtsey to his smart bow. Frederick was of a similar age to herself. She had watched him and his sister Charlotte antagonise each other, although she had never seen him up close before. He gave her a friendly grin and she responded in a similar manner.

Intending to write a quick note to Sophie for Frederick to take it back with him, Michael disappeared, leaving Corinna alone with their guest. Awkwardly she stood in the middle of the room, not knowing quite what to say or what he knew, whilst Frederick, on the other hand, seemed perfectly at ease.

"Gosh Corinna, Mama told me all about your adventure. I do wish I had your courage. What spunk! I do hope we can become good friends, now we are neighbours." Frederick chatted on, his mischievous eyes reflected his enthusiasm and leaning forward confided. "I think you are marvellous. We are going to have so much fun. Charlotte is no sport at all. Oh, she is going to be so jealous. Serves her right!"

Then Frederick laughed, an infectious laugh which made her giggle as well, without knowing what they were laughing at. This younger Metzger was nothing like she expected and her initial disappointment gone, she was pleased that at least one of them was ready to be her friend. The first hurdle was over.

"I can't wait to tell Etienne. He will be so surprised."

Etienne! Corinna could well imagine his reaction to the news.

"Don't you dare go teasing your older cousin. He has had enough to contend with over the last few years. You forget the war has left him battle weary, although he may not admit it. Show him a little consideration, let him have some peace. I think you had better leave Etienne to me or your mother."

Michael had entered the room again, and now he interrupted. I don't want Corinna's position here jeopardised by you making Etienne angry."

Frederick turned to beam at her, promising to be good, although he couldn't promise the same for his sister. But as recompense he was willing to take her riding whenever she wanted, to prove himself her friend, and she willingly smiled her silent acceptance.

Late autumn had arrived and in the evenings by a roaring fire, Uncle Michael entertained her with stories. There at his side she learnt about the villagers, his own childhood and travels, his mementos, her mother's visits and even the Metzgers.

It seemed the Metzger family had always lived across the valley. The eldest son, Gerard, had naturally inherited the house amongst other properties before giving the family home to Etienne years ago, when he moved to Vienna. Then Sophie, the widow of their father's younger brother, and her two children had come to live there, a convenient arrangement, since Etienne had his army commitments to attend to.

Corinna hung on to every word about Etienne, learning all about his early short tragic marriage to Eva, his subsequent army career as a captain and his long friendship with Lieutenant

Lietner, a fellow officer. Corinna sighed, wondering when she would see Etienne again. Would they ever become more than properly acquainted? She could only dream. Although in her heart she knew it to be a useless dream and one she could not afford, since he would always remain the one most capable of discovering the truth. The one to ruin her position here.

Autumn and winter also brought their own surprises, both unexpected and in stark contrast. The first came when a cart arrived at the front door to deliver a small trunk for her. The carrier, muffled against the weather and impatient to be back home, departed with little conversation and few clues to its contents or sender. A baffled Corinna instantly snapped open the clasps and threw back the lid. Inside she found a letter from Aunt Theodora placed prominently on top of the folds of material. She knew the writing and nervously opened it, quickly scanning the contents. Her dear aunt had not only sent some of her lovely dresses to her, but the most treasured item of all, her mother's precious wooden carved jewellery box.

She nearly wept for joy. Immediately she delved deep into the layers of clothes, tossing the carefully-arranged garments aside, to find her box safely hidden in the centre. A lump swelled in her throat as she lovingly fingered its surface and hugged it tight to her chest. This was the best present of all. Nothing could be more perfect.

Besides this, she had two guardians to watch over her, plus a whole new range of friends, including Etienne's warm-hearted widowed aunt Sophie, who adored her, and Frederick her son, who had become a regular visitor to the lodge. Predictably, Frederick's sister Charlotte was the only one who remained truculent, refusing any sign of acknowledgement or friendship; not that Corinna minded one minor hiccup in her present happiness.

Corinna's next surprise, however, was less pleasant. Her eldest brother Leopold's arrival sent shudders down her spine. He was the image of their father, and he made no bones about the reason for his visit, explaining this was no social call. He did not understand how Theodora could sanction this arrangement of allowing Corinna to be harboured under Michael's roof, of all people. Especially, he continued, after what had happened here before with Theresa, as a result of Michael's treacherous encouragement.

Corinna gasped, fearful of whatever complicity Michael was being accused of. What had her Uncle Michael done? She refused to believe anything bad of him.

"This was Theresa's only place of refuge from your father's tyranny and Corinna shall have the same protection" Michael interrupted sharply. "I shall provide all the love and affection you failed to give her in Gmunden."

His deep voice boomed out, send his rich tones echoing around the room and drowning Leopold's words under his own angry retort. Michael drew Corinna to his side, put an arm firmly about her and squeezed her hands gently in his. Corinna relaxed. So this was behind the rift with her father, the reason why they had never been allowed to communicate with him. There was nothing to worry about; her dear uncle Michael remained her protection and was her strength.

They had both expected Leopold to leave after being put in his place, but he remained looking from one to the other, clearly displeased by their unity.

"There is something else?" Michael enquired.

Leopold nodded solemnly and Corinna knew in that instant before he spoke what was coming – Max! After all this time, she had to face the truth. Realistically the news about his flight would have had to come out eventually, although she hoped that was all.

"Maximillian," he began.

"Is he well? When will he be allowed to come to visit?" Corinna gushed excitedly.

"He has disappeared" he finished, focusing his attention on her.

"What do you mean, disappeared? How?" she demanded angrily.

Leopold kept up his intense study of her as he told her that Maximillian had run away from the Cadet Academy in Vienna. He was wanted by the military authorities for absconding and they were still searching for him.

Corinna was prepared. She was full of questions and concern; when had he gone? Why had he gone? What had happened to him? What were the family going to do to help him?

"Help him? Father has disowned him!" her brother snorted.

Corinna stared at him. Poor Max, they could not mean to just abandon him, could they? But she knew full well that that would be their precise attitude. They were heartless and mean – all of them.

Apparently Max's flight was common knowledge in the family, not that they were likely to publicise the shame of it. The authorities had been to Gmunden and at their father's suggestion, even to Innsbrück, to see if Max had been there to see her. Trust her father to support the military rather than his own son! She hated him even more now. The only thing that made her smile was the account of the response they had received from her aunt, who had sent them packing in a very short time.

"A very convincing act, Corinna, but have you heard from him?" Leopold demanded.

She looked shocked, but wondered if her guilt could be read in her face.

"That is enough, Leopold. I will not have you bullying Corinna" Michael declared.

"Did you see him before you left Aunt Theodora?" Leopold continued, refusing to be swayed.

"How could she? I think the facts speak for themselves" her uncle answered for her.

Michael gave her hand a little squeeze of reassurance and then continued his own defence of her brother, insisting that this was all their own fault, since they were to blame in the first place for sending Max away to such a harsh environment. To which he added that their family should not expect help from anyone here, in harassing another of their father's victims.

"Poor boy. Disappeared, has he? Good for him!" her uncle exclaimed proudly. Leopold cleared his throat in defence.

"If the authorities haven't found him by now, he must be safely out of reach, otherwise none of you would be clutching at straws" Michael concluded merrily.

Seconds later, their guest was ushered abruptly from the lodge. Once gone, Corinna melted into Michael's strong supportive arms, suddenly weak, her nervous energy spent. She was not as brave as she pretended.

"My dear, there is nothing to worry about. Such stories do not usually reach these parts of the country and would mean nothing in this isolated area anyway. And I for one will not be mentioning it to anyone."

"Max isn't bad" she insisted amid the large gulping sobs which overcame her. Her lip trembling, she wiped away the last trickle with the back of her hand. This incident was bound make Michael wonder if her running away was connected to her brother's vanishing act. She hung her head; she did not want to lie. It must be obvious she had seen him before she left her aunt's home and she waited for him to ask, yet he did not. He simply comforted her, telling her she had done nothing wrong. Nothing wrong! Except deceive everyone.

Surprisingly, as the weeks passed, everything continued as normal and the rumours and speculation never occurred. Her life continued in its pleasant manner and Corinna stopped worrying about what other people might be thinking. Frederick continued to take her riding, whilst in exchange she taught him to dance properly, both of these activities to the annoyance of Charlotte. On the practical side, Corinna set to making the necessary alterations to the warm and practical inter clothes she happily accepted from Adela, Martha's daughter, who had outgrown them. She embroidered a beautiful waistcoat for her uncle, learned to cook with Martha and joined Adela dancing in the village. The traditional regional folk dancing was like nothing she had ever experienced before, but it was exhilarating and she loved it. Here, with no pretence to keep up, no restrictions and no responsibilities, she enjoyed her unchaperoned solitary walks, exploring the woods, the freedom to skip or run or twirl around, whenever she felt like it. She would laugh and sing and listen to the birds on her journey. This was another new kind of happiness.

Her familiar smile was still evident on her way back to the lodge from Adela's cottage and she could not help singing the last tune she had heard being played there. Even the message from Frederick about Etienne's unexpected arrival home yesterday had not made any difference to her contented mood.

"So Miss, you have found your voice at last." came a voice from nowhere. A voice she recognised instantly.

"I admit I am surprised at what has been happening in my absence" said Etienne. "You have found a new home, Sophie has fallen under your spell and Frederick shows every sign of being bewitched by you."

Corinna wanted to say so much; she wanted to thank him, to explain, but felt tongue-tied.

"I presume you are not going to run away again, are we?" he almost laughed.

"Run away? Why should I?" she stuttered.

"You ran away from your aunts, by all accounts."

The way he spoke, he sounded as if he did not believe the story. Corinna had not been prepared for such a direct challenge, nor the familiarity with which Etienne strode along beside her to escort her home. Her natural chattering had deserted her and she was far from confident or calm as she reached the front door.

"If you would care to come in?" Corinna offered, with a small bobbed curtsey. Etienne purposefully strode in through the front door of the lodge without any polite response. Astonished and indignant at his lack of manners, she indicated for him to sit, only to be met with a brisk refusal, forcing her to remain standing herself, as they faced each other.

"I have been waiting for the chance to, er, thank you for helping me," Corinna began.

He ignored her attempted politeness. "I was intrigued, I knew you must belong somewhere in society, especially with such expensive hand-made riding boots. To be found in the middle of nowhere, in that state, does not happen every day."

Corinna clutched at the furniture in front of her for support and waited, but he did not mention the uniform jacket. She could only wonder what he knew – if he knew anything. Her mind raced in preparation for any accusations. She held her breath while Etienne smirked, satisfaction gleaming on his face. He began to prowl the room, stopping only to look at her directly when he spoke.

"I have no doubt you are Herr Holbach's niece, but what else are you? You are no innocent little runaway from Innsbrück society, afraid of being sent back to your father."

She gulped. He knew so much already, but what else?

"What were you up to? If I didn't know better, I would suggest it bears the marks of some secret romantic entanglement or a failed elopement, although I expect you will never admit to either."

So that was what he thought! She felt safe. She slid into the nearest chair and had to hide a smile. She had almost stopped listening to him, pleasantly pleased at his mistake.

"Am I mistaken?"

"You surely do not expect me to answer," she smiled coyly.

"You play the lady well enough" he admitted curtly, his narrowed eyes retaining the glimmer of suspicion. This was no compliment, and she knew it.

"I hope I will always behave properly" she continued sweetly, prepared to match his tone.

"Mmmm. Your recent scandalous little adventure does not support that claim" he purred.

Then as he hesitated to continue, her Uncle Michael entered the room, busy, bustling and completely oblivious of the tension between them.

"At last, Etienne! I have waited impatiently for my chance

to thank you personally for saving my darling niece" Michael gushed, making a great fuss of Etienne and grabbing his hand warmly.

Bubbling over with enthusiasm, he overwhelmed Etienne with tireless conversation, all about Corinna. Etienne's eyes were on her all the time and Corinna enjoyed his predicament as he was forced to listen to her uncle.

"My dear Etienne, It is an extraordinary coincidence after all. This painting is of her mother, my sister. I don't expect you would remember her very well. See how alike they are" he purred, indicating the portrait on the wall and drawing Corinna to stand beside it. Reluctantly Etienne glanced at the portrait and back at her, forced to acknowledge the truth of her uncle's observation.

"Theresa loved coming here" Michael sighed.

"Theresa… Schopenhauer" Etienne muttered, almost to himself, as she easily read his lips.

Etienne made no further comment and swiftly made his excuses to leave, although Corinna feared the discovery of her actual surname was now ringing very loud alarm bells in his memory. He was bound to be curious.

"Was Etienne well acquainted with my mother?" she asked Michael, hoping that any consideration for valued family friends might make a difference to any actions on his part. Michael looked quite surprised at the suggestion.

"No, not at all. He might have met her when she was visiting here. It was Gerard, his elder brother, who became her friend. Quite a good friend," he sighed wistfully.

Oh well, that was another theory crushed, Corinna concluded. She would just have to wait to see if Etienne would yet be her downfall.

CHAPTER FOUR

As it was, Etienne did nothing at all to challenge or worry her as the weeks passed. Although still at home, he did not enter her company, and Corinna gradually accepted that her fears were probably groundless. He was absent on and off during the winter and now Frederick reported that he had gone with his friend Lietner to visit his brother Gerard. Apparently his brother's bad health and recent letters were of great concern. Meanwhile, he declared, as he sat with her at the lodge on another visit, his dear mama had been busy arranging her own social calendar for the year, which included her latest idea of hosting a soirée in the next few weeks.

Frederick grinned and slipped the envelope from his pocket, waving it teasingly in the air, while Corinna gasped and flung herself at it. A proper printed social invitation with her name written on it! She was effervescent, overjoyed and delighted, because she meant to look her best. The elegant ball gown included in the chest of clothes from her aunt would still be the finest they had ever seen in these parts. Corinna's eyes sparkled.

Michael turned her round and round as she paraded in her dress, commenting that it was wasted here and should be gracing the palaces of Vienna. Corinna laughed. She did not want Vienna or any glittering capital, all she wanted was for Etienne to admire her just once before he dismissed her totally from his association.

"The dress is beautiful, except it lacks the finishing touch" he teased. He had only recently presented her with a fringed silk shawl to match the gown, so Corinna was mystified, because she knew the dress was perfect.

"A piece of your mother's jewellery would complement it" he explained, tweaking her chin. "The little necklace of blue and white stones will do perfectly. I bought it for her years ago, so I know it will suit you." He patted her hand knowingly.

Corinna went to fetch the carved wooden box from her room and she sat showing him all her treasures, each in turn, including the necklace he had remembered.

"Where is the gold and enamel brooch?" he asked. "It was a gift on her last visit here, she set such store by it." A puzzled expression lingered on his face as he looked in the box again, hoping to find it. Then he slowly closed the lid and gave a little shrug of disappointment.

"I am not sure," Corinna answered thoughtfully. How could she say she had given it to Max? She could only hope her uncle would believe it was lost.

Sophie had been kind enough to send a carriage for them, refusing to let them spoil their clothes on such an occasion. Her silk dress rustled as Corinna fidgeted expectantly during the short journey to the Metzger house, her spirits soaring and her dark brown eyes shining at the prospect of the evening ahead. The softness of the silk shawl arrayed about her shoulders, in this lovely gown and with her hair in the style which suited her best, she knew how pretty she looked. She had also regained that special air of elegance she had acquired before in Innsbrück. She could not fail to impress her hosts and especially Etienne.

Politely she bobbed a curtsey to his smart bow in the entrance. Although he took her gloved hand briefly, his lack of a compliment made her realised that she should have known better than to expect anything from that quarter. Frederick, on the other hand, made it all worthwhile, barely allowing her minutes to dwell on her disappointment before he whisked her away to the small ballroom. There, transported into that other world, she laughed and twirled the hours away. On and on she glided about the floor, so light on her feet, loving every minute. While she had never expected Etienne to ask her for a dance, his friend, Lieutenant Lietner, who had been introduced to her earlier, had done so several times. He had proved to be a very fine accomplished dancer, making her evening even more enjoyable.

"I am delighted to see you are so well recovered," he told her.

She blushed. Of course he would have been with Etienne when she was found.

"May I call you Corinna?"

"If you allow me to address you as something other than Lieutenant or Herr Lietner."

He laughed. "I hate my first name. It is never used. I would prefer you just call me Lietner, everyone else does, even my own family."

She looked surprised, but pleased to share a confidence, she accepted his request.

"Then Lietner it is."

She had been the perfect young lady and she was convinced her polite performance of social graces would be noticed eventually by Etienne. As it was.

"I regret my duties as host have deprived you of my attention. Am I forgiven?" he commented at the end of the evening. Her heart almost missed a beat. She nodded, not forgiving the man who had captivated her heart with his handsome looks, not grasp at this opportunity to improve their tentative acquaintance.

"I am sure you enjoyed yourself this evening" he murmured softly, and actually grinned. His manner remained mild and light-hearted, his voice kind and his whole demeanour affable. It left her in awe of him as he personally escorted her back to the carriage.

Etienne's conduct was to continue to surprise her even more, since he now frequently began to join the family during her visits at his home. At the end of their afternoon refreshment, he would slide into the chair opposite her and pour himself the last cup from the pot. He enquired casually what Innsbrück was like and her aunt's home, to which she proudly expounded with great enthusiasm descriptions of all the marvellous theatres, concert halls and gardens, beautiful buildings and large squares. She found herself chatting away as naturally as if he had been her friend for ages, his slight smile and interest encouraging her.

"I was surprised to learn recently, from the carrier of all people, that one of your brothers had come from Gmunden to visit you. You seem to have family all over Austria," he remarked as he leaned forward to replace his cup on the tray. Corinna gulped and nodded. Clearly he was waiting for more of a response, but she remained silent. He sighed a few times as if to prompt her, but when no answer came he rose slowly from the chair.

"A most interesting silence" he concluded softly to her ear, his sarcasm not unnoticed. With a slight bow of his head, he sauntered into the hall, his manner conveying the impression that their conversation had meant nothing except idle curiosity on his part. Yet Corinna felt uneasy at his mention of Gmunden, for it could hardly be a coincidence. He had been there before; she had seen him on the hotel terrace. She wondered if he had been there recently and what else he might have learnt about her family. Thrilled by his attention and in her eagerness to talk to him, she realised she could have so easily ended up admitting more than she should. She would have to be more careful.

Why was it that every time he seemed friendly, he said something to worry her? Privately she could not help wondering if he already knew the name of the missing cadet and had made the connection that Max Schopenhauer was her brother the moment he found out who her mother was.

To be honest, Corinna would have preferred to avoid the Metzger residence for a while, but her sudden absence might have aroused Etienne's curiosity, if not his suspicions. So she continued crossing the valley from the lodge to the Metzger house, carrying off her visits as normal. At least she had survived the winter and the rigours of its long cold spell with very little hardship, and soon she would be returning to Innsbrück and her Aunt Theodora.

With Etienne gone to see his ailing brother once more, Corinna relaxed; a few more weeks and she would be on her way as well. So she couldn't believe it when her uncle received and accepted an invitation from Etienne to spend a week in Graz with the Metzger family. Lietner and his sisters were included. Etienne had arranged a house for them and a small staff was engaged.

Corinna did not know what to make of it. A vacation with the Metzger family! Michael might be old friends with them, but that was no reason for them to be included. It was not as if they had ever done this before. It did not make sense. Her uncle thought it a marvellous idea and was so much in favour of it that he thought it worth putting off her intended stay with Aunt Theodora for another month.

"You don't understand, my dear" he explained. "I want to go to see my old professor friend, to reminisce and visit all the book and curio shops while we are there." He assured her it would be a great excuse for her to visit somewhere new. He had made up his mind; this vacation would benefit them all and he enthusiastically set about preparing for it. Besides, he teased, with her clothes more than adequate for Graz, she would keep her antagonist Charlotte on her metal.

Corinna smiled weakly, as if she had ever been bothered about Charlotte or what she thought of her. She did not want to go; she preferred to stay here, but she knew she was being selfish. How could she spoil her uncle's plans, after he had done so much for her? She would just have to make the best of it, for his sake.

Arriving at Graz, they found Etienne already in conversation with Lietner and his sisters. Smiling, he extracted himself temporarily from their custody to welcome them.

"This trip to Graz would not be the same without you with us," he told them warmly.

She could not believe it as he held her arm and gently squeezed her hand as he guided her the short distance to his friends, who also confirmed the delightful merits of sharing their company in Graz.

"I am pleased you came" Etienne added.

Corinna nodded, struck dumb at his few words echoing in her head, his bewitching voice and his eyes, which seemed to search hers. She blushed at his closeness and quickly smiled towards his other guests.

"So Corinna, do you think you will like Graz? Not as grand as Innsbrück, I expect, but tolerable enough for us all to enjoy ourselves," Lietner began.

"And something of an adventure too, since you have not ventured far afield since your arrival in our community," Etienne continued, keeping his attention focused on her.

Indeed Etienne and Lietner had contrived a fine selection of diversions to occupy them all, a blend of cultural and the less serious, suiting everyone's tastes, plus the traditional promenade of the parks and gardens to provide a sedate form of exercise. Everything had been allowed for and nothing left to chance. Corinna eagerly fell in with the unfolding programme, enjoying every new entertainment which came along as they explored the city. Her eyes were everywhere, thrilled with inquisitiveness and often stopping in mid-conversation or amid their progress to cause a sudden collision with those behind her as she stopped to read the many theatre posters they encountered. Even Frederick confessed his fascination as he dawdled with her, before they were both rebuked for delaying the group and forced to catch them up.

During one of their obligatory afternoon strolls, Frederick suddenly nudged Corinna, drawing her attention to the occupants of the adjacent pathway, where the leading lady from the play last night paraded herself, together with her excessive entourage of admirers, through the park. It was impossible to miss, and the more respectable pillars of society turned disdainfully aside as she approached. Her loud peals of laughter rang through the quiet avenues, interspersed with giggles and shrieks of pleasure as one or other of her retinue either flirted with her, flattered her or presented her with some token of their affection. The flamboyant Nadine was obviously the centre of attention everywhere she appeared.

Corinna, agog at the proceedings, could not resist having a closer look. She hissed at Frederick to come with her. Almost, running, she dragged him along the next path, declaring that no one would notice once they were hidden from the others by the tall hedging. The actress was strikingly dressed in oriental silks, a black silver threaded cloth twisted into a turban covered her head, one length dramatically thrown around and over her shoulder, to frame a wonderful face. Her big eyes fluttered from one suitor to another, never resting. They were magnificent, with long black lashes and brushed with bright theatrical make up. She flapped her fan at them or shook her shawl, her movements exaggerated and provocative to keep the undivided attention of her escorts.

Corinna had never seen anyone like her, and when the woman stopped momentarily across the flower bed in front of her, Corinna found herself staring straight back. The stranger smiled at her and Corinna returned the acknowledgement, immediately blushing at her own forwardness.

"And well you might colour, Corinna Schopenhauer, when I am sent to prevent such folly," Etienne commented loudly from behind her. "You look like a naughty child who does not have the slightest twinge of guilt at her behaviour."

Corinna grinned, not answering, and danced her way back to the others with light, skipping steps, displaying her natural enjoyment. This led her straight into an outburst from Charlotte for her undignified manner.

"You need not fear, Charlotte. Corinna will not show you up any further, she shall walk with me." After which Etienne slipped Corinna's arm through his and ushered her on past their little gathering, whispering to her as he did so. "And you, miss, will do well to accompany me if it's the only way to keep you out of trouble this afternoon. This imprudent side to your nature is not a characteristic to admire in a female, let alone a young lady. And you are supposed to be a young lady, while you are here."

She did not argue, her rueful grin widening to a smile in accepting his recommendation. She did not mind in the least having his undivided company and walked on, her head held high and her arm in his. Thus they continued, Corinna moving elegantly and sedately at Etienne's side as required of her new position at the head of their party. It was Etienne's turn to smile.

"I will never know what to make of you, Corinna. A wide-eyed country girl one moment and a sophisticated educated young lady the next!"

Corinna accepting his gentle teasing, happy enough at his brief attention. For an instant they had almost become friends. In fact by the time they had reached the waiting carriages, they were well ahead of the rest and found somewhat unexpectedly that their arrival coincided with the return of the actress and her party to their coaches. Etienne cleared his throat and pulled Corinna smartly to one side, as they were about to be engulfed by her followers.

"I think it would be prudent for our own safety, Corinna Schopenhauer, for us to enter the carriage until the others catch us up," he remarked curtly, displaying his disapproval more for the benefit of those close by than for Corinna. His displeasure had an immediate effect, as the people closest to them parted, to bring the actress face to face with Corinna again. Having heard his tone, she ignored his presence and concentrated her almost genuine concern towards Corinna.

"Please forgive my friends, my dear," she murmured softly,

taking hold of Corinna's gloved hands in her own and patting them kindly.

Corinna looked to Etienne for help and found none. His aloof expression and straight face indicated that he would not condone any association with this stranger. Lost for words, Corinna glanced hopelessly from one to the other, not daring to offend Etienne and hating to be impolite to this woman, however unusual she might be. The actress, however, was aware of her dilemma and swiftly led the clamouring crowd away, although she did make one swift turn of the head to give her a departing smile.

"Whilst Lietner may admire your ability to mix with every level of society, Corinna, you seem unable to discern between the acceptable and less suitable of acquaintances," Etienne commented, opening the carriage door. His stern tone made no difference to her resolve and she cast him a cool look of defiance as she sat down in the coach to wait for the others.

As a form of punishment, Etienne ignored her and devoted himself to Lietner's sisters for the remainder of the afternoon. He made a particular point of attending on them in the evening as well. Corinna shrugged off his petty attempt to make her feel she had done something wrong and refused to feel put out or jealous.

The next afternoon a reluctant Frederick confided that he found this town life was not for him, until the small crowd opposite indicated that Nadine, the actress, had drawn her faithful admirers once more, allowing Frederick to smile his own hallowed admiration from a distance. The others too engrossed by a band of young hooligans who were creating a nuisance on the pavement. Whilst most of them were avoiding two of the boys scuffling on the ground, Corinna found a small fold of paper thrust furtively into her hand by one of the other children. Although surprised, her fingers instinctively closed around the paper before concealing it in her buttoned cuff without a flicker of betrayal on her face. Then she nimbly swept her skirts aside to bypass the rolling bodies and continue her path towards their coach, noting there was no sign of who might have sent her this clandestine message. The strange occurrence was made more curious when the gang of impish boys then vanished from sight as swiftly as they had appeared.

As soon as she reached the privacy of her room, she tugged the paper from her cuff and quickly scanned the scribbled words. It was from Nadine Brunn, the actress she had seen in the park, explaining that she had overheard her name and wondered if Corinna was the sister of a young man she had met in Vienna. Nadine had purposely not mentioned his name, but considering her obviously arranged distraction to ensure the message arrived in secret, it indicated only one possibility, her acquaintance to her darling Max.

Corinna scanned the rest of the short note. It requested that if Corinna was the person Nadine thought she was, she would be pleased to have her come to the theatre whenever she could, any day a few hours before the performance.

Tormented, Corinna stared at the note, her mind in a whirl, wondering how she could get to the theatre unnoticed and remain undetected. Amid a household of strangers and with an itinerary accounting for nearly every moment of their time, she saw little chance of sneaking away.

The following morning Corinna found that the hand of fate had miraculously presented a solution, for Etienne regretfully told them of the cancellation of the recital planned for later that day. After each excited individual promoted their own preferences, the majority voted for a visit to the fair erected in one of the parks.

Frederick was determined to make Corinna join them, but she stubbornly refused, guiltily aware how her declining of his companionship hurt him. Instead she could only make the excuse that she preferred to rest.

"I think you are making a big mistake. You are missing a great opportunity" came Etienne's comment as they left. Not far as Corinna was concerned, because she had a much more important excursion in mind.

Corinna watched them all leave in the carriages and impatiently forced herself to wait for a while to make sure that the staff had retired below stairs for a few hours before setting out herself. She was going to have to find the theatre on her own and on foot, not that the latter bothered her, since she was well used to walking these days. She headed briskly towards the centre of town and after hurrying along the now busier streets, she dared to ask for accurate directions.

It did not take long to find the theatre, and then with no one taking any notice of one more person on the premises, the correct dressing room. Tapping on the door, she entered to receive an enthusiastic welcome as Nadine rushed to greet her and squeeze her hands between her own, before sitting next to her on the sofa.

"My dear, you are Max's sister aren't you? There cannot be two people with that name. Goodness, if it had not been for your escort's disapproval, I might not have taken much notice. I can't believe you are in Graz. To see you in the flesh after Max had told me so much about you. You don't mind that I wanted to see you, do you?"

"Do you know where he is? Have you seen him?" Corinna pleaded, hopefully.

"Not since Vienna. Maxie was a lamb, a sweet charming lamb, and although he enjoyed the entertainment of the city, he was never meant to be a soldier. It was not in him."

Nadine poured her a little wine, chattering on as she did so to complete the picture of Max in Vienna, restricted and bored, hanging about the various halls, cafes, inns and theatres, teasing the chorus girls, flirting with any pretty face and generally trying to make the best of his wretched situation.

"Poor Max, he does not deserve what has happened to him," Nadine went on. "I saw him before he fled Vienna. I have never seen anyone so desperate, so wretched and distraught. I did not know how to advise him and he was intent on seeing you. I thought it a foolish risk, but that was Maxie, he would never listen to reason! Did he find you?" Her words were sincere, earnest and secretive.

Corinna could only grasp Nadine's hand in gratitude at the warmth, friendliness and devotion the actress had expressed for her brother. Here was someone who cared about him with nearly as much devotion as she. They were bound together by the burden of her brother's protection. It came as such a relief to have someone to confide in.

Her pretence of control failed and she let go, burying her face in her hands, crying as she had not done for a long time. There was no stopping the deep gulping sobs which shook her body, or the relentless torrent of tears which flowed down her face as her heartache and despair gushed out. She missed his charm, his voice, his company and his support. She could not lessen the onslaught and soon the handkerchief she had borrowed from Nadine was reduced to a small wet rag screwed up in her hand. Blowing her nose, sniffing and wiping her eyes, she felt no comfort in this release of her emotions. Sadly there were no answers for her, only a weariness and an emptiness of spirit, where she had expected hope.

"There, there, my dear. I'm sure he is safe," Nadine soothed.

"He had no money, I gave him some of mother's jewellery." she confessed, remembering that night. Corinna had come desperate for news and instead had found a woman, a friend, merely seeking the same information. She walked back with her mind full of Max.

That evening during the varied conversation, Etienne mentioned the recent rumour that Nadine and her company would be touring in Germany soon. A shiver went down Corinna's spine, Germany! If only she had known that before she had left the theatre, she could have warned Nadine to look out for Max, or given her a letter to take with her. In a few days they would be returning home. She had to try to get back to the theatre a second time, although it seemed impossible. Drat, drat and drat!

Corinna had planned ahead. She carried a neatly folded letter, tucked safely in her purse, and its very presence at her fingertips made her pulse race. Her one chance came when they visited the large market square and they dispersed to browse among the rows of stalls. It was only a few streets from the theatre. She had passed it yesterday. She could not believe her luck.

She waited to see where everyone was, or if anyone was watching her. Etienne had settled down with his friend outside the inn and lazily stretched out, savouring the wine at his fingertips. From there he could tease Sophie about the carriage, showing signs of strain if she bought anything more. Frederick had done her the favour of retreating to sulk by the stone water fountain, and the rest were preoccupied with the contents of various stalls.

She carefully separated herself from the scattering group and made her way around the back of the stalls before turning off out of the square and into the next street. She barely needed half an hour; she only had to leave a letter, that was all. Then, putting her best foot forward, she set off, knowing she would have to run both ways. Immune to the curious glances of passers-by, she did not stop until she reached the stage door. There, panting, she regained her breath to rush up the stairs to Nadine's room, to burst in, much to Nadine's surprise.

"What on earth is wrong?" Nadine began.

"Nothing. Is it true you may be going to Germany soon?" she gushed impatiently.

"Possibly" the puzzled actress replied.

"Max intended to go there. He mentioned Heidelberg. If he sees any of your posters, if he contacts you, would you give him a letter?"

"Oh, Corinna, a letter? I am not sure of the wisdom of this. We will only be touring in a few cities," she told her with true concern.

Corinna felt crestfallen. She knelt, pleading with Nadine, burying her head in her lap; it was so little to ask. This letter was her only opportunity to let Max have some words from her, something tangible he could keep. Corinna produced the envelope from her purse, eagerly handing it over to a doubtful Nadine and desperately insisted she must try.

"What if the letter was stolen or lost? If someone finds out?"

Both of them became locked in their own private thoughts. Their conversation died away, leaving the hushed room disturbed only by the soft tick of the wall clock and the muffled sounds of the outside world beyond.

With that the clock struck loudly behind them, causing Corinna to panic and make a swift and unceremonious departure. She flew out of the theatre; she had been here far too long, and the others were bound to have noticed she was missing. How the devil she was going to explain her absence she could not imagine. Her footsteps echoed as she ran down street after street, oblivious to the people who moved aside to avoid her and often darting across the road without a thought to her personal safety. They were a blur and insignificant to her present demise. Soon she had a pain in her side from the running and her shoes hurt.

Corinna eventually reached the top of the street next to the square, where, out of breath and in some disarray, she stopped to compose herself before rejoining the others. Cautiously she peered around the corner into the square, to discover to her horror that most of the stalls had been cleared away and the carriages were gone. There was no one there! What was she to do! Surely they would not have left without her.

She walked slowly around the square, trying not to draw too much attention to herself, and sat down on the stone steps by the fountain to think. She would have to walk back, which would take ages, and she would be so late. She would never be able to explain this!

Suddenly Etienne appeared from nowhere, grabbed her arm forcibly and swung her around to face him. "And where the devil have you been?" he growled. "Luckily enough, Lietner noticed your disappearance in time to let me slip away to give you an alibi."

She snatched her arm from his grasp, only to have him grab

hold of her wrist again and drag her towards a secluded recess. She tugged useless against his iron grip, almost tripping as he hauled her along.

"I did not bring you here as my guest to have you flout convention and abandon all sense of propriety" he snapped. "Now where have you been? And don't say you wandered off merely for a breath of fresh air when it's obvious you have been running."

"I got lost!" she hissed at him.

"Liar!" he bellowed. "To wander the city unchaperoned secretively was not mischievous or thoughtless, it was deliberate. What are you up to?"

Flinching only slightly at his outburst, she stood her ground. Having a bullying tyrant for a father had taught her to remain stubbornly dumb. They stared at each other, Etienne waiting for her next excuse, which never came, until eventually he let out one long, exasperated sigh.

"Ever evasive. So Corinna, since I am supposed to have taken you to some fictitious shop to help you buy a present for your uncle, we had best go and buy something, to corroborate the story."

He marched her down the row of smart shops, where she selected a gift and had it wrapped. Then he made her walk all the way back to the house with him, with barely a word spoken.

Back at the house, Lietner had been waiting, peeking out from the porch in search of them. He smiled the instant he saw them and gave Corinna a quick wink of reassurance. He related the commotion their little apparent saunter had caused, fearing the subterfuge had given the wrong impression in some quarters. Frederick was annoyed and Charlotte was jealous that they had been together.

"Charlotte sees Corinna as a rival for your affections," Lietner warned.

Etienne laughed. Having lived with his younger cousin's infatuation long enough, he had become a past master at diverting her unwanted advances. He scoffed, ushering them all towards the door. They walked on inside as if nothing had happened, but Etienne gave her a last rebuke. "I had expected you to grace me with the truth. I had asked you to accompany my family, out of the goodness of my heart, but mark my words, Corinna, it will be a long time before I make the same mistake again."

She regretted offending his generosity. She quite liked Etienne; more than liked. But although she had not wished to alienate herself from him, at this precise moment his whole attitude towards her really did not matter one bit, because her spirits were keyed up by hope, her mind full of Max and the letter he would receive. Dear, darling Max was more important than anything, and the secret satisfaction at having managed to send him correspondence more than outshone any harsh words from anyone. It had been worth the risk, she concluded.

The incident however had concerned Michael to such an extent that he felt forced to issue a warning to her, telling her not to get any romantic notions over Etienne after such a short while in his company. Corinna assured him his concern was unnecessary. Even if she had any feelings for him, she knew they would not be reciprocated, since he had made no secret of his other pleasurable late-night company elsewhere in the city. His dancing eyes and his roguish grin had remained betrayingly on his face when Lietner had challenged him the next morning.

Soon they had returned home, each with their memories, some more than others. Corinna was happily mulling over the unexpected developments of this trip. Etienne had not pressed her again for an explanation or made any further reference to that day. Michael was feeling pleased to have everything back to normal. Even Frederick, with their previous harmony restored, had resumed his regular visits to make the most of the time before Corinna was due to leave for Innsbrück. His eager chattering relayed the recent arrival of some boxes from Gerard, which had since remained stacked unopened around Etienne's study, together with accompanying documents from bankers and family lawyers concerning his brother's estate. The latter had for some curious reason put Etienne in a distinctly unsociable mood.

Herr Metzger's frame of mind was of little importance to her, although she was curious at his visit to consult with her uncle, especially when he strode smartly out of the Holbach lodge in silence. Michael explained he was upset by the correspondence from poor Gerard. Michael remembered Gerard with affection, as he had been a natural protector to Etienne during their youth. Gerard, the perfect country gentleman, had encouraged the then worthless Etienne back into the family fold despite his continuing military career. Gerard had forced Etienne to take over their country home or see it neglected, knowing he gave him no choice. Then later Gerard himself became a recluse to hide his own unhappiness.

There was no compulsion for him to explain further and Corinna did not expect him to. She merely understood that the episode had also made her uncle a little unhappy when he remembered his old neighbour.

Corinna having arrived at the Metzger house as arranged to go riding with Frederick, the footman prudently ushered her into

Etienne's empty study to avoid Charlotte's tantrum in the drawing room. Corinna idly ran her fingers along the shelves as she wandered around before slowly returning to the doorway to listen out for Frederick, so she had not heard Etienne enter through the open French windows from the terrace behind her, and it was only the sound of the bureau lid being slid back that made her turn.

Etienne sat down and pulled forward a box from which he took a handful of letters, tied together by a faded blue ribbon. Carefully he undid the ribbon and after turning a few of the envelopes to one side, he selected one. Removing the folds of paper from the envelope, she saw him read and re-read the letter. The letters were old and could only be from one person.

The effect of the letter's contents were clearly apparent. His shoulders sagged, his head slumped forward and there was a tremble in his hand as he stared at the pages. Finally he folded them, his hand pausing to rest on the box for a while, until he thrust it back into the desk and locked it again, to stride out the same way he had come.

Why she had stood there simply watching him, with no compulsion to make it known she was there, she did not know. But having done so, she now felt a terrible pang of sadness at seeing his soul laid open and witnessing his pain. She felt marked by the depth of feeling Etienne had exposed for Eva, the letters he kept and the obvious memory of her he treasured even after all these years.

That evening she asked Uncle Michael to tell her more about Eva and Etienne. He shook his head wistfully.

"Poor Etienne. No one will replace the magic of Eva in his heart. She was his life, vivacious, tantalising, very pretty, and with fire in her eyes. Living in Vienna they indulged themselves in the city. They loved the concerts, playhouses and opera. Maybe they were too much in love, because Eva's death, an accident after a year of marriage, left him in the blackest of despair, silent, sombre, eating little and sleeping less. He was determined not to be hurt again and lost himself in the military world with its own medley of madness. Vienna meant Eva – they were one and the same. Even now you will find that he hates Vienna as much as he loved it. He is torn in half by its memories and never free of its ghosts. If it was not for the fact the army headquarters is there, he would avoid the place at all costs. As a soldier, experiencing battle and its death and suffering have naturally changed him. Maybe this has allowed him to put everything else into perspective. Who knows?"

Corinna embraced him, laying her head comfortably on his shoulder, and fingered his waistcoat thoughtfully.

"He may love the company of the ladies, but his devotion to the memory of Eva always prevents him finding any real happiness again. Which is why I hoped you would not fall for Etienne. You are so young, too young for such heartache," Michael concluded.

The memory of that scene in his study, put together with her uncle's revelations of his past sadness, had touched her beyond reason, making her heart beat so loud she could not control it. Her uncle might be right about the folly on her part of any deep affection for him, but the sympathy and love for him could not be denied. Oh, Etienne! So much for common sense. Thank goodness she was leaving for Innsbrück tomorrow, with all its distractions.

CHAPTER FIVE

Corinna had been nervous about her return to Innsbrück and her reception, despite all her aunt's letters of encouragement. In fact it seemed she need not have worried so much, because she had not taken a step from the coach when she was engulfed in her aunt's arms. Corinna had never seen her Aunt Theodora so animated or so excited to see her. She was swamped by her affection and her incredible capacity to make everything as pleasant as it had been between them before.

In the days that followed, any scolding or recriminations were swept away by kind conversation, new clothes, new dances and a host of outings. Indeed Innsbrück society itself surprised her most, for instead of shunning her for her past indiscretions, she was feted and in demand, her days made dizzy with invitations.

After two months in the city, two months of exhausting socialising, Corinna expected her aunt to prepare to follow her normal pattern of retreating to her house in Tyrol to avoid the summer heat in the city, so she was startled when her aunt clapped her hands and announced a change in their next agenda – they were going to visit some friends in Salzburg. Corinna was delighted at the prospect, knowing the timing coincided with the folk festival; her friends, Adela and her sisters would also have travelled to the event, to perform and represent the village. It might be a long journey and a little too near Gmunden and her father, but the idea of Salzburg also meant an abundance of playhouses and theatres, and most importantly the possibility of seeing Nadine.

Yes, as the recent months had passed, how often had mind drifted away as her thoughts had been preoccupied with Nadine finding Max. She kept wondering if Max had received her letter yet and if he had, if it had given him some comfort. Surely he knew how much she still loved him and missed him? She wanted to know he was well. Would Nadine be back from Germany and would she be in Salzburg? Had she seen her brother? She hoped she would have time to scan all the billboards and posters around the city to find out if she was there.

Theodora easily made the transition from one city to another, having asked her late husband's lawyer to lease a suitable property for her. Salzburg was a beautiful city in the Salzburg Alps, the fortress palace of Hohen-Salzburg, and the cathedral and many fine buildings created an impressive aura, enchanting Corinna. Enthusiastically she toured the exclusive shops with her aunt and listened to the music in the parks, both women determined to take advantage of their new location.

The festival was wonderful, Corinna and her aunt sat in the auditorium surrounded by banners, ribbons and flowers and they enthusiastically clapped each participant as the singing and music filled the air. Everything was so colourful and Corinna bubbled with happiness; she was so eager to find her friends and introduce them to her aunt. She just had to make them show off their charming regional dress, whirling and swirling their skirts to full effect, with white stockings and low-heeled buckled shoes, their hair plaited and garlanded with flowers. Her aunt was enthralled, to such an extent that they were soon all invited to share afternoon tea at the conservatory in the park after the gala.

It had been lovely to catch up with the latest news from the valley, but there was no forgetting her real purpose. In the days that followed Corinna resumed her daily routine of scouring for news of Nadine during their journeys about the town, her head always turning this way and that. So far the lists had not mentioned either Nadine or the theatre company, but Corinna never gave up hope.

On one of their journeys about the city, the carriage jolted to a temporary stop, as often happened, and in that second, Corinna discovered herself staring straight into the face of a man on the pavement. The man who stared back, as surprised as she was if not more so, was Etienne. Politely she made to lift her hand in recognition, to see him quickly turn away and hurry down the street to disappear down the nearest alley. Of course, what he was doing here was none of her business, except that she knew from Frederick's latest letter that he had told the family he would be absent and out of the country for some time. So much for the military changing their plans.

Indeed Corinna would not have given it any more thought, had she not been surprised by her next sighting of him. It came one afternoon as she and her aunt were crossing through the vast park gardens to return to her carriage, and her bonnet blew off in a sudden gust of wind. Giggling, Corinna quickly grabbed at it, only to miss it and have to run a few more steps to catch it by the steps of the bandstand. Then, as she stood up, a man on a park seat near the pond caught her attention. There was no mistaking that curl of hair at the back of the neck, she knew it anywhere; Etienne. There he sat with his arms around the shoulders of a woman.

Tempting as it was to stand and watch for a while, she resisted and turned away. The setting for his latest dalliance, however unusual, was nothing to do with her.

On the next occasion when her aunt had business matters to attend to, Corinna was allowed to please herself as to her own activities, as long as she was suitably accompanied if venturing out of the house. With a maid at her side for the sake of propriety, she viewed the various shop windows to find gifts for Adela and her sisters. It took some time, but they were both savouring their chance to dawdle amongst the tempting articles on offer.

"What the devil are you doing here in Salzburg, Corinna?" growled a man's voice at her shoulder. She froze on the spot, unwilling to turn around. Leopold!

"Well, what do you have to say for yourself?" her brother demanded in his usual domineering tone. The maid looked quite frightened at being accosted in the street in this manner and crept nearer to Corinna, sidling silently behind her charge. At moments like this, Corinna herself would have been glad of her aunt to protect her.

"Father will be surprised," Leopold went on. "He would be interested in seeing you, as you are so close to home."

This was more than a simple suggestion, and as she made to pass him by, he stepped into her path, making her realise the ease with which she could be dragged off the street at any moment and taken home to Gmunden. She was not strong physically enough to resist. She had no defence except to cause a scene and send the maid running home for help, by which time it would be too late. Her heart was pounding, and she was scared.

"Can I be of any assistance?" Lietner enquired politely, having appeared by magic from nowhere. There in his officer's full military uniform, he stood at her side, his imposing presence making it perfectly clear that he was quite capable of defending any damsel in distress. Corinna had never been so glad to see anyone; suddenly she felt completely safe.

"This is none of your concern Sir. I am her brother," Leopold instructed, hoping to dismiss any interference. But Lietner showed no sign of taking his word for anything, his expression remaining firm. He had only to look at Corinna's face to see she was glad of his help.

"To the contrary, sir. It is very much my concern, since I know this lady is the ward of her aunt and I propose to escort her back to her guardian this moment, thus ensuring she does not have to endure this unpleasant, unwanted and unnecessary barracking in the street, even from a relative," Lietner replied sternly. He clicked his heels smartly, gave a slight bow to end the confrontation and turning to Corinna smiled kindly and offered his arm to her, which she gladly accepted without having the words to thank him. Then, with the maid falling in quickly behind, the three of them strolled off as if their association was all perfectly normal. Corinna's hand still trembled on Lietner's arm, and he reassured her by placing his other hand over it and smiling even more.

Lietner proudly walked her back to the house, content to have her hand resting on his arm, until he was forced to hand over his responsibility. He introduced himself to her aunt and explain the circumstances of the afternoon. Her aunt was astonished that any attempt to remove Corinna from her care had been made and was grateful for his intervention. Indeed she declared she would now consider it a wise precaution to have one of the grooms in attendance at all times when they left the building.

"Frederick had mentioned you would be in Salzburg," Lietner told her. "I hope you do not object to my calling upon you while you are both in the city. I am in town with my sisters."

Her aunt seemed quite pleased at his courteous overtones and readily agreed, especially since he was already associated with Corinna, Michael and the Metzger family. Corinna had no objection to his request, her only concern lay in the words he used. As if Frederick was in the habit of corresponding with Lietner! Besides which, how could her own letter have reach Frederick in the few days they had been here, for him then to write to Lietner? No, this convenient appearance had nothing to do with Frederick, this was more to do with his older cousin.

"Will Etienne also be calling upon us?" she asked suspiciously as he made his departure.

"Etienne? Why should he? He's out of the country, isn't he?" he responded, giving her a rueful, wide-eyed grin.

Corinna fully understood his far from obscure inference, but she would play along for a while, she decided, if that was the way he wanted it.

"Then why aren't you with him?" she mused.

"I'm on leave. Which is why I am here with my sisters."

From that moment on, her search for news of Nadine came to a standstill, for when her aunt wasn't keeping her days filled, Lietner and his sisters seemingly were. She was invited here, there and everywhere, until after a while Corinna began to realize that the numerous and enjoyable outings were completely occupying her time.

"Surely you have more pressing military matters to return

to, rather than spend so much time entertaining me?" she asked him.

"Oh, Corinna, I am on leave, remember. Besides I love being in your company," he insisted. Although he sounded genuine, Corinna gave him a sideways look. It was hard to believe he had nothing more important to do during his stay.

Corinna would stare curiously at him when they were attending functions, while he managed a continual bright smile in response. Without comment, they faced each other, each of them keeping the secret. Each of them was clearly wondering what the other was thinking. Finally one day she drew a deep breath and exhaled slowly, shaking her head. This was so annoying.

"I am of the mind that all these invitations to keep me busy are at the instigation of Etienne, for some reason," she said.

"How on earth could that be? You are with your aunt and he is engaged in military business."

"Military business? And 'out of the country', according to his letters home, but we both know he is here in Salzburg. He saw me and I saw him. I am of the impression that you have orders to make sure we do not meet. And I don't believe it is because he is still peeved with me after my behaviour in Graz."

"Oh, Corinna. Please do not let your imagination work so hard," he whispered. She knew perfectly well what he actually meant and raised a sceptical eyebrow.

"Why won't you tell me what he is doing?"

Lietner offered no explanation.

Corinna remained suspicious, her mind considering every conceivable probability and every plausible and satisfactory explanation as to why Lietner had been engaged to keep her occupied. If Etienne was here on some secret assignment, then all they had to do was tell her that.

The next day her aunt was absent on a private visit somewhere, and Corinna was trapped indoors by intolerable rain. All she could do was peer endlessly up and down the street and let her mind wander from one topic to another, before finally returning to Etienne. What was he up to? She could not help being curious, and the more time she wasted on the problem, the more she wanted to know. Lietner was never going to tell her anything, because it was obvious they were in league together. So how was she ever going to find out?

Outside the rain had eased. Lacing up her boots and finding a good outdoor coat, she ventured through the house, which luckily was still quiet of servant's activities, to slip out the back way. Lietner was the key, and she fancied there would be little harm in maybe following him. Besides, she had nothing else to do for the rest of the day.

Corinna walked along the still wet cobbles through the rear mews towards the house where he and his sisters were staying. Of course he might not go out at all, or if he did it might simply be an errand on his part, in which case he would most likely leave by the front door. She decided to wait at the back. If he appeared there, it would indicate that he was up to something secretive.

Then, all of a sudden, there Lietner was right in front of her, leaving from the servants quarters and closing the iron gates without even looking around. He strode off at such a fast pace and so suddenly that Corinna had to run hard to reach the corner so as not to lose sight of him. She soon found the task of following him was harder than she had anticipated. It became a game of alternate moves, hanging back at a distance, walking slowly, watching which turn he took and then rushing to that point, where she would stop to sneak a careful look around the corner to ensure she had not lost him. There she would wait, watching for his next diversion, before she started the whole process all over again.

She had no idea where she was heading or which way she had come. Deeper and deeper into the less-known areas he went, never once turning back to check behind him. Through the various squares, archways, and streets, this way and that he led her. Corinna became increasingly nervous as she hurried doggedly along in his footsteps. She was frightened of falling too far behind, and ignored the dull rows of buildings, yards and back alleys as she continued to hurry through the uneven ground and puddles in her path.

She stopped to find herself facing an expanse of waste ground and a mass of muddy ruts. Still panting, she glanced at her elegant boots for a second and pulled a face, but she had little choice. She plunged on ankle-deep across the squelching ground. Her feet were soon wet and she struggled to keep her skirt hems out of the mud to cross the open space. Once clear of that hurdle, she faced an empty wood yard, which she rushed through to get into the next road, to find Lietner was nowhere to be seen.

After all she had been through, all that trouble, she had lost him! She was so angry with herself and now, fearing, she was lost, she began to look around. Ahead the cobbled road clearly led into a wide avenue, from where she could see one of the formal parks. She hurried towards it, to discover she recognised the distinctive railings and gates; it was the opposite entrance to one near their own residence. She was almost back where she had started. He had deliberately led her in a circle! He must have known she was following him. Drat! Her only choice now was to return to the house.

Luckily no one was at the rear door awaiting her, so twisting the handle, she pushed the door until she could squeeze in between the narrow gap she had made. Removing her muddy boots to prevent any telltale marks, she crept up to the quiet, empty main hallway of the front entrance. Her heart was beating like a hammer. There she stopped and listened. Everything was as it should be and thankfully the muffled voices remained behind the closed doors as she tiptoed across the marble floor.

She had not reached the bottom step of the main staircase when Lietner, of all people, peered from the drawing room and quickly stepped out to join her, pulling the door to behind him.

"Did you enjoy your afternoon walk?" he whispered, pointing at the ruined boots in her hand.

Corinna nearly choked, "How long have you been here?"

"Only a few minutes," he answered. Then in a louder voice, he informed her that he had been waiting to confirm her acceptance of an invitation to spend the evening playing cards.

"I am surprised that your aunt let you go out unaccompanied. Or didn't she know what you were up to?"

"I can walk as far as you lead me. Wherever it is!" she hissed back.

He smirked broadly, informing her in a louder voice that her aunt had expected her to join them in the drawing room shortly. Corinna smiled sweetly. 'Most certainly', she agreed at similar volume, whilst inwardly seething at the perfectly-arranged wild goose chase he had deliberately led her on through those awful and muddy parts of the city.

"You owe me a pair of shoes!" she snapped.

"You should curb your curiosity. Touring the city alone is dangerous. I thought you would have learnt your lesson from the incident with Leopold. Besides, it might lead you into doing something… inconvenient."

He was warning her. Inconvenient for Etienne, he meant. Well, despite this unconventional form of deterrent, Corinna still meant to find out what was behind this.

"If you had the common sense to tell me what Etienne was doing, none of this would be necessary," she said.

"That is why you were following me?"

"Yes."

"Corinna, this has to stop. I will admit it is a highly sensitive military assignment and your family being here is making it difficult. I cannot tell you any more. Please don't do anything to jeopardize the situation."

"You should had said that in the first place and saved us both a lot of wasted energy." She smiled at him, indicating her complete satisfaction at his explanation, and quickly left him to skip up the stairs and change from her damp outer clothes before anyone else appeared.

Corinna felt perfectly content to let the whole matter drop and was quite prepared to concentrate simply on her other task of seeking out news of Nadine, except that there were still no posters or announcements anywhere. They were due to return to Innsbrück soon, and Corinna regretfully accepted that she would have to abandon her ideas about the actress. Nadine and Max – the two were clearly bound together.

Maybe she had been thinking about Max too much; there was even an odd moment when she had imagined that she had seen his face at one of the windows overlooking the street. But she had immediately dismissed the illusion, knowing he was safe in Germany. Dear, dear Max.

With time on her hands as she began some of her packing, she found she could not quite dismiss Etienne and Lietner's recent behaviour. Etienne could not possibly consider her a threat to anything he was involved in. It seemed so ridiculous! Inconvenient, Lietner had said. In what way? It would be no good asking him. Neither could she believe that anything connected with the military would make her and her aunt's presence in the city an inconvenience. They had no connection to anything military. Except… no, she did not want to even consider the one link there was.

But a few days later, during a carriage ride with her aunt, she saw that face again at the window overlooking the street. She felt more than just a little unsettled. She did not dare to stare too long, in case her aunt noticed. It was so like Max; but it could not be. There was no reason for him to be in Salzburg. Why would he come back to Austria?

But now her mind would not let it go, it was no good. What if it was Max? What if this other secret intrigue was to do with Max? Heavens, it was too frightening to think about. She tried to convince herself she was being silly, but deep down she knew she had to make sure. Which meant only one thing - to follow Lietner again.

The night hours were the obvious time for clandestine meetings, which meant there was only one course of action left to her, to attempt to steal out after dark. Corinna had no qualms about attempting her secret foray into the night. It was too important not to. After everyone had retired as normal, she waited patiently, then slipped down the back stairs to the servants' entrance once more and made for the street. Dressed more suitably for her vigil in an unflattering drab plain dark dress and her damaged out-of-shape laced boots, with a large dark cloak pulled tight around her, she merged into the darkness. The back way through the mews offered plenty of recesses to retreat into. Dodging the occasional traffic of delivery carts and servants using the lanes, she arrived at the rear of Lietner's building once more.

She walked slowly up and down for ages, dragging her feet and scuffing her heels deliberately and rubbing her hands together against the cold night air. Time passed, and she heard the church clock chime several times. How much longer, she wondered, beginning to think she had been wasting her time. The first sudden heavy spots of more rain made her head for the nearest shelter, where she drew herself into a corner under the dark shop canopy to peer out into the gloom once more at the occasional damp passing figures.

Then, bent against the rain, his collar turned up as if he also wished to avoid being seen, Lietner eventually crossed the square. He hurried onwards through back alleys and strange surroundings, although she felt sure she knew where he was heading. Corinna felt increasingly nervous, and despite the litter and dirt which cluttered her path through the various passageways, she hurried after him, trying to ignore the shadowed obstacles lingering in every doorway. She saw him pause only once before entering a passageway at the corner of a building. From where she stood, she could just about see him open a door and disappear inside. She looked around her and even in the darkness it was easy to recognise the place she had identified earlier. This was exactly where she had seen Etienne disappear that day.

Strangely, not long after that, Lietner left the building again and strode back towards her, forcing her to dart into the nearest recess to let him pass by. Now she had to make a quick decision.

Since she did not want to be left alone here, should she follow Lietner back or should she take a look at where he been? The rain had stopped briefly, although it would soon resume, so Corinna flew across the street and rushed up the last few steps before halting to gazed down that long passageway. She screwed her eyes into the dim light, feeling uneasy and a little unnerved. What did she expect to find? Goodness, why was she even here? She did not need to be. Why was she doing this? The quietness was quite frightening. She tiptoed down the narrow alley, not knowing what to expect.

It certainly wasn't the dirty drunken vagrant who suddenly lurked from the blackness to face her. There was no avoiding the smell of drink which reeked on his torn old clothes, the stench so obnoxious she had to put her hand over her mouth to prevent herself throwing up. He leaned against the brickwork in front of her, blocking the way, belched, swore and tottered from one wall to the other for support, making Corinna freeze for a moment. Then he lurched towards her and raised his ugly hands, bound in strips of rags, to her face, waving the bottle at her.

"Very pretty," the man cackled.

Corinna shuddered, turned and taking a deep breath she ran and kept on running for all she was worth, the sound of her feet echoing on the cobbles and her own panting, gasping breath drowning everything else out. She was not sure which way Lietner had gone, but she did not dare look back. On and on she ran, oblivious of the spectacle she made or the witnesses to her flight. She did not slow until she reached the calm normality of the wider avenues. There, thankfully, she knew she could find her way back to the house. It could have been so different, she really had been in danger from all sorts of unknown things. She was still shaking as she trod the last few steps to the rear door, where even the safety of locking the door against her awful experience failed to quell her pounding nerves.

It was several hours before she felt calm again. The vagrant had scared her so much that she never wanted to go back there, except that she knew she had no choice. Instinct told her she could not let this rest; she must return to that alleyway. She had to retrace her steps. It was only the awful idea that Max might just be there that persuaded her.

In daylight it would not be so daunting, she convinced herself, mustering the courage to try to slip out before her aunt was up that morning. This absence would not be approved of. She had no excuse ready for her aunt, but then common sense was never one of her virtues. She made some vague explanation to the maid on the way out about an errand she had forgotten, and before she could be reminded not to go out alone, she was gone.

This time her journey was uneventful and the way decidedly empty as she tiptoed down the long narrow alley. Please don't let Max be here, she prayed as she approached the hotchpotch of doors in the walls on both sides. Why would it be Max anyway? She stood there in the dim shadows, unsure of her next move, when the creak of one of the doors being opened made her turn towards the sound.

"I saw you from the window. Come inside quickly." a voice whispered from the dark interior. Corinna peered into the entrance. Max! It really was him. Yet he should have been safe in Heidelberg. This was a trick of the mind, it would pass in a moment, she told herself, shaking her head to rid herself of this insanity.

The figment reached out and took her hand, coaxing her inside and locking the door behind them before quickly guiding her up a narrow and rickety flight of stairs to the first floor. Hugging and holding her, he kept her wrapped against him. With a lump in her throat, unable to speak, she clutched at his hand for reassurance, trying to understand, wanting to believe this wasn't happening. Why was Max here? All she could do was look at him. Max, Max with a stupid grin. Her handsome reckless brother, looked perfectly relaxed. There was no sign of the terrible fear she had last seen in him.

"Do you like my lodgings? It has been my home for weeks," he teased, indicating the drab surroundings of the shabby, dimly-lit room. "I did not think you would come on your own, although I suppose it is safer not to attract too much attention," he continued, completely at ease with the situation and without any indication of concern.

What did he mean - on her own? Who else did he expect? Panic surged through her veins.

"What on earth are you doing here?" she eventually managed, wondering why he was here, when he was still a fugitive. She was concerned for his safety. What foolishness had brought him back?

"Goodness Corinna, you have become a most exceptional young lady. I have heard so much about your adventure." Max beamed at her, ignoring her question.

"What are you talking about? How?" Corinna could not take this in, he was talking in riddles.

"Don't be so modest. For someone who was always so timid, and not surprisingly so with our father, you have proved to be very brave in adversity. And all of it for my sake. I did not deserve such sacrifice and loyalty."

"Stop, stop you have lost me. Where did you get all these ideas?" Corinna was puzzled as to who knew or could have told him.

Max laughed and patted her hand in his, as he confided that Herr Metzger was the source of his information. The same Herr Metzger who had promised his protection and kept him in touch with present events. What events, she wondered briefly, overwhelmed at the ease and normality with which he used Etienne's name, as if it was perfectly commonplace to him. Alarm began to jangle every nerve in her; even as the fearful questions sprung to mind, her brother was eagerly confirming the worst of them. Corinna stared at Max, fresh horror filling her. All this time Etienne had known about the uniform and Max, right from the beginning. He had been so clever, so deceitful. She hadn't fooled him one bit despite all her efforts.

"How do you know Etienne Metzger? When did you meet him?" she pleaded.

"Goodness Corinna, you act as if you do not know what is going on."

"But I don't." she shouted wildly at him.

"Herr Metzger is a friend, isn't he?"

Now it was Max's turn to grow silent, his face changed as she shook her head. He was far from being a friend.

"Did Nadine, your flighty actress friend from the theatre in Vienna, find you? She was going on tour in Germany and promised to look out for you." The words died in the telling, for Corinna already knew the truth before she had finished the sentence.

"Nadine?"

"Oh Max - she persuaded me she was your friend. I entrusted her with a letter for you."

"I have the letter. Herr Metzger brought it."

Corinna stared at Max, his words sinking home. How could this be any worse? Etienne had the letter; he could only have acquired it from Nadine. Nadine, who knew where to find Max. Nadine and Etienne! That was where he had spent those late hours the night before. Etienne had planned it all. He had set up the whole elaborate plot, everything from the carefully-arranged meeting with Nadine in the park to the absences to allow her to reach the theatre, including the cover-up for her disappearances to the others. How convincing Nadine had been! What an accomplished fraud Etienne had proved himself. All those lies!

The enormity of the whole elaborate scheme stunned her. All the expense of taking them to Graz! Her heart sank. She could not believe he had done all this, just to find a deserter.

"What persuaded you to trust him?" she asked, now desperately pacing the floor and snatching a look out of the window. Corinna was angry, angry with herself for being so gullible, angry that Etienne had Max in his clutches because of her stupidity.

"I didn't, at first!" he argued fiercely, "I swore to die right there rather than return to Austria. I was sceptical of how he came by the letter. It was only when he revealed the full extent of your use of my uniform to protect me, that you wore it with the intention to mislead any authorities that came, by sending them in the wrong direction."

Her mouth dropped open with surprise. That had not been her intention at all. She hadn't even thought of it. Trust a military mind to interpret her simple actions differently from the truth.

"He has promised to help my case."

Why should Etienne help? He was a soldier through and through, he obeyed strict military discipline, there was no reason for him to promise help to any deserter. It was not within his code of conduct, although she found it very strange that he had not so far turned Max into the authorities. What was he up to?

"Why did he want you to come back at all, here, to this city?"

As far as she was concerned there was no good reason whatsoever for bringing Max back, unless he had something else less pleasant in store for her brother.

"Etienne is investigating Klaus Mahler and his family who live here."

"Sorry, Klaus? Who is Klaus?" she interrupted.

"He is that cadet I had trouble with. The one who pushed me to the limit. The one I would willingly have killed, if I had not absconded. Anyway, apparently another officer was already suspicions about his behaviour; they think he might be involved in more serious activities. If I can identify some of Klaus's associates from Vienna, the military may be inclined to reconsider the charges against me."

"And why bring you here?"

Corinna did not like the sound of this, more lies. It did not make sense or ring true. Her mind was in further turmoil.

"Klaus came from here, so his friends might also be local to the area. We can hope." Max shrugged philosophically.

"And how precisely are you supposed to identify them, whilst you are hidden away up here?" came her sarcastic question.

"I don't know. I expect they have something worked out." He was rather peeved that his little sister was throwing up all these obstacles to the scheme. Max was astonished at how she was now logically pinpointing the mistakes.

"Max, I doubt the authorities will forgive your serious act of desertion that easily, even if you can identify these men. That does not sound very feasible, even to me. Max, I'm sorry, but I don't trust Herr Metzger. I doubt he represents or has approval of the hierarchy of the military command in this. We have both been totally misled."

Corinna hastily related her side of the recent events and the discrepancies in this drawn out tangled web, which naturally alarmed Max, forcing him to doubt those he had previously thought as his friends and protectors. They had to be careful, she warned him. At all costs he must pretend that he had not seen or spoken to her, unless they discover that he had found out the truth behind their devious manipulations. For the moment he must try to placate the situation until they could think this through properly, because they must find a way out of this.

She hated leaving him, but she had to get back to the house quickly and promised that whatever happened, somehow she would return tomorrow. Her silent plea was that he did not do anything silly in the meantime.

She had not even noticed the stern figure who waited on the corner for her return. Thus before she even reached the vicinity of her front door, she suddenly found herself confronted by Lietner.

"And where have you been this time?" he challenged her.

Corinna had no intention of answering, although she was instantly relieved that he clearly had no idea she had found Max, thank goodness.

"What possessed you to follow me last night?" he went on. She could see he was really angry, indeed as he clutched his hands into a fist, she sensed it was all he could do to stop himself from shaking her by the shoulders, right here in the street.

"What makes you think I followed you last night?" she asked, too innocently.

"Because..." he began, leaning close so they were eye to eye, "you were seen doing so."

They could be mistaken, she wanted to argue, but felt she needed to be careful not to antagonise him any more. So Lietner had not seen her! Well, who had? Etienne? Not that it mattered, as long as they didn't suspect she had found Max. She stayed tight-lipped.

"You may be used to roaming around as you want in the countryside, but it is different here. Cities are not safe. Why didn't you listen to me? Didn't you know how dangerous it was? You could have been attacked, raped, killed or kidnapped. You are stupid and irresponsible. Have you considered you are putting other people's lives in danger, not just your own?" He obviously meant Etienne again.

"What is all this shouting? What is going on out here?" her aunt demanded, appearing at the door.

"Ask your niece. She needs keeping under lock and key" Lietner stormed, before turning on his heel and leaving her. Theodora looked at her niece, her head tilted, her expression sceptical.

"Well? What mischief has resulted in such an outburst?"

"He was reprimanding me for walking about unchaperoned and without an escort. He thinks my country ways should be kept for the country."

"Then he is correct. And since he has delivered such a stern reprimand and saved me giving you the same lecture, I won't say any more. Now come inside and tidy yourself up. We have a lot to do today."

Corinna could not concentrate on the rest of the day's activities, much as she tried. How was she to hide her preoccupation from her aunt? She sat lethargically on the upholstery and conveyed tiredness, by yawning and closing her eyes as the coach rattled around the city. This way she could concentrate on the problem without giving anything away.

She needed a plan for Max. He was trapped in that room. How could he escape again? What would she have to do to help him? Whatever they did was not going to be that easy, but together, and this time it would be together, she promised. She was prepared to sacrifice everything, her whole future, to go on the run with him. They would need horses and money. How were they to get out of the city without being stopped? Where would they go? What on earth could they do to provide for themselves? How would they survive?

They would be all right, she tried to convince herself. It could not be too difficult. Look at Max, he seemed to have managed. He wasn't starving, he looked fit and well. Her head ached with the futile hours she spent thinking over everything. By the end of the day she still had no answers and no plan. She simply did not know what to do. She wanted to cry with the frustration of her failure.

Corinna did not sleep at all that night. She lay looking at the ceiling until the first rays of dawn filtered into the room, and still she had not found a solution to their problem. Tired, she dragged herself out of bed and dressed to sit on the window seat, desperate to find inspiration. Below she heard the staff going about their normal routine. But then came an unusual banging at the front door, then voices and the light running steps of one of the servants going up to her aunt's room. A little later there was a tap on her door and one of the maids anxiously informed her that her aunt had sent for her to join her downstairs, due to Lietner's unseemly early arrival. He had demanded to see Corinna urgently. She shuddered. What could he possibly want, what was wrong? Max had promised to be careful.

"Why didn't you stay out of this? Max has gone, no doubt urged to do so by your influence." Lietner told her sharply, the second she entered.

"But - he can't have!" she stuttered.

"What is this about Max?" demanded her aunt, who remained seated in utter confusion, trying to make sense of the strange conversation taking place in front of her. Looking from one to the other as if the younger generation had gone mad.

Max had gone! Where to this time? He had left without telling her, he had deserted her, abandoned her again. How could he, how could he! She was hurt and bitterly disappointed in him, to steal off like that, without a word. Although annoyed with Max for leaving her, maybe he had taken the only chance which presented itself to escape. She could not blame him for that. Etienne must have frightened him, since he was responsible for all of this subterfuge, in the first place. Yes, she blamed Etienne Metzger; she was furious and she meant to have it out with him. Her anger exploded as she demanded to see Etienne.

Lietner did not even blink at her ear-splitting outburst; the feeling apparently was mutual. Etienne had sent him to fetch her, he informed her. A carriage waited outside.

CHAPTER SIX

Tight-lipped and still seething, Corinna marched purposefully behind Lietner through the corridors of the municipal building, her mind bursting with exactly what she wanted to say to Etienne. Once inside the office, she was left alone facing an Etienne who appeared as mad as hell, his own eyes darker than pitch and narrowed by the fury in him. A shabby, unshaven and a seething Etienne, who could hardly wait for the door to close behind the departing diplomatic Lietner.

"You have just ruined months of subtle investigation. What do you have to say for yourself?" he raged.

"You deceitful manipulator!" she snarled, her eyes levelled unflinchingly at his, her anger equalling his own. "How dare you blame me for anything . You are the one who has used everyone, betraying family friendships and companions. To go to such lengths to track my brother down is beyond belief!"

"I could only find Max through you. It became obvious that you were the only one who knew anything. I did what I had to."

He made no apologies for his actions, nor gave any sign of regret. He was obviously merely a soldier doing his duty as he saw it.

Corinna remembered their first meeting at the Holbach lodge, which now proved to be another prime example of his talent for allaying her fear of discovery by making her believe he had guessed her reasons for running away were other than they were. He had even sent her battered expensive riding boots back to her the next day, without any reference to the other clothing she had been found in. This man was too clever; all this time he had been playing games with her.

"Why was it so important? Why couldn't you let him be? To trick him into coming back to Austria was mean of you. He could be arrested at any minute. For what good reason?"

"A military reason. And one I do not need to explain to you, Corinna. This is a military matter and none of your concern."

"Max is my concern!"

"Actually he is also my concern," Etienne said very sincerely and calmly.

Her eyes blazed again briefly, before she took a deep breath to continue.

"You are only using him because you think he is useful to your other investigation." she growled.

"I am not going to spend the rest of the day arguing with you," he told her. "As if I don't have enough to contend with. Why in the devil's name did you scare your stupid brother into disappearing again? He was in no danger! I had him protected and safe. I had men watching over him all the time, which is how I soon knew of your visit."

"How dare you pretend you will help him? You don't mean it. Why should you? All this intrigue to find my brother. I can hardly believe it was worth all the effort."

"The military has important concerns."

"So you keep saying. Are you investigating Klaus or saving my brother? Which is it?"

"Both."

"Fiddlesticks!" she snapped.

They stared at each other for a tense moment before he slowly smirked and his eyes took on a mischievous glint. Then he let out a fearful cackle. The sound was so distinctive that she recognised it immediately. That dreadful tramp who had frightened her so much had been Etienne.

He grinned, obviously having enjoyed the performance.

"I hate you!" was all she could manage to say.

"Hate me as much as you like, Corinna. All you want for Max is a safe life, probably in exile. Believe me, that is not enough. I want him free to return home. The sooner you recognise that I am your only hope for eventual success, the better for all concerned."

She resented his lecture and the dismissive way he was assuming all the responsibility for exonerating her brother from his present predicament, as if she was no longer important. Did he really think she would take any notice of his high-handed manner? As if she would ever trust him after this! She wasn't that foolish, now he had shown the real side of his character.

"I knew you would never dare tell anyone, not even your closest relations. In fact the one advantage of your silence has been that their ignorance has kept them from complicating or disrupting my inquiries until recently. Goodness, do you realise, if you had not turned up in Salzburg, if your older brother had not turned up, if your aunt had not started to ask unnecessary questions in the wrong quarters, I might just have found out enough to help extradited him from this stupid mess altogether?"

Her aunt? What on earth had her aunt to do with this? She was astonished. Her dear aunt, who had not ever asked or said a word to her about Max, had quietly been trying to help during their stay here.

Corinna left his office, having learnt one very important lesson – never to believe anything at face value again. Her aunt by then had arrived, and was storming around the corridors outside and naturally demanding her own meeting with Etienne. After it she came away completely baffled by the man.

On her return to the house, Theodora sat Corinna down for a talk, admitting that after having realized her father's letter might have been the catalyst for her flight, it was Leopold's visit to her home which had made her suspect that it also involved Max, especially since she understood the devotion between them. Theodora had long intended that Corinna should not bear the burden alone and had been ashamed to have waited all this time before acting. The only reason she had kept the real reason for this visit from Corinna was that she had not wanted to build up her hopes, only to have them dashed by failure, as had just happened.

"Your faith in Max was enough to know what has to be done, Corinna," Theodora confessed.

She had come to Salzburg, in the hope of finding out if there was any other reason for the deliberate bullying of her brother by Klaus Mahler, herself firmly believing it could be because of a family grudge against their father. The idea was not beyond reason and she had begun discreet enquiries, without success.

Theodora further astonished Corinna by assuring her that despite Etienne's instance that everything should be left in his capable hands, this had only made her the more determined to pursue her own course of actions. Indeed she was not the type of woman to be dictated to by anyone, especially by those in authority or one Etienne Metzger.

Corinna could only hug her aunt to display her enormous gratitude, while her aunt patted her softly and said there was no need for such fuss. Corinna did not agree. There was every need. To think her aunt would do so much for her sake. People constantly surprised her in one way or another.

Theodora's first course of action was to extend her stay in Salzburg rather than return to Innsbrück, for she would not be forced into leaving the city until she was ready. There were matters to organise, important correspondence to her own circle of influential friends in the capital and the need to bring Michael Holbach here. Two heads were better than one, and she also felt that his presence here would be most beneficial for Corinna. Therefore at Theodora's invitation, Michael travelled to Salzburg, eager to mull over the pros and cons of her campaign. Both of them were quietly hoping that Etienne would be recalled to active duty soon, to keep him occupied and well out of the way. For once they appreciated the emperor's policy of moving his army move to different areas in an attempt to unify the many different states and nationalities of his realm.

Indeed Michael could hardly contain his annoyance with Etienne for his devious behaviour towards Corinna in the guise of friendship. He stated that he doubted he would ever speak to Etienne again, let alone ever forgive him, despite their long family friendship, whatever the excuses. He had already written to Etienne informing him of this.

As for his dearest Corinna, how could he not lavish even more affection on her? How he missed having her about the place. How could he have been apart from her for so long, he exclaimed many times, sweeping her up into his arms.

Only a few days after Michael's arrival a card was left at the door by Lietner, asking for permission to converse privately with Corinna. Her aunt and uncle were against the idea, but Corinna agreed.

"If you have come on Etienne's behalf…"

"No. Corinna, I would not be that foolish. I come for my own purpose, to ask your forgiveness in this recent matter. I feel as guilty as Etienne for deceiving you."

"Dear Herr Lietner, I don't blame you for anything. You never lied to me, you never denied that Etienne was in Salzburg, you just refused to tell me what was happening. That is completely different."

"That's a great relief. You are very understanding. I would hate for us to fall out because of this. I hope we can still be friends."

She nodded and smiled, to which he returned a grateful sigh before taking his leave.

"Max is safe in Germany again. You do not have to worry. The investigation has been put on hold until everything has settled down again. We are both recalled to military headquarters. No doubt to be reprimanded and posted elsewhere." He bowed and left by the front door.

She gasped, glad of the information. How kind he was to have bothered to tell her at all. How unlike his best friend, who would have kept her from knowing anything.

Although Etienne and Lietner had both gone, which allowed them all to relax a little, Theodora had done with waiting. Anxious at the passing weeks, she complained that they had achieved nothing here. The next source of enquires could only be at the source of this trouble – Vienna. Yes, Theodora intended to go to Vienna to see the Secretary of Internal Affairs herself and engage whatever lawyers were necessary.

Unfortunately, she had learnt from her contacts that his schedule would not bring him back to the capital for some time, as he had various business commitments and appointments elsewhere. This meant that their plans were merely delayed, not abandoned. With no indication of when she might be able to arrange a meeting and with the winter months ahead, the decision to postpone their further travel plans was hard, but practical. Both parties had been away from their homes too long and there were matters that had to be attended to. While Theodora declared that she much preferred to be in the comfort of Innsbrück and the winter festivities there, uncle Michael was eager for Corinna to go back with him, to which she eagerly agreed.

Once home, she had hardly drawn breath at the lodge when a familiar head peeked around the door. His beaming face, mass of fair hair and blue eyes appeared bewitching. Frederick was clearly eager to resume their old ways. Yes, she had so missed his energetic exuberance. She promised to ride with him whenever she could, but first she had to deliver the presents she had so carefully brought with her, for Adela and her sisters.

A day later Corinna wandered through the fields, enjoying the prospect of seeing their reaction to the surprises she carried in the basket. Then she stopped, unsure if her eyes were playing tricks or not. The more she looked at the person by the stile ahead of her, the more convinced she was that it was Etienne.

She should have expected as much. There he was, standing casually waiting, when he should have been on his way to join his men. She could feel her anger grow within her. If he had come for another confrontation or to give her another lecture on her inadequacies, she was in the right mood to give as good as she got.

Her eyes fixed on his face and not watching the uneven path, she made the mistake of stumbling ungraciously for several steps before regaining her balance. It was just the impression she had not wanted to give, as it ruined the effect of her new assertiveness. She scolded herself.

"Why are you here?" she asked curtly, in a far from friendly tone.

"I took a slight diversion – to make peace. To put things right, if I can. There must be some way to end this animosity between us."

"Animosity! I find myself barely able to be civil to you!"

"So I have wasted my time." Etienne was silent for a while, looking shrewdly at her. This apparent civilised apology was not going as he had anticipated.

"How can I apologise to you or your uncle or explain, if neither of you will listen?" he said.

Explain what? It was a military matter and none of her concern, he had told her that himself. She doubted any such explanation would be forthcoming.

"Is there anything else?"

He shook his head. Corinna turned on her heel and resumed her intended errand, climbing over the stile and walking across the next field, leaving Etienne alone. She did not even look back. In her opinion, Herr Metzger was completely untrustworthy.

As expected, Etienne had returned to active duty and the winter passed with its merry hustle and bustle of Christmas festivities, the magical spirit of bonhomie and cheerful greetings. Frederick rode back and forth when the weather permitted, but with a lack of other items of gossip, he often referred to the topic of his cousin's continuing absence.

"Etienne again! Why does everything centre around your cousin?" she grumbled. He countered swiftly by questioning her lack of interest in Etienne, when he had always known of her slight fondness for him. She had always liked Etienne, hadn't she? She pulled a rueful face and shrugged.

"He is too dangerously handsome. You could never trust what he meant."

Frederick laughed out loud, admitting he had often admired his cousin's gift with women. Etienne's dark looks and roguish charm had attracted females for as long as he could remember. It was refreshing to know that Corinna, for one, was no longer under that influence. Charlotte, however, would never be cured.

Corinna gave him a weak smile and wondered if his assessment of her feelings was really correct. If only she could work out exactly what she really thought of Etienne. It was not easy; sometimes she made excuses for him, yet at other times she hated him.

All too soon it was announced that Etienne would be home on leave for a month, and Corinna knew the next encounter with him would be even more difficult. As expected, he sought her out when she was alone, for what they had to say to each other could only be said in private. Sitting on a low stone bridge by her favourite stream, she had heard him ride up, but did not look around as he dismounted to approach her.

"This atmosphere is far from pleasant for us both. May I talk to you? Please."

"There is nothing left to say, is there?" she said sadly.

"I am sorry I deceived you. I am sorry I raised his hopes. I am sorry I failed."

If he was trying to make amends, it was not working.

"Max is nothing to you. Why pretend you intended to help him?"

"For Gerard's sake, for a man who never forgot your mother. For someone who loved your mother. If it were not for my brother, I would not have become involved in this. He begged me to see justice done. He was in Vienna at the time when he became aware of Max's plight. Gerard wanted me to help him because of his fondness for your mother. That is the simple explanation, nothing complex or devious, whatever you think."

Everything sounded so plausible, almost too plausible, but then he had had months to think this one up. She wanted to believe him and simply accept that this man would protect Max for no other reason than that his brother asked it of him. But she found it very difficult.

"So however you judge my actions, remember I am equally capable of such devotion and loyalty to my brother, as you have already demonstrated towards yours," he went on. Her silence to his declaration was taken as a signal to continue. "My brother thought that the desertion seemed too obvious, it bothered him. Although after my initial look at the papers for the missing cadet, I dismissed the idea, but he made me promise. It was only later when Kronmeier, another officer, began to suspect that Max's desertion had been forced to divert the authorities' attention from suspicions of a larger scheme. So far we cannot prove anything. In the meantime I wanted Max close, to take care of him. I did not want him to disappear again and to be unable to find him."

"For which you are still blaming me, no doubt?" she stated, remembering his initial accusation.

"You hindered my plans, but I should not have blamed you. I am not infallible. I regret the way events turned out. "

"So do I" she sighed.

"Corinna, you are a remarkable young lady, I did not appreciate having such an unusual adversary. It took time to fit all the pieces together. I identified the tattered remnants of your clothing as a cadet uniform, but the uniform made no sense - why seek to attract attention if you were running away? Once Gerard had mentioned the desertion, it did not take much guessing. Then your stubborn silence made sense. The uniform was a key to something else, the secret of your brother's escape. I knew you would protect him at all costs. You showed remarkable single-mindedness and quick wits to fend off any intrusive questions. I had to find him, if I was to help him. Even if it meant tricking you."

"How did you persuade Nadine to play her part?" came her question.

"Nadine! We are old friends. Very old friends."

A grin lit his face at the memory, a grin which only aggravated Corinna, although she showed no outward sign. Why should she be jealous? Etienne was a man with all the foibles of any human being. He was no saint and no devil, just a mixture of both.

"I am sorry Corinna, I had to - there was no other way to find Max. I hope you can forgive me, some day."

Try as she might she could not deny his justification for his behaviour. She believed he had meant well; not that she was willing to acknowledge that to him any time soon.

"I have endured an unwelcome visit from my estranged

grandfather to rebuke me about my interference in military matters. But he will not alter my attempts to help Max," he reassured her.

Corinna knew about her mother and his brother being friends, but she silently wondered why anyone would have gone to all that trouble for an old friend who had died fifteen years ago. Of course, with her uncle being the only other source concerning Gerard's regard for her mother, she could not wait to ask his opinion.

"Tell me uncle, do you think Gerard would have asked Etienne to help Max, because of his feeling for mother?"

"I think he might well have done."

She did not see the sadness in her uncle's eyes, nor his shoulders drop slightly, until he drew Corinna to his side, held her close and squeezed her hands gently in his.

"The ghosts of the past, my dear. I suppose I must tell you. Your mother was a pretty, enchanting girl. Poor Theresa, so in need of love in a loveless marriage. I regret to say your father was not a considerate or sympathetic husband, she deserved better. It was no wonder that she preferred to visit me whenever she could."

There had been little need to tell her what her father was like; her own experience confirmed the truth her uncle reluctantly spoke of. She had always loved her mother; although she had never known her, she had always imagined her to be special. Now to discover her father had been responsible for making her mother so unhappy as well, made her angry, hurt and very sad.

Michael stopped to kiss her swiftly on the forehead, as was his way.

"And Gerard?" she prompted gently.

"Gerard became well acquainted with your mother during her visits at the lodge. She met him a few years before Max was born. They were so happy, so content in each other's company. There was an undemanding depth of esteem for each other. I cannot explain it." His voice broke; he could not speak for a moment.

"Just to see each other, was to know how the other felt. Yet there was such terrible pain in their happiness, both of them wanting to be together and accepting it was impossible. Every time she came back to the lodge, it was as if they had never been apart, there was no reference to the time they had spent away from each other. There were no desperate useless promises, Theresa knowing she could never be free. It was a hopeless situation, there was nothing I could do. Nothing anyone could do."

Corinna bowed her head and twisted her hands together in her lap, trying to hide her tears.

"And I was an unhappy witness to the suffering it caused the both of them. I saw my sister torn apart emotionally. That carved wooden box you are so fond of was a gift to your mother from Gerard. She had to pretend it was from me, so that she could take it with her when she went home."

It was all so real, Corinna leaned against her uncle's lap, Michael stroking her hair as he held her until they both slowly restored their composure. Her lovely mother.

Later that night, Corinna sat in her bed, the mellow lamplight reflecting her mood as she nursed the treasured wooden box in her lap, her fingers lingering over its surface. It meant even more to her now, because it had been given as a simple token of love and it held her in a spell.

In due course the differences between her uncle and Etienne

seemed to be resolved, Etienne having finally convinced Michael he had acted for the best. Although not pleased about his behaviour, Michael had finally forgiven him. Yet whether their acquaintances would ever be as affable as before remained to be seen.

Etienne left soon after on his trip to see the ailing Gerard, which was overdue. He had not been away long before Frederick came over to tell them that Gerard had sadly passed away, which had left the house in a sombre mood. Etienne and Lietner had attended the private funeral, after which, once everything was settled with the lawyers, they would be bringing the last of his brother's personal effects home. Then Lietner would be staying briefly to put some relevant papers in order, while Etienne had to go straight back to Vienna.

Corinna and Michael were just as saddened by Gerard's death. He had been quite dear to them both, although in different degrees, and Corinna wished she had met him, if only the once. To see the man who had meant so much to her mother and to thank him for trying to help Max. Yes, that most of all, to thank him; she wished she could have done that. The regret of not ever being able to do so made her even sadder.

Corinna was pleased to see Lietner arrive at the lodge. She now rather liked him, maybe because there were no secrets between them, nothing to keep hidden from each other. As their friendly conversation proved.

"I hope you do not mind that I came to see how you were. Salzburg was such an awful mess, wasn't it!" he said frankly.

Corinna nodded, unwilling to press him too much, only to find he had no qualms about expressing his opinion about the whole affair.

"Maximilian was as difficult, stubborn and as unpredictable as you," he teased. Corinna laughed, easily acknowledging her own faults, and was relieved to find that there was no sign of any awkwardness between them.

"I do not blame your brother for being suspicious. It was quite a risk to come back. It is just a shame nothing could be resolved. Anyway – at least we are all safe and in one piece, thank goodness."

Yes, there was that, Corinna agreed.

"Etienne has been summoned to see his grandfather. Now there is another fine mess! With Gerard passed away, the Count Bardolph von Hetsch-Radberg sees Etienne as his new heir, despite having originally disowned their mother for marrying their father. I expect he will want him to take his rightful place in the capital, with an illustrious future among the important upper nobility."

"What?" spluttered Corinna, her eyes wide and her mouth dropped open. She had not realised Etienne was so well connected. No one had ever mentioned who their grandfather was before.

"Does that mean Herr Metzger will refrain from interfering in our family again?" interrupted Michael, who had been sitting there quietly reading.

"I wish I could promise that, but I cannot," Lietner sighed sadly, looking at them both in turn.

The conversation diplomatically lapsed into gossip for a while, until Lietner hesitated, clearly considering whether to say what was on his mind or not. He wondered if he might relate something about Gerard to her, something he thought she might like to hear, since it concerned her mother. Corinna could not wait, although Michael coughed nervously.

"I am sure Etienne won't mind me telling you. Apparently Gerard had kept all your mother's letters and he had carried the last letter she had ever sent with him every day."

Michael cleared his throat deliberately to catch Lietner's attention. His eyes widened at their guest and he gave him the slightest shake of his head, indicating that the topic should be dropped immediately. Not that Corinna had noticed any of this, because her own emotions had already made her catch her breath. All the recent revelations of her mother's unhappiness made her want to cry, and as she stifled her tears, her reaction alarmed Lietner considerably. He apologised profusely for upsetting her; he had not meant to, he declared. "Please, please forgive me," he urged her. Despite her insistent protest to him that he had not upset her, that her tears had merely been out of fondness for her late mother, Lietner decided it would be best if he made himself absent.

Corinna could not forget his words. To think that Gerard had kept her letters all this time and that he had been so steadfast in his love. Just like Etienne and Eva's letters, it must be a family trait, she concluded. Now more than ever she wished she could have met Gerard or seen him or his likeness. She immediately asked her uncle if he knew of any portrait of Gerard anywhere in the Metzger house. She should have thought of it before; she might have passed it by without knowing, all these times she had been to the house without even looking. Michael pondered the matter for a moment before saying that there might be one in the study or the library.

"I must try to see it," she said.

Corinna had her tactics all prepared when she arrived at the Metzger house a few days later. Slipping away from the rest of the family, she made her way to the study and quietly entered the room. Lietner sat lazily at the large desk, unperturbed by the mass of scattered papers on it, idly staring into space. He was glad to be distracted, he told her, quickly pushing the papers aside into a heap as she approached, his voice genuine and warm.

She soon found herself eagerly explaining her inquisitiveness concerning Gerard. She wanted to get some impression of him, she said. She tugged him to his feet and dragged him with her to examine the portraits on the walls. And there it was, directly above the locked bureau where Etienne had sat that day. Where else would it have been but here, with all his personal memories, here to face him?

Corinna stood absorbing the man, his features so like his brother, yet with the blondest hair and the bluest eyes, just like Frederick. He was everything she thought, the kindness in his eyes, the slight smile on his face captured to such an extent that she could imagine everything else about him. She could have stood there for ages, locking him into her heart, but Lietner gently interrupted the spell.

"Come, we had better join the others for afternoon refreshment, otherwise your lengthy absence may create suspicious rumours," he laughed. Grinning with an inner satisfaction, Corinna placed her hand purposefully into his offered arm and they both stepped merrily out of the room to make their way casually through the house to rejoin the other inhabitants.

Frederick smiled as his mother passed him a few pages to read for himself, as had become the habit of late. Etienne repeated his excuses for his prolonged absence.

"He says not to expect him back for a considerable time," said Frederick. He passed them on to Corinna, who flashed a glance at Lietner.

"All this journeying about, first here and then there, as if he has trouble making up his mind where he wants to be," Sophie complained at this continued disappearance.

"I'm sure he will be home soon," Lietner offered, trying to pacify her.

Not necessarily, thought Corinna, while Lietner refused to enlighten them either.

"He could be entertaining. There are plenty of beautiful heiresses in Vienna," Frederick teased. Charlotte pulled a face at him, sulking at the idea, jealousy colouring her face.

"It could be a delicate if not risky attachment, an affair, a married woman, a mistress even. Let's be honest, a grand passion of the heart is not Etienne's style," said Frederick wickedly. For which he received a stinging blow from his mother.

Lietner escorted Corinna to the door and proceeded to accompany her personally to the pony and trap. A little secret smile was exchanged between them.

"How do you think Etienne is managing in Vienna?" she asked.

"Not well. They have never got on. They are both strong willed. There will be nothing except arguments and angry words from dawn till dusk. I'm glad I'm not there."

"I can't imagine anyone daring to interfere with Etienne's plans," she said in impish sarcasm.

She tossed her hat upon the seat and jumped up beside it, happy to be on familiar terms with Lietner. He leaned on the framework, his eyes as bright as hers, then confirmed he was reluctant to see her go and regretted he would be leaving in two days' time.

None of the family had quite believed that Etienne's absence would last long, yet the contents of several communications finally revealed him to be firmly established at his grandfather's resplendent residence. Sophie and the others were nervous of his association there, unwilling to voice their thoughts too often in public, although many questioning looks betrayed their doubts about this unwelcome development. They could only conclude that Count von Hetsch-Radburg, having tired of Etienne's lazy excuses, meant to bring his philandering to an end. It was obvious the old man had taken matters into his own hands. His heir was about to take his rightful place. He was to be seen, presented and recognised amongst the highest of society, including the royal circle, and earn the respect of his fellow peers.

"I do not understand. He values his independence," Frederick declared during Corinna's next visit.

"Etienne never confides the whole of himself," Corinna conceded affably, unwilling to say too much. The extraordinary behaviour did not ring true and had already caused considerable speculation between Corinna and her uncle, although naturally neither of them were willing to enlighten his family with their own suspicions.

Corinna's reunion with aunt Theodora came earlier than expected in the year. She was escorted by Michael as far as Salzburg, where they had arranged to rest for a few days before the completion of her and her aunt's prearranged journey to the capital. Yes, Vienna, was still on the agenda, with Theodora's resolve and determination to tackle the authorities, no less than it was before the winter. Vienna - oh, how Corinna wanted to go! Not just for Max's sake, but to see the place itself. She had heard so much about it that she longed to see its splendour, to walk the streets and feel the city's heart, just once. She could not imagine how her wonderful aunt had arranged it.

Corinna and her aunt had barely settled into the hotel in Salzburg when Theodora received a letter from one of her private sources, her clerk at the lawyer's office. He reported that Etienne was in fact staying in Salzburg at his grandfather's other smaller palace, not in Vienna at all. The letter also confirmed that Etienne had been preoccupied in dutifully entertaining the other house guests, a certain unknown female Elizabeth Brecker and her family. They were accompanying him everywhere of late, according to rumour, and Etienne was clearly enjoying himself.

So much for his supposed commitment, Corinna huffed, while Theodora remained nonplussed at this latest information. Her response was more practical; she pointed out the advantage of his being safely engaged elsewhere. It would keep him from finding out about their impending journey to Vienna. Corinna would still have preferred to personally rebuke him for apparently shelving his promise to his late brother, although she doubted the opportunity would arise before they left.

After a morning touring the exclusive shops in preparation for their journey, Corinna had deposited her parcels into the coach and gone ahead into the hotel to take lunch, only to discover Etienne on his own, dining at the same hotel. Corinna smirked as she sat down and took up the menu card, her eyes demurely lowered, wondering if he would deliberately pretend he had not seen her. She did not wait long to find out.

"Corinna, I did not expect to see you here," he said, stopping on his way to the door.

"Nor I you," she countered in fake surprise. "How delightful to see you. I am here with my aunt." She smiled pleasantly at him, moving her purse out of the way on the plush buttoned upholstery, in case he wished to sit, though she knew he would not.

"How long are you staying in Salzburg?" he asked quietly.

"Don't worry, I will not intrude in your arrangements!" she said softly. He cleared his throat in annoyance.

"No doubt you will be the toast of Innsbrück society again soon."

She smiled and shrugged. If he was trying to find out her plans, he would have to do better than that.

"I thought you were staying with your grandfather, but here you are in Salzburg, enjoying yourself," she said, with deliberate ambiguity. He might have wondered exactly what she meant, but her aunt's arrival heralded his quick departure, to her amusement. Little did he know that if, he wished to speak to her again in the foreseeable future, he would have to travel a long way to do so.

So go to Vienna they did, to stay with Theodora's sister-in-law, while Michael remained discreetly in Salzburg at the lodgings with an old friend, prepared to send word if anything important occurred. As Corinna sat in the coach she could not believe she was there. Vienna was vast and spectacular, the palaces, the churches, grand promenades, tree-lined avenues, the gardens and the sheer size of everything making her stare wide-eyed, trying to take it all in. She made no secret of enjoying every minute. She was both overwhelmed and spellbound by the surroundings.

Theodora of course had more in mind than a simple visit of the sights while they were in the capital, but one of the other advantages of being in the city at this time was a series of royal birthday celebrations and parades. How exciting, Corinna exclaimed, although it was hard to see how they were to fit everything in, with the gala concert and other entertainments already arranged by her aunt's relations. But no doubt they would do their best.

It was day two of the royal processions and the city seemed bursting with people and the wide avenues and squares seemed to be filling with more and more crowds. It became so difficult to move easily about the streets that the coachman advised that they abandon their normal morning drive altogether and find some safe vantage point from where they could also watch the parade instead. Common sense prevailed and Theodora decided to remain in the coach, insisting she could see everything perfectly well from there, while Corinna was allowed to walk down the nearby flight of steps for a closer view, provided she stayed in sight. The people waved and the excitement grew with the noise, forcing Corinna to stretch on her toes to see the brilliant splendour of the cavalry over the heads of those in front of her. The spectators started cheering as more people lined the route, then she heard the band in the distance and the sounds of marching boots. Waving back to her aunt, she deliberately took a few more steps into the increasing crowds below, hoping to get closer to the spectacle.

People surged forward as the main part of the procession reached them and Corinna felt herself being hemmed in on all sides as the crowds were increasing into a solid mass, edging the pavements and every vantage point. She tried to push back against the surrounding throng, to force her way back to the steps, but they were reluctant to move. Despite her frantic efforts she found herself trapped against a very solid stone wall and as the people leaned more and more against each other, crushing her, she began to feel faint.

Suddenly a space was cleared and she sensed strong arms supporting her and guiding her away. Dazed and the world a little grey, she was glad to sit down, her legs felt like jelly. Cold water made her open her eyes wide, to focus on Etienne poised at her side with a sodden wet kerchief in his hand.

"Is that better? Anything could have happened in that awful melee."

Etienne in Vienna! Impossible! She was stunned to see him. By now she was sufficiently recovered and found herself flinching away from the cold water as he, instructing her to keep still, resumed his task of dampening her face.

"I had better get you back to your aunt immediately."

They were in a small quiet courtyard with a water fountain, just off the main parade route and through the archway at the other end of the courtyard. Beside them waited a coach finished in expensive black lacquer, with gold coach lines and a crest upon the door. Even the coachman and outriders were all in smart livery. Etienne did not even defend his retinue or its presence here.

"I suppose I should not be surprised to find you in the glittering grandeur of Vienna, enjoying yourself," she offered, nodding towards the coach.

"I accompanied my grandfather to Vienna, because I had to. Tedious as it is," he growled quietly.

"And your other companions - are they still in Salzburg or travelling with you?" Her curiosity could not be contained.

"If you mean Elizabeth and her family, they will come to Vienna in due course."

Corinna pouted, wondering how long this attachment would last.

"Jealous?" he queried.

"No. Just disappointed. I had expected you to be honouring your promise to your brother."

"Corinna, I will never forget my obligations, however it may appear," he snapped, standing up sharply.

With the crowds thinning on the street, Etienne took her back to the bottom of the steps, bowed smartly to take his leave of her and then, looking up towards the carriage, pointed out that her other knight in shining armour had arrived to take care of her. Lietner, in full dress uniform, was talking to her aunt, the small core of soldiers standing a little way off waiting for him. Hurrying up the steps, her aunt expressed her relief to find Corinna had survived the scenes they had just witnessed.

"I was about to send one of my men to find you. I am in town with my regiment and my sisters have come to watch the parade," Lietner said.

Of course he was! How convenient! If Etienne was here, then Lietner would not be far away.

"I have acquired a balcony at headquarters tomorrow to view the next parade for them, it is much safer. If you would care to join them?" he continued. A suggestion her aunt eagerly accepted, before Corinna could think of an excuse not to. This left Corinna with no other choice except to smile and thank him. Whilst Theodora had happily endorsed tomorrow's arrangement, Corinna merely saw this as a repeat of the previous ruse to keep an eye on her.

"Did you know Etienne was in Vienna?" she asked softly, to one side.

"He has duties here. I do not think we will see much of him," was all Lietner would say.

The next parade was even grander than the first and with a much better view, Corinna could see everything, the spectators lining the roads, the band, the grand military parade of marching uniforms, best of all the monarchy in their splendid carriages waving to the people. The colour and the atmosphere were all so exciting, and she could not help but enthuse about it, all the way back through the marbled halls of the large government building towards their carriage. She had not taken much notice of the other occupants in the other balconies, the officials in the building itself or the stewards who kept them away from the cordoned-off sections.

Corinna had assumed she had seen the last of Etienne for a while, so she was more than surprised to see him here with an older statesman, who could only be his grandfather by the startling resemblance they bore to each other. The pair of them were descending the main staircase, neither of them talking or looking at each other, their eyes focused straight ahead, a grim set to their jaws and both barely acknowledging the officials who respectfully parted as they approached.

All of them could sense the hostile atmosphere between them. The instant Etienne saw the Lietner party, he abandoned his relation, leaving an indignant, scowling aristocrat glaring after him. Etienne's expression had changed to one of enormous relief as he asked how they were all enjoying themselves and with Lietner's sisters one on each side he strode out into the daylight, Corinna, her aunt, her sister-in-law and Lietner following.

"You certainly know how to upset your grandfather," Lietner joked.

Etienne laughed.

"I dread to think what the atmosphere is like at the Radberg Palace," his friend continued. Etienne glanced at Lietner, his eyes narrowing, his humour subdued.

"You could be a little more discreet about my private business."

"It is no secret," Lietner replied in a similar tone.

"We have not settled our differences."

Then, dismissing the subject, Etienne exchanged a few pleasantries with everyone, led them to their coaches and bade them farewell. He took Corinna's hand for a moment to help her into the carriage and smiled at her.

"I hope you can persuade your aunt not to suddenly whisk you away from Vienna, too soon. There is to be a Gala Ball at the Radberg Palace next month. I pray you will all accept the invitation when it is delivered."

She found it hard to ignore his gaze or to be free of his charming expression, which refused to be diverted. To attend a grand society ball, in one of the most opulent palaces in Vienna! He was being too considerate, so thoughtful and altogether too nice.

"You still like dancing – don't you?"

"Dancing, of course!"

CHAPTER SEVEN

Of course the whole purpose of this trip to Vienna had been for Theodora to meet with the Minister of Internal Affairs, to discuss the matter of Max. Although they made the most of enjoying the city during the frustrating delaying tactics Theodora unexpectedly encountered in trying to secure a meeting with government officials, this had remained her prime objective. Thus, when her aunt had finally left for a lengthy private meeting with the Minister, Corinna could think of nothing else as she waited impatiently in the house for her return.

All her hopes, all her anxiety, expectations and doubts, churned in her head as she paced the room. She would rush to the window at every sound of a carriage passing and then just stare into space, praying for the authorities to be lenient, kind and forgiving. The hours dragged by, but she could not settle to anything.

The first glimpse of her aunt's face as she descended from the carriage, her deep frown and grim set of the jaw as she shook her head, told its own story. It was not good news. Her dear aunt had failed to influence them, despite being renowned for achieving anything she set her mind to. Corinna could not hide her disappointment, nor wait to hear what she had to say.

They sat together clutching at each other's hands as an exhausted Theodora bemoaned her failure. She had done her best, but her efforts had proved inadequate. She told Corinna that the Ministry fully accepted that Max had been bullied and that Klaus Mahler hated Max enough to deliberately make him flee, but they still considered that no excuse for Max's act of desertion. Max had run away, plain and simple; the warrant for his arrest would remain. Nothing could exonerate him. The hard truth was, there was no hope at all.

Corinna could not believe the outcome. She had always assumed they would find a way to achieve the impossible, but it seemed there were no miracles. All her optimism vanished in that moment. She went cold and she buried her head into her aunt's arms. And all Theodora could do was hold her, gently trying to console her.

"I can't believe it," Corinna whispered.

"Sadly we are in no position to find any evidence which might make a difference. And to be honest I doubt that Herr Metzger, for all his influential connections through his grandfather, will be able to alter the situation either."

"If he really wants to any more" Corinna mumbled.

Metzger's recent infatuation with Elizabeth had certainly put his dedication to their cause in question, as far as she was concerned.

A quietness settled over the pair of them and the next few days saw a variety of moods encompass them both, fluctuating between despair, acceptance, and bewilderment.

"Meanwhile, Corinna, you have a life of your own. We must carry on," Theodora reminded her. Corinna put a brave face on as they fulfilled their arranged engagements, although in her opinion there was nothing to keep them in Vienna any longer, nothing to stay for. Even the remaining glittering celebrations held little fascination.

Which explained why Corinna felt no excitement or pleasure when the gold-edged invitation for the ball arrived. Although her aunt tried to persuade her that it was a once-in-a-lifetime experience and not to be missed for any reason, she had no heart for the mad whirl of dress fittings which swept through the city as the ladies exhausted nearly every shop of its finest goods. Theodora and everyone else had all acquired the grandest ball gowns their finances could afford, and a collection of shoes and other accessories lay waiting in the various houses for the final choice on the night. In Corinna's room a beautiful dress hung in its soft wrappings, tantalising and extravagant, yet she had no desire even to touch it. It held no fascination or expectation for her. She had no wish to attend another charade.

Corinna lay looking at the ceiling, her mind flitting from one thing to another before settling once more on Etienne. If only he had not been so handsome, so distant and so in love with Eva. She had accepted that his affection for any other female would always be fleeting, so the idea that this Elizabeth might end his devotion to the late Eva made her angry. Angry enough, she decided, to show him precisely what an exceptional woman she could be, a woman to rival Elizabeth. Tonight she would give her own performance. She looked at the hanging dress with new interest.

Corinna had never taken so much trouble and special care over her appearance as tonight. The smallest detail had to be perfect, since she meant to dazzle Etienne despite his affections being elsewhere and prove she had become a lady who could handle anything he threw at her. Her dress was white, the only colour for evening. It had a tremendous full skirt with a tight-fitting bodice and a low, off-the-shoulder neckline. She surveyed the expensive dress, the immaculately-styled hair, the jewellery and the satin shoes from every angle in the mirror to see if she had achieved the effect she had tried to create. She could not have been more pleased. She knew full well she looked spectacular. Her gentle features shone with radiance and her eyes sparkled. Amid an aura of pure happiness, she floated on air. At last, draping the fringed silk evening shawl wrap around her shoulders, she descended the stairs.

She received gasps of admiration from those who waited below.

"Good gracious Corinna, you look stunning - absolutely stunning!" exclaimed her aunt with pride before she swept her into her arms and hugged her. "I shall have to post sentries at the door to keep the admirers at bay!" Corinna laughed, and they all set off in high spirits to enjoy the ball.

The Gala Ball promised to be a glittering occasion. An endless line of carriages drew up before the magnificence Radberg Palace, the brilliance of its interior spilling out to greet the host of guests. It seemed not only the whole of Vienna but half of Austria had come to pay homage to the man. Entering the wide white marble staircases on thick velvet carpets, they were met by gilded ceilings, immense sparkling crystal and gold chandeliers, gigantic galleries and corridors festooned with huge mirrors. In the high-ceilinged drawing rooms people talked, plucking glasses from an abundance of footmen in splendid livery and waiting for the entrance of the Count and his party from the private apartments.

There was a great hush of expectancy as the elderly

statesman appeared. Few men carried such an impressive aura. His air of absolute control and authority caused conversation to halt and heads to turn during his progress amongst the assembly. The honour and reverent respect shown to this personage had been clearly extended to Etienne, who accompanied him.

Graciously the Count greeted his important guests, chatting familiarly with other dignitaries and exchanging further pleasantries as he made his way through the lesser ranks of society. Corinna nodded demurely and curtsied respectfully as he passed on, leaving her to come face to face with Etienne when she stood up again. His dark eyes curiously surveyed her and with a simple nod of silent acknowledgement, he also moved on.

In contrast the select group of other house guests were whisked passed them by the secretary to take their place at the far end of the room. Shortly after, the orchestra broke into music and the initial formalities officially over, the evening progressed with dancing. Young girls danced quadrilles with young officers, carefully watched by their chaperones, and others gradually took to the floor. Glamorous dresses rustled about the floor and jewels glittered upon every head, neck, ear and wrist. Officers wore full dress uniform, while the generals and other officials wore their sashes and decorations, while the court dignitaries wore black with gold lace. The brilliance of the occasion was overwhelming and Corinna understood why her aunt Theodora had advised her not to miss this experience. It was breathtaking beyond imagination.

Corinna soon lost herself in the whole magical atmosphere as she melted into the pleasurable swell of the melodies. The exhilaration pulsed through her and had her head spinning; she had never known such a fantastic sensation. She had never danced so much or so well. She glided in a dream, partnering anyone who asked her for her arm to take the floor, including Lietner, who held her so lightly, his touch guiding her subtle movements and showing off her tiny graceful figure. She wished the music could last forever. It all left her breathless, glowing and thrilled inside. She had never sensed such a feeling of pure contentment and the smile on her face proved she was enjoying herself beyond all expectation.

The Count and his party settled at the far end of the room, where Etienne devotedly focused his gaze upon the attractive young lady on his arm, displaying an attentiveness she had not seen before. The girl was slim and blond and there was no denying she was beautiful, Corinna noted as she silently watched the pair of them. Corinna did not want to admit the twinge of jealousy she felt and turned away, intent on ignoring this distraction.

Tirelessly the hours passed until, as was the custom, the next interval came, when an excellent light buffet supper was served in the adjacent rooms, bringing another temporary halt to the dancing. Some guests preferred to sit and watch, others strolled the grand halls and terraces, whilst many adjourned for refreshment. There was much intrigued whispering behind fans, light laughter and amicable, relaxed conversation.

Lietner's errand to fetch a glass of fruit punch for one of his sisters allowed Corinna to edge quietly away through the crowds. Preferring some air, she made for one of the terraces, where she strolled the stone flags, idly touching the balustrade and running her fingers over the plants which adorned the decorated terraces, heedless of what else went on around her. So when Etienne appeared, not unexpectedly, to seek her out, she was determined to retain the inner contentment this perfect evening had brought her. She was in such a relaxed mood that his own over-cheerful manner and his elaborate, too-polite bow had no effect on her.

"Good evening Corinna. I can see you are enjoying yourself."

"It is such a wonderful evening, Etienne. You were most kind to send us such an invitation."

"It was my pleasure. It was the least I could do to recompense for my previous behaviour. I could not have you miss this occasion, knowing how much you adore dancing. Your charming presence here has captivated every partner so far. I should know, since I have been studying your progress for most of the evening."

"Have you?" she beamed, secretly please by his admission. Then, to her utter surprise, he swiftly leaned forward, took her face between his hands and kissed her on the lips, an impudent kiss which was so light and so brief that it barely registered any sensation at all. She could not understand why he had bothered.

"I could not help myself," he laughed. "Thank goodness, I am as immune to love as you are."

He continued to gaze into her eyes, and just for a moment she had the awful feeling that he was tempted to repeat his lack of judgement. She dug her closed fan hard into his chest, making him take a step backwards.

"Please do not let me keep you from your other guests. I would hate for them to be deprived of your company for one more moment," she declared wearily, shaking her head.

"You are dismissing me, after I made a special effort to find you?" he said, pretending to be hurt. She did not answer him, ignoring his exaggeration. She had had enough of his company, preferring instead to study her bent and battered fan.

"Oh, Corinna! I am aware I have been under your scrutiny tonight, having suffered your constant gaze to add to my burden. You are not impressed by my association with Elizabeth. Tell me, why should Elizabeth want me? I do not deserve her hand. I do not deserve anyone's hand, do I?" His eyes twinkled brightly.

Corinna still remained silent, she was not about to express any opinion; she refused to give him that satisfaction. She wished he would leave.

"You may have every right to think the worst of me, judging by recent events, but nothing is ever what it seems," he pointed out more seriously, his voice repentant, as if to excuse his faults.

Then a fanfare sounded from within, a loud bellowing salute heralding the arrival of the Emperor Franz Josef. This drew a scurry of activity behind them and made Etienne turn. He bowed smartly and hurried away to attend to his more pressing formal duty. Corinna quietly cursing him, watching him, wondering if the evening had been worth all the effort or if she had merely proved her inadequacy to deal with him again.

She heard the Grand Master of Ceremonies tap his staff loudly on the floor. There was an immediate hush, followed by the rustle of hundreds of dresses as the ladies sank to the floor in a deep curtsey. Then the music began inside again and with hours more to lose herself in the sheer pleasure of the dancing, she shook herself free. Nothing was going to dampen her happiness tonight, not even Etienne.

Corinna returned to the gaiety of the huge assembly, to soak in the atmosphere of the proceedings. The Emperor and Count von Hetsch-Radberg sat together talking, the royal entourage positioned protectively around them. What amazed Corinna most as she looked around was the sight of Etienne and Elizabeth now happily dancing together. Poor Elizabeth, she thought, so unaware of Etienne's lack of commitment.

Corinna danced as she had never danced before, beautifully poised, every movement elegant, with every partner. She caught Etienne watching her more than once. She smiled to herself. She was woman enough to know when her campaign had worked. She had made her point; there was no way he could have failed to notice her new maturity. More than satisfied at the subtle effect she made, she also noted that in these last few hours he rarely moved from his position at the far end of the enormous ballroom.

Constantly surrounded by an ever-changing number of people, Etienne seemed outwardly calm, with a pleasant smile and a nod to those who passed near, but as the hours passed Corinna was not the only one to notice the frequent glares between Etienne and his grandfather.

"That looks ominous." she whispered to Lietner's ear as they danced.

"I am sure Etienne has it all in hand," Lietner whispered back.

Indeed he had, for there were no other signs of animosity in front of the Emperor; they were obviously to be saved for the quieter and private moments outside the main ball room.

Corinna, naturally intrigued, looked at Lietner, her eyes silently seeking an explanation, although she suspected her companion would not tell her even if he knew. And she was right.

As soon as Franz Josef and his entourage had departed, during the next interval, Etienne, the Count and his secretary retired from the public rooms. Corinna, watching from the landing, saw Etienne return, then move almost invisibly and equally inconspicuously amongst the invited guests to escort a certain gentlemen back across the marble mezzanine to where the private secretary waited. The man was certainly not one of the guests, since he was dressed in ordinary outdoor clothes. Glancing around before they disappeared through the doorway into a private wing, Etienne found Corinna staring directly and intentionally at the man, which caused him to hesitate. What was it about his look, his strange expression? It seemed to indicate that he was torn between the need to come and talk to her or follow this stranger. He started to purposefully stride towards her and then changed his mind.

Curious, very curious, Corinna considered, staring at the vacant space. What wasn't he saying? Whereas earlier she had not considered this occasion to be anything other than it was supposed to be, she began to suspect differently. She shivered suddenly - how could she have been so slow? What was the one thing he had not mentioned for a long time, the one promise he had made to his brother? This meeting was nothing to do with just another private argument with his grandfather - it was to do with Max! She had misunderstood this whole situation.

Corinna looked at the solid, forbidding doors for some while, pondering. Then, noticing that there was no one else around, she made her decision. If she was lucky, no one would even notice her disappearance from the throng in the ballroom. With an air of quiet detachment, her steps treading the carpeted floor, she swept down the stairs and across the still-empty hallway. Then, like a naughty child, she took her chance to open the heavy doors and enter the private section.

Pulling the doors closed behind her quickly, she was relieved to find there was no one else in sight, not a servant to be heard or seen, and no one to challenge her. Although as she crept along the corridor in front of her, she was ready to pretend she had every right to go where she was heading. Now all she had to do was listen for the sound of telltale voices to guide her.

It did not take long to find the door she wanted. Creeping close, she stood with her ear pressed to the door. She knew she should not be doing this; she could get caught, she could get into a lot of trouble. Heavens, it was too late to turn back, she chided herself.

"I trust, gentlemen, this will not take long," said an unfamiliar voice.

"We are both in an awkward situation," she heard Count Radberg remark calmly.

"Caused by your grandson – who refuses to accept the obvious," replied the stranger.

"The obvious being that Klaus Mahler is important to both of you, more important than justice." That was Etienne's voice.

"We did not sanction his action at the Academy, if that is what you are suggesting. Klaus Mahler is a hothead, and for some reason he has a personal grudge against the Schopenhauer family. Aren't the best types of revenge the simplest? Some people enjoy the pure satisfaction of destroying something, whether it is a life or a reputation. We all understand that. His actions were nothing more sinister than that," said the stranger.

"Nothing more sinister! Klaus remains unchecked because he is too useful, because he can supply information to certain people."

"Everyone needs information," the stranger reminded them.

"I acknowledge your dedication to your ideals," Etienne's replied sarcastically.

"You wish to damage our association?" the distinguished man asked too casually, clearly without expecting a truthful reply.

"Not unless you become a threat to the Emperor and his

Empire," the Count replied. Corinna heard him tapping his cane impatiently. She was getting stiff, but she did not dare move.

"So Klaus is protected. At the expense of the individual!" Etienne snapped.

Corinna straightened up, her back aching. There was no need to stay any longer.

Corinna scurried away down the long corridor, frequently stopping to check behind her, but unbelievably she remained undiscovered. Her mind racing, her nerves alert, she appeared the exact opposite as she calmly and gracefully crossed the mezzanine once more to waltz sedately up the stairs and settle into one of the recesses, with all the outward signs of being completely at ease. Behind her battered fan, she let out a deep breath. Her eavesdropping had only confirmed what she already knew. She should not have listened, because it only made her sad again.

She remembered how her aunt had explained the seriousness of her brother's plight. This had all become much too political to understand. This was no longer about Max at all. Everyone had their own agenda. Everything had become far too complicated, beyond the simple fact of a cadet being bullied.

Not long afterwards she heard purposeful footsteps approaching, footsteps she knew. Etienne. She pulled her full skirts in towards her, out of the way to let him pass, but the steps stopped, making her look up. A serious expression met her.

"Did you overhear enough?" he asked flatly.

She did not blink or make any excuse, not even when he casually uncurled his hand and dropped a small silk tassel belonging to her fan into her lap. He must have found it in the corridor. She had not even noticed it was missing.

"I would have known it anywhere," he whispered.

"I heard enough to accept I have been very foolish. I do not expect anything to be achieved against such immense opposition," she sighed sadly, ignoring the tassel.

"My grandfather simply refuses to use his influence on my behalf" Etienne muttered. She put her hand gently over his to confirm her acknowledgement of his struggle. She felt slightly sorry for him. Even Etienne was getting nowhere. These other men with their grand schemes were too powerful to be persuaded by mere sentiment. How could he change the official view?

"Oh, Etienne. I appreciate your efforts on our behalf, but the government and its ministers are too powerful to fight. The matter may never be satisfactorily resolved."

"I thought I was better placed to help him. So much for leaving matters in my very capable hands. Who was I kidding!"

"I apologise for criticising you. I had thought you were too busy with all your personal amusements, when that was far from the truth," she said softly.

"Please Corinna, don't be so nice to me. I am not whiter than white in this deception."

"Mmmm. Were you ever, I wonder?"

"You seemed resigned to defeat."

"The authorities have already told my aunt that it is a lost cause and although difficult to accept, I think we must," she said calmly.

Then Lietner burst along the landing. The dancing would resume at any moment, he said, and not only was her aunt fussing over her absence, but his own junior officer was in a fit of anguish because Corinna had not returned for the next dance which he had booked with her. Corinna reluctantly left Etienne to his own deep thoughts.

In the remaining, testing hours, Corinna danced on until she was exhausted by the physical exertion and the growing tension of trying to keep up her sparkling performance. Her heart was no longer in it. That aura of pure happiness she always felt when dancing had deserted her, although she continued to smile politely. Her head began to ache. Unable to enjoy herself, she was forced to admit that she could not dance any more. From her distant position she watched Etienne, who also seemed to be enduring the event without enjoyment.

Midnight passed and people were beginning to drift off and leave. Others wandered about for refreshment or sprawled about the more comfortable furniture. A tired Etienne made his way around the room, avoiding trivial conversation and insincere company, glad to stretch his legs. He strolled lazily along the landing until he stood alone by the window in the supper room. A brief moment of peace was all he needed; time to rest and time to think.

Corinna smiled at the figure of Etienne by the window as she went to join her aunt, ready for her own departure. Quietly she tiptoed away. There was no need of further conversation between them, enough had already been said tonight. She had nearly reached the outer door when he followed her to request a favour, not for himself, he hastened to add.

"Elizabeth has not had much female company of her own age to talk to while she has been here" he said. "Would you be kind enough to let me introduce her before you before you leave? I think it would do her good."

Corinna's jaw dropped. His consideration for Elizabeth came as a surprise. She opened her mouth, but did not know what to say. Her silence made him widen his eyes.

"Surely Lietner's sisters…?" she asked.

"Oh, but she wants to meet you."

Dumbfounded by the prospect and without any formed argument to put forward, she found herself escorted automatically into another room.

Corinna could not help cringing inwardly as she managed a polite and gracious greeting to the sweet Elizabeth, introduced by Etienne. The outward calm and smile were a sham, as both she and Etienne knew. She caught his eyes on her, but frustratingly Etienne deliberately left them alone together. She glared at his disappearing frame. What was he playing at?

But she found it hard to remain angry for long. The exuberance of this bright-eyed, pretty young thing was impressive, and she seemed genuinely eager to become friends with Corinna. Her sincerity and enthusiasm bubbled over, astonishing Corinna, although it also made her feel sad for Elizabeth, for it was obvious from her cheerful manner that she was fond of Etienne and had no idea that he was about to break her heart.

Elizabeth was keen to hear all about her, her aunt, her uncle and the places she had been. "Herr Metzger has mentioned you so often," she said. Corinna blushed, wondering just what Etienne had told her. No doubt he had elaborated on all her mistakes. That would be typical.

Then, fortunately for Corinna, they were interrupted by Lietner and his sisters, whose appearance soon drew Etienne back into the room to introduce them all to each other, thus enhancing the cordial mood of the whole gathering.

Etienne was smiling, again. He leaned towards her. "You will be pleased to learn that Elizabeth already loves another. Like you, she has more sense than we give either of you ladies credit for. Besides I am a soldier at heart and not good husband material."

Corinna sighed, unwilling to debate his failings. She did not have the energy.

"What are you going to do now?" she asked.

"Go home for a while, have a rest from society and rethink my strategy. I expect I will need to exercise my thoroughbreds to keep them in condition, despite the fact that Frederick has the habit of regularly letting others do that for me in my absence. It takes a good rider to handle them."

She noticed his tired eyes crinkle and fully understood his meaning. Pulling a rueful grin, she retaliated, she could not help herself.

"That would be less dangerous than risking your neck by jumping fallen trees on hairpin slopes?"

"You saw?" he asked, knowing immediately what she referred to.

She nodded. It was hard to forget the sight of his disastrous landing. She had been the only person who had seen the horse and rider sailing out over the large fallen tree, to land with a jolt further down the slope, then slide sideways downhill to hit the track at the bottom amid a cloud of dust and flying gravel. He gave her a repentant grin.

In the days after the ball, the various residences started packing up for their visitors to return home. Elizabeth and her family had already left the city, without Etienne. Corinna and her aunt were making preparations for their own departure from Vienna, although Corinna found she really did not mind what her aunt had planned.

Corinna and her aunt made the long journey back to Innsbrück, where Corinna glided through the rest of the season without a hint of the lack of enjoyment she felt in public. She continued with her schedule of engagements and passively endured the endless rounds of society functions without protest. Indeed there was no faulting her performance, and when Corinna prepared to return to her Uncle Michael, Theodora hugged her long and affectionately, for she was loath to let her go. Theodora expressed her admiration of her courage and strength in adversity and told her niece how proud she felt of the rare young lady she had matured into.

Heartened by her aunt's compliments and eager to go home to the countryside she had missed, she could not wait for the coach to reach her uncle, who would be waiting to meet her in Salzburg. Although the pattern of her journeys now included being escorted by a maid and a footman for safety, at her aunt's insistence, Corinna found her spirits lifted with every mile closer they travelled.

When she arrived, Uncle Michael's jolly face beamed as wide as ever in greeting. His arms drew her against his chest and then swung round and round while both of them giggled delightedly. Michael had so much to tell her. He had news from home, with Sophie's letter reporting the surprising romantic attachment of Frederick to Irene, one of Adela's sisters. The letter went on to say how well they fitted together and how they suited each other. Their obvious happiness was apparent to all as they strolled arm in arm in the garden or sat in the small arbour, idly discussing their confidences, doing silly things and laughing like any young couple.

Sympathetically Corinna smiled. Although pleased for Frederick's happiness and not wishing to appear ungracious, she was fully conscious of another change in her life. Here was just another adjustment as she realised he would no longer be there to keep her enjoyably amused. Growing up was not always as pleasant as it seemed, she decided.

They had already expressed their opinions in a lengthy exchange of letters between herself, her aunt and Michael concerning the overheard conversation at the Ball. The knowledge of the utter futility of their hopes had been a bitter blow, and they were loath to discuss it any more. So they walked and talked as it suited them, and hardly mentioned Max.

Their departure was delayed for a week because of Michael's interest in a book auction, so they took in the sights of the city, but as they ambled back from one of their walks, they were both surprised to find a liveried coach and outriders outside in the street. They were further shocked to find a messenger from Count von Hetsch-Radberg standing at their door, requesting their company at his home outside the city as soon as possible. Apart from the fact that they had assumed that his grandfather had remained in Vienna, they could not see any reason for such an invitation, since they were not even properly acquainted with his lordship.

The messenger confided that it was to do with the Count's grandson. After the ball, Etienne had returned to his grandfather's summer home. There was only one conclusion to this request, that there was much more going on than was being said. Somehow it must be connected to Etienne's continuing battle with his grandfather over Max. In that case they had little choice about going, although it was a journey neither of them really wanted to make.

"How can Etienne stop Klaus being useful to Count von Hetsch-Radberg and his colleagues?" Michael pondered, voicing aloud Corinna's own thoughts.

The nearer to the aristocrat's residence they came, the more Corinna found her energy draining away. From everything she had learnt in Vienna and even verified by Etienne himself, the Count had proved over and over that his loyalty was to the state and not the individual. He was after all a member of the Imperial Council, that inner circle of Austrian society revered for their politics and diplomacy. Etienne was wasting his energy. Sadly she knew his grandfather would win. How long did Etienne intend to try? Months, years? He would have to give up at some point.

The secretary met them at the entrance and led them through the magnificent rooms and hallways of the fine palace. He invited them to freshen up and then escorted them towards the private quarters. They were shown into an enormous study, where they were cordially greeted and made welcome. Then they were told to sit, while he himself remained standing.

"Tell me miss, is there anything between you and my grandson?" he asked calmly. Corinna and Michael blinked, shocked at the question.

"I beg your pardon?" Corinna managed to stutter.

"I am sorry to be so blunt, but I wish to know if there is any romantic liaison…"

"Certainly not!" she said indignantly.

"No secret pact between you?"

"I'm sorry, I do not understand. A pact about what?"

"Then pray can you explain why when he is not engaged in his army manoeuvres? He is back at my heels, plaguing me to do something to help your brother."

Corinna could only shrug and remain silent.

"If it is not for you, then why is he so obsessed in this matter?"

"Because he promised his brother he would do so," Michael offered.

"Yes, yes. I have heard that every time from him, but I fail to see why Gerard would ask such a thing in the first place."

Corinna and Michael looked at each other. It was not for them to divulge the personal details of Gerard's private life, nor his reasons for such a request. If Etienne had not felt it necessary to inform his grandfather, then they certainly weren't about to either.

"I really do not see why we are here. We are no longer involved in this doomed enterprise," said Michael. The awkward silence which followed was interrupted by a tirade of angry words from the next room, shattering the normal hushed reverence of this residence. Etienne's voice declared that he did not care who heard him, he had dragged himself here against his better judgement and he was prepared to continue this confrontation for as long as it took to get results.

One of the liveried servants tapped on the door, then opened it and announced the arrival of Etienne. The look of utter shock on Etienne's face could not have been more explicit.

"What are they doing here?" he growled, glaring at his relation.

"I sent for them," his grandfather answered.

"How dare you inconvenience my neighbours or embarrass them by having them witness our arguments!"

Etienne turned to Michael to apologise for the unnecessary journey they had made. He had not realised what had been happening, or he would have prevented it.

"Your grandfather thinks I am responsible for your continuing to pursue Max's cause. He does not believe that your loyalty to your brother is enough to explain your actions,"

Corinna pointed out, before anyone missed the whole point of the visit. Etienne turned to his grandfather, his face distorted with anger.

"It does not matter who instigated my quest. I mean to win this battle."

"Are you saying that Fraülein Schopenhauer has nothing to do with your intrigues?"

"I am!" Etienne shouted into his face.

"Yet she is his sister and you are neighbours, you are well acquainted. You invited her to the Gala Ball."

"For heaven's sake! How many times do I have to tell you? How many times have we had this conversation? Gerard simply wanted something to be done for a cadet who had been maligned. He hoped for better justice from the military, or some offer of clemency. That has not been achieved. Therefore I must do what is necessary to make you change your mind about the present outcome of the case. I am disappointed at your reluctance to use your influence on my behalf. You ignore the truth and deliberately suppress its existence when it suits you. You and your associates refuse to lift a finger to help one man."

The Count merely raised one eyebrow. "One man? I do not deal in individuals. For the guardians of this realm, there are more important issues. To preserve Austria, there must be sacrifices sometimes."

Corinna was shocked to hear it put so bluntly. This was her brother they were talking about. Max was a sacrifice for the good of Austria.

"I cannot allow myself to be swayed by sentiment," his grandfather concluded.

Radberg turned dismissively to his desk, a clear indication of his wish to terminate the interview. The gesture was not lost on Etienne, but he was not one to comply with mere hints.

"None of this is going to help Max. You are wasting your breath, Etienne," Michael stated quietly.

Corinna was tired of listening to all the hints and veiled threats. The anxiety and stress had left her worn out. Her face dejected, she could only manage a pitiful glance as she shook her head. Didn't Etienne realise he would find himself thwarted again and again? This was the whole of the government he was fighting.

Corinna saw the exchange of looks between Etienne and his grandfather, recognising that neither could win the other around. Her instinct told her that these men were never going to resolve anything. For all her young years, she could see it was futile. Max would never come home. He was safe, that was all that mattered, safe and well. What more could you ask or expect?

Dragging herself to her feet, she stood to face them, composing herself as her aunt had taught her before beginning.

"There was absolutely no purpose at all in bringing us here, Count Radberg," she said. "I do not understand why we are expected just to sit here and listen to you two rant and rave at each other for hours. What is the point? You have no intention of ever agreeing to Etienne's demands or of helping my brother."

She paused to get her breath, while everyone else remained speechless at the sudden outspoken outburst from such a young female.

"And you, Herr Metzger, enjoy the game of cat and mouse too much. You are exhibiting every sign of becoming exactly like your grandfather. You are well suited. You deserve each other. Well, enough is enough. I want to go home. I do not want to have anything more to do with either of you. I do not want to speak to you, see you or hear from you ever again. If you cannot help Max, then leave him alone. I will be out in the courtyard until you can provide a coach to take us home. However long it takes to arrange."

She drew a breath, cast Etienne a meaningful glance and marched into the sanctuary of the other room, where she sank down quickly onto a chair to recover. She had never put so many words together before. She might have spoken out of turn, even been impertinent, but she did not care. Had she said too much, or not enough? Well, it was done now.

Etienne would have retaliated, but Corinna had stormed out of the room and he was left to glare at the door. Michael smiled to himself, Corinna had expressed herself very well and he was in complete agreement with her. So much so that he added his same assessment of the situation and told them he intended to join his niece in the courtyard.

Meanwhile Corinna had collected her cloak, hat and gloves, and to the astonishment of the staff she walked out of the grand entrance and plonked herself down right down in the centre of the front steps to wait. They could arrange a carriage or she would walk every step of the way back, she really was past caring.

As the two of them arranged themselves comfortably in the coach, Etienne was rushing down the steps to speak to them. His hands seized the door to delay their departure.

"He has played his hand well," he said. "He thinks he can make me give up, because he has made you declare you have. It makes no difference. I can make him change his mind. I promise."

"Your promise is too late." Corinna replied. "I refuse to endure the trauma this always causes. It is time to let go, to move on. Good day, Herr Metzger."

The carriage left with no more said by anyone. Inside the occupants pulled the rugs around them, glad to be leaving. Etienne walked slowly back inside, unsure of his next move.

CHAPTER EIGHT

A few months after their return home, Michael came back from his walk with the news that he had encountered Lietner during the afternoon. They knew he was visiting the Metzger home on the way to his next posting, to deliver letters for the family from the absent Etienne, who had been assigned elsewhere. "He seemed to have an unusual distracted mood about him," her uncle commented.

Only mildly curious as to this odd behaviour, Corinna concluded that these peculiar antics were nothing unusual. Soldiers were a strange breed. No doubt there were days when even they doubted they were doing the right thing, she mumbled philosophically. Which made her uncle look at her, startled at her worldly observation and a little put out that his vulnerable niece had become such a worldly-wise cynic so easily.

Needless to say, Lietner was bound to call upon them. Since he was unlikely to see them again in the near future because of his military commitments, he had come to see how they were now they had returned home. A polite enough excuse, Corinna concluded, allowing him to continue the mundane conversation for a while so that she could compare her own observations of his manner to those her uncle had made previously. She let him struggle on, noting that he deliberately made no reference to Etienne, which prompted her to tackle him with the one obvious question on her mind.

"So where is the elusive Etienne this time? You look worried."

Lietner let out a long, exaggerated sigh. He had been promoted to acting captain and taken temporary command of their unit, while Etienne had taken extended leave. He admitted that they alone might as well know that Etienne had resumed his investigation in Salzburg. Against all advice, he had entered into the seedy backwaters of refugees and criminals alike, once more to search for any information he could use against Klaus Mahler.

"Such stupidity," Michael voiced sadly. Corinna pursed her lips together, frowned, put her head on one side and looked at Lietner. They could easily have been kept in ignorance.

"It was kind of you to let us be privy to what must be military intelligence."

"It is only because you are safely here at home Corinna, and far away from Salzburg. Otherwise I would not have told you anything. At least with you here, there will be no repeat of your previous escapades. There will be no creeping about the streets, no following people, no secret night-time exploration, and no involvement whatsoever which might endanger Etienne."

Corinna pulled a face at him and screwed up her nose. "Protecting your brother in Salzburg last year was one thing. With Etienne deliberately frequenting taverns, getting drunk with servants and turning the heads of the housemaids, it was an acceptable deployment. This latest venture of his is beyond comprehension."

"And his grandfather's reaction?" Michael enquired.

"He blames everyone except himself for Etienne's present disappearance."

"What do you mean by 'disappearance' exactly?" Corinna queried.

"His whereabouts are not known."

"You really don't know where he is?" Corinna asked.

Lietner was a disciplined soldier. He gave no indication; he stared her out, unwilling to expand or divulge anything further. Nothing is ever as it seems, she reflected, remembering Etienne's own words.

"There will be no sudden long journeys in that direction, will there? I want your promise," Lietner asked Corinna.

She reluctantly agreed, if only to make him relax his grip as his fingers unwittingly pressed hard into her flesh, until thus satisfied he abruptly stood back, releasing her, for past events had proved her ability to keep her word.

"We have nothing planned which takes us away from the country for a while. I am sure I can keep her out of trouble," Michael joked. Lietner coughed deliberately and looked at Corinna, one eyebrow raised quizzically, indicating he was not so sure. Then, appearing more relaxed, Lietner left them to ride back across the valley, his task complete.

Corinna sat quietly and thought some more about it. Her silence caused Michael to sense the unease the news had created.

"Now Corinna. Stop worrying about Etienne. He is a soldier and more than able to take care of himself." he instructed softly.

Was he, she wondered? He was only a man after all.

Life returned to its normal routine and the weeks passed, with Corinna occasionally persuading Frederick to let her ride

Etienne's thoroughbred horses again. She loved the rush of the wind in her face and the feeling of pure freedom which soared through her veins as she raced ahead across the estate. Moments like this were rare, but so exhilarating, and she would turn back, to thank her friend for his kindness. After which they would idly walk across the fields towards the village, for she had no wish to deprive him of his dearest Irene's company for too long.

On her way back from the village Corinna had thought she had glimpsed Lietner watching the track from the trees near the lodge. Then he wasn't there. She must have been dreaming. Such a silly illusion, she decided, when she knew he was far away. Dismissing the incident, she did not even mention it to her uncle. Thus she was surprised when as she and her uncle were in the middle of sorting the boxes of books to be sent to auction, Lietner arrived breathless at the door.

"Why were you hiding in the lane?" she queried.

"I did not want anyone local to see me. I really do not want any of the Metzger family to find out I have been here. Or why."

A huge smile over his face, excited and relieved, he eagerly volunteered his good news. It had only taken a month before he was suddenly instructed by one of his military superiors to return to Salzburg. They wanted to locate Etienne as soon as possible. He had written orders for Etienne to return immediately to headquarters, with no excuses or delay; these orders coming from the highest authority. Clearly Count von Hetsch-Radberg had used his power to impose his own very different solution to the whole dilemma. Etienne would be brought back into line, like it or not.

"I have been ordered to return Etienne, by force if necessary."

"So you know where to find him?"

"I have a good idea."

Lietner smiled very broadly without admitting anything, as usual. Diplomatic as ever.

"You have always known!" she challenged him kindly.

Of course Corinna then wanted to know why Lietner wasn't setting off that minute; he did not need to waste time here, she gushed all in one breath, eager to persuade him to be on his way. To which Lietner merely returned his half-hearted laugh, reminding her of her own past experiences where she had learnt daylight was not the right time for any secret movements. Later this evening would be the ideal time to slip across the valley.

Corinna shrugged forgivingly. Lietner's unswerving loyalty to his friend should be enough to save Etienne from any disaster. Automatically he became part of this same intrigue, but she felt they could depend upon Lietner in every circumstance. There was nothing to worry about.

"At last we are free to go to Kuchl," her uncle chuckled.

He had dutifully put off his visit, because the town was quite near Salzburg and he had not wanted to risk complicating anything for Etienne or even put Corinna in the slightest of danger. Now the restriction was over, they were both anticipating the journey, since Michael felt they both deserved a few days away and a change of scenery would do them good. Apart from leaving the books with a dealer, there would be plenty to interest them, including the small unusual shops to explore in the quaint town.

Several days later they had arrived and settled in their lodgings. The boxes of books disposed of, Corinna set off with her uncle to enjoy the various landmarks. In particular there was a pretty little church in the most extraordinary setting. A row of trees edged each side of the winding path, forming a soft columned guard to its front entrance, and the hallowed hush of the place could not fail to inspire an appreciation of these surroundings. Halting by one of the massive trees, Michael had turned her to point out something about the roof decoration when she suddenly tugged him aside. Positioned behind a wide tree trunk, she nodded towards the further end of the path.

"Look, look!"

"What is it?" Michael whispered, not understanding.

"That is the Count's private secretary," Corinna dared to whisper.

"What if it is?" he shrugged.

Peering carefully from this position, she then saw a second man who walked slowly up and down, across the front of the church, his head turning sharply in every direction, scanning the scene, ever watchful, before approaching the secretary. After a quick conversation, the secretary and his acquaintance disappeared inside the building.

Corinna's every instinct was to dash across the grass and follow them, but she made a determined effort to keep her curiosity in check. Maybe it was not as important as she thought.

"Why would he be meeting anyone here, of all places?" she asked her uncle.

"It has nothing to do with us" he replied firmly.

A short time later the two men retraced their steps out of the main entrance, where the secretary left first, now walking casually around the building to the rear with all the air of knowing his own importance and showing no sign of any duplicity on his part. The other man eventually followed the same route and made his way down to the small rear gate, where he signalled for a carriage, which must have been waiting further down the lane.

Corinna frowned, considering the situation. She stared at the ground, studying her shoes and wiggling her toes as she thought, when a shadow crossed close in front of her and stopped, making her glance up. The man startled her. She recognised the secretary immediately. Obviously he had not left.

"Fraülein Schopenhauer, Herr Holbach." he bowed slightly. He gave a little chuckle and grinned. "Since you have unfortunately witnessed my meeting with Herr Mahler, let me reassure you, I do as I am bid in my service to my master."

Herr Mahler! Klaus's father?

"I am sure it is none of our concern," she bluffed.

"I hope Herr Lietner is doing his best to find his friend, because there are those who do not appreciate his presence in their midst."

Corinna had barely taken the words in or even assembled a question before Michael interrupted. "If that is all, I bid you good day sir."

The secretary understood her uncle's hint and was instantly gone. "I think we should go back to the house immediately and finish packing." Michael declared.

Once back at the lodgings, Michael confessed that he was concerned. "I don't like this, Corinna. Although the secretary must be aware that Lietner is already off on a mission to fetch Etienne, he implied an urgency to the matter. If Herr Mahler is ignorant that Etienne will have to abandon his plans quite soon, Mahler might contemplate other methods to influence Etienne's departure."

"Such as?"

"I'm not sure."

Michael's frown deepened and his sigh made Corinna's alarm grow worse.

"I think Henri Mahler could be dangerous. Thank goodness we are going home tomorrow."

The next morning they were ready to leave. Everything had been carefully arranged in the hall. There was a set of boxes to be collected by the carrier and some personal luggage which they would take with them. A small carriage stood outside ready to take them to the pick-up point for the post coach. Corinna was in her plain and practical travelling clothes and Michael was busy bidding his landlord farewell when another carriage drew up nearby. Instantly a very smart young and handsome soldier stepped from the carriage and bowed gallantly towards her uncle.

"Herr Holbach. I am sorry to inconvenience you, but I have been sent to fetch you by Lieutenant Lietner," he said. "He requires a private word with you."

The pair of them were taken aback by the appearance of this man presenting himself here and his strange communication. They must have heard him wrong. But then he repeated the words exactly.

"I did not realise that Lietner knew where we were staying," said Michael.

"I only know he has sent me here, so he must have some knowledge of your progress."

Michael and Corinna exchanged a silent look, both aware that Lietner was in Salzburg and would not have had time to achieve his assignment yet. They could not understand this diversion to his mission. It seemed very strange.

"Does he expect me to travel all the way to Salzburg?" was all Michael could think to ask.

"That is not necessary. He proposes to meet you a few miles out of town. It should not delay you long. The carriage is for your journey and with your permission I am to remain here to protect your niece." He smiled and gave a little shrug.

"If he is that close, why can't he just come here?" Michael demanded.

"I am not in his confidence. I simply carry out my orders," the young man replied. He leaned against the coach, offering no other explanation, and seemed unconcerned and unaware of any problem concerning his instructions.

Michael gave it due consideration. Lietner would not have sent for him unless there was a good reason, and since he had sent a soldier to guard Corinna, Michael did as was suggested and hastily clambered into the coach, promising to be as quick as he could.

The coach rattled gently along out of sight, whilst her new companion stood by their belongings on the pavement and occasionally smiled pleasantly at her to reassure her that she had adequate protection if needed. The owner of the lodgings appeared at the door a little later, to mention that he had to leave for a prior appointment, but that the house was open to her if she wished to wait inside. She thanked him, but insisted she preferred to stay where she was.

Impatiently she fidgeted on the spot, continually looking up the street. Then she began to pace, her bonnet now swinging by its ribbons in her hand in time with her marching. Why was her uncle taking so long?

"I think we should wait inside," the soldier suggested.

The young man accompanied her inside the building and into the first room, where she settled into a chair with a sigh to wait for her uncle to reappear and explain what on earth this was all about. "I wish I knew what was happening," she ventured.

"I'm sure everything is fine," he reassured her, his face continuing to crinkle kindly at her, which was quite pleasant.

A little later the housekeeper popped her head around the door of Corinna's room to inform her that she was going to do some errands and would not be long. Corinna did not mind, since she had the company of such a fine young man, resplendent in his uniform. Indeed she could not stop looking at her companion. He was really quite handsome. She even blushed as he looked back at her, wondering if he could tell how much she admired him.

Her admiration was not allowed to last long, for at the sound of approaching footsteps outside in the hall, the young soldier headed for the door to see who was there. Peering outside, he quickly turned back to her and bowed.

"I am no longer needed here, Fraülein Schopenhauer. I must take my leave." Corinna could not think of anything to stop him going, only managing to voice her thanks for his diligence on her behalf.

"It has been a pleasure," came his departing remark, the delightful betraying smile on his grinning face indicating his own interest, which made her blush again.

The door closed behind him and she was left staring at the door, realising she did not even know his name. Then, rather than her uncle entering as expected, the stranger who appeared in his place was – Henri Mahler!

"Good afternoon Fraülein Schopenhauer. He is charming, isn't he, my son? He was so keen to meet you and keep you company."

It took moments to shake the foolishness from her senses and to realise that the handsome young man who had tricked her and her uncle had been Max's enemy – Klaus Mahler. It had been so easy to be taken in by his charming looks. How could she have been that naïve?

"Your uncle will be delayed, it seems. And your host and his housekeeper are absent."

"Sir, you were not invited into this room. Please do me the courtesy of leaving," she bravely declared, attempting to dismiss him.

"Unfortunately I cannot do that. I just need a few words with you. You are the sister and Metzger's neighbour. Quite a coincidence! I will tell you it has been inconvenient to have Herr Metzger in our midst, we will be glad when he leaves," he said in a sarcastic tone.

"That is nothing to do with me."

The man laughed, its dry crackle sounding harsh.

"Maybe not, but I think you might be able to assist in my plan. A short stay with us would provide a little insurance to persuade Herr Metzger to abandon his quest."

"What? But I have no part in this," she pleaded, aware her show of bravery was fading fast.

"Nevertheless, I have associates waiting at the rear to take you somewhere safe."

Corinna gasped, as her true predicament dawned on her. She shivered; she was in no hurry to go anywhere. How long had it been since her uncle had left the house? How long before he found out it was a false message and returned?

"There is no need to abduct me. Etienne is recalled. He has already been forced to give up. His grandfather has ordered his return."

"We shall see."

Henri Mahler ignored her argument. He obviously did not believe her.

"Now, if you would care to accompany me to…"

"No. This is ridiculous. I am of no use, it won't influence anyone," she continued. Her heart thumped furiously as she stared out of the window, wondering if anyone in the street would hear her if she shouted for help. How could she escape?

"There is no intention to harm you. If…"

His words were interrupted by heavy footsteps running into the hall and breathless voices exchanging information. Then there was an urgent knock on the door and Klaus reappeared to beckon his father out of the room, where in low tones a message was conveyed. Although she could not hear it, by the expressions on their faces it seemed to change everything. Herr Mahler returned to the doorway, but came no further.

"It seems there has been an incident and discretion dictates my swift departure. There is no longer any need for your company. I apologise for the inconvenience. Let us hope that Herr Metzger is not too badly injured, for I fear the wrath of Count Radberg on all concerned will be immense."

She heard their feet running through the hall, as they left very quickly. Orders were shouted from the back yard before a coach raced away. Leaning against the door, she quickly locked it, half expecting the men to return. Then it was so quiet, so eerie, the illusion seemed peculiar, and her fear refused to be lessened by this silence. She was cold and shaking and felt weak at the knees. She was all alone and now Etienne had been injured. She burst into great gulps of tears. She sank slowly to the floor and sat still, leaning against the door.

A cold fog had settled through her body. Etienne! What were his injuries, how bad was it? She had never imagined him being hurt. She tried not to panic, whilst the thought that he might even die tore at her heart. His precious life; his voice, his very being, his anger, his kindness. It was as if she could not breathe. She did not care about anything except Etienne, nothing but his safety.

By the time the housekeeper had returned and tapped on the door, to see if she was all right, Corinna was a quivering mess.

"Miss, Miss! Are you in there?"

Nervously she mumbled that she was still waiting for her uncle to return and would stay in the room until he had reappeared. At which the housekeeper, satisfied, went about busying herself with other duties in the house, the sound of her contented humming giving some comfort to Corinna.

Then there was a slight tap on the door and a different voice, a man's voice, one she did not recognise. "They have found your uncle," he said. "He is safe. He instructed me to hurry ahead to let you know."

Corinna was not about to believe any stranger, nor unlock the door. He obviously understood her reluctance and told her to come to the window, where she could see him coming down the street for herself. Slowly she did so. She looked up and down the street, her nose pressed against the glass, until there he was, walking a little unsteadily, supported by a second man.

Surely these men were genuine? It could not be another trick. Mahler and his men were long gone, but still she waited. She wasn't about to trust any stranger, however good willed they seemed.

"He was so worried about you," the young man reported, looking up at her from the pavement, mouthing it slowly so she could understand. He uncle looked tired, dusty and slightly the worst for wear, but his face when he saw her lit up with relief. She saw him thank the men most heartily and offer them some reward, which they refused, then, shaking hands all round, the good Samaritans departed. Only then did she force her tired, wobbly legs to move, but she would not unlock that door until he had reached it. Her uncle burst into the room and swept her into his arms before she could speak, begging her to forgive him for believing the message and leaving her. He should have known better.

"Oh my dearest. You are here! Thank goodness you are still here. After they deposited me so abruptly in the middle of nowhere without a word, they turned back towards town. I was terrified they meant to kidnap you."

"They tried," she confessed softly.

"Oh, no! You're not hurt, are you?"

She shook her head, unable to tell him the rest or to voice the terrible reason why she had been spared that fate.

"Oh, my dear child, the sooner we get home the better." He sank into a chair, exhausted by the whole drama. "I should have realised that if Herr Mahler learnt of your presence anywhere near Salzburg here, he might just try to gain some advantage. He must have seen us yesterday. I cannot believe you are safe. Forgive me for putting you at risk."

Corinna clung to her uncle, her face still pale and drawn.

"What is it? What is the matter?" he asked, now aware that there was more to come.

"They left me behind because they were told Etienne had been injured and feared reprisal from Count Radberg." There, she had said it out loud.

Michael could not speak, he was so shocked. He just stared at her. His mind now whirling, as hers had a short while ago. Eventually he drew a long breath, regained control and stood up.

"Home Corinna, right now," he said. Within seconds he was ushering her into the coach and issuing orders.

"What about Etienne?" she managed.

"Oh Corinna. Will you please worry about yourself for a change." he was not about to brook any delay in leaving. "No doubt we will be informed. The military look after their own. He will be in good hands."

As they travelled home Corinna attempted to quell her nerves, not knowing which had frightened or frustrated her more, the confrontation with Henri Mahler, the close proximity to Klaus or the awful worry about Etienne.

"I think we have both been naïve in this," Michael confessed. Corinna nodded; she did not like these complicated ruses. She had long tired of these games men seemed to relish in.

"All this travel is much over rated. I believe this journeying to and fro across the country is unnecessary. I much prefer to be amongst a community I trust," said Michael. Corinna was inclined to agree. All she wanted was to go home; nothing else mattered. Home was the answer, home with Uncle Michael, to be safe in his comforting arms and to have dear Martha fussing over her once more at the lodge. To relish their beloved surroundings and to be with people she knew; to see her friends and never leave the valley again.

It was less than a week later when the news that Etienne had returned home seriously injured and very ill from army manoeuvres spread through the valley, horrifying everyone. Corinna and Michael, who had been expecting it, knew the story was an attempt to conceal the truth from the family and the locals. Indeed they could hardly wait for Lietner to call to relay the facts of the matter.

"How bad is he?" Corinna asked, the moment Lietner entered.

"He has been shot in the top of his shoulder. He will recover, but he wasn't in the best of health anyway and it will take time. At least he is in the best place. Sophie will take good care of him."

"How did it happen? Please tell us all the details," Michael requested.

They sat gathered together while Lietner relayed the incident to them both

"We had an arranged procedure, despite the month having passed without contact, our meetings alternating between several places to avoid suspicion. As Etienne ambled along the cobbles towards me, when he finally appeared, I could not believe the change in him. He looked really ill. The short time of living in filthy alleys and rat holes had already made its mark. His health was clearly now as imperative as his safety. But before he reached me, he was approached by two people who drew him aside, then they all moved off together to a hostelry. Clearly, retrieving Etienne would need more assistance than I had thought. I withdrew briefly to find my adjutant to have him bring my men closer and to remain inconspicuous.

"Eventually Etienne and his acquaintances rolled out of the front door, seemingly ready to go their own ways, and Etienne disappeared into the wilderness of hovels close by. I delayed following immediately because of the possibility of other eyes in the dark watching. Besides, I knew where to find Etienne's lodgings. When I reached the place, I noticed men lingering on the corner, their conversation low and sinister. One of them even nodded towards the building in question. I was worried.

"As soon as the men had wandered off, I tapped at his door and found myself dragged inside and the door kicked shut again. You can imagine the reception I received when I told him why

I was there. He was furious, fervently cursing his grandfather and the military hierarchy for sanctioning the order. He hated being forced to give up and promised it would take more than myself to make him, at which I told him that that too had been arranged. There was no persuading him and I left him to fetch my men, because it was obvious we would have to take him by force despite any commotion it would cause.

"On my return I found the door was open and an awful scuffle was taking place inside. Etienne's face was grim and sapped of energy, and he was struggling and stumbling. I heard the shot being fired and the adversary ran out of the door, leaving Etienne lying on the floor as pale as death. I could not believe it."

Corinna cringed, her fists clenched tight, as she imagined the scene.

"Luckily by then my men arrived, we plugged the wound and delivered Etienne to the barracks for the proper medical attention he needed. After which it was agreed that he should be sent home to Sophie as soon as he was fit enough to make the journey. We knew that once Count Radberg heard of the incident, he would insist on Etienne being placed under his own care. Indeed his grandfather had been determined to take control, despite any refusal, but we were prepared to detach the whole unit to make sure Etienne's wishes were carried out. Every one of his men was prepared to risk their careers, prepared to disobey any orders to the contrary. Their loyalty is extraordinary. I am very proud of them. Anyway, Etienne has survived the ordeal, it is all over now and he is home."

At the end of Lietners' long story they all sat in silence, each exhausted by the drama and lost in their own thoughts.

"What on earth was Etienne thinking of?" Michael could not but ask.

"I think he had hoped that his prolonged absence would make his grandfather act in some way to protect Etienne by putting pressure on Mahler's dissident organisation. But his grandfather had recognised the scheme and instructed his retrieval instead. Of course after the shooting, who knows what will happen."

Corinna hardly slept that night. The story had been much worse than she expected. A mass of visions filled her mind; there was Sophie fussing over his absences, Frederick teasing him about his flirtations, Etienne with his horses and making that infamous jump. Then Etienne laying on the ground, the dark red blood beginning to cover his shirt, his expression incredulous and his eyes staring briefly at the world before they flickered closed. She could not sleep at all after that.

Despite all the reassurance she had been given, she knew she would not feel any relief until she saw him for herself. As she picked at her breakfast, she attempted to persuade her uncle to let her visit Etienne.

Of course he was going to agree, if only to prove Etienne was tougher than she imagined. So while Michael went to speak to Sophie, Lietner arranged for her to be ushered quietly up to the room where Etienne lay. Corinna caught her breath as she entered, for whilst she had not expected a miracle overnight, she had been unprepared to see him look so drawn, so pale or exhausted. Even the bandaging around his shoulder and arm, well padded, came as a shock. Her heart now pounding heavily, thumping in her ears and her head and tears swelling in her eyes.

"It looks a lot worse than it is," Lietner whispered.

Etienne groaned and slowly opened his eyes, staring at the ceiling, unaware of his visitors.

"Hell's teeth, I survive a war to be shot by some maniac," he complained, holding his arm. Lietner grinned sympathetically and helped his friend to sit up, at which point Etienne caught sight of Corinna.

"You should not have allowed her in here," Etienne grimaced.

"I had to see how you were," she explained.

"Do not expect conversation. I do not feel particularly affable at the moment."

"I understand, I will go," she said, but Lietner shook his head. Etienne winced and shuffled about, trying to find a more comfortable position.

"You shouldn't have put yourself at risk. I wanted you to give it up," she whispered.

Etienne actually managed a forgiving smile. "We do what we think is right at the time, don't we?" he said. Corinna nodded, reflecting on how something so simple in the beginning had become so complicated.

"All of this because of Max. - for Max," she sighed.

"Because of Gerard. For Gerard!" he corrected her.

"Whatever!" she exclaimed. Goodness, this was not the time to argue over trivialities. He sank back into the bed and glared at her in silence.

"We - I - have to see this through, however long it takes," he said.

"Please Etienne. I don't want you risking your life again," she pleaded softly.

"I will not be dictated to!"

"Would there be any point? Oh, this is all my fault."

"No Corinna. Listen to me, did you ever ask me to help you, did you ask me to interfere? No, I managed to get in this mess all by myself."

"I told you it was madness. So did Kronmeier," said Lietner.

"Don't give up," Etienne whispered to her.

"I am only being realistic."

The past few minutes had already left him worn out, exhausted mentally and physically. His eyes closed as he gave into necessary sleep once more.

Michael popped his head in to see the invalid with Sophie, then, satisfied, they all quietly made their way downstairs again. Lietner informed them reluctantly that he would have to depart the next day. He had to return to duty. Unfortunately this left Etienne at the mercy of any unwelcome visitors. They all knew whom he meant. He begged Michael to be on hand to assist Sophie if his grandfather came. Michael naturally reassured Lietner that he felt sure they could manage between them, but Corinna secretly wondered if any of them had the strength to handle Etienne's grandfather. She hoped it would not come to that.

Michael, as a concerned neighbour and an old friend, made frequent visits to the house, which passed without any unusual comment. Their many calls were of some relief, since she had so much to say to Etienne.

"I haven't given up, I just don't expect miracles any more" she confessed to Etienne. "Max will always be here, in my thoughts, in my heart. I can hope, I can dream, but not at the expense of such sacrifice."

"You worry too much."

Just then Frederick came to inform him that a messenger had arrived with a letter from Vienna. It was perfectly clear who had sent it. The man, in dark clothes and gold braid, appeared in the doorway, stepped forward smartly, nodded and handed

Etienne the letter. Etienne took one look at the handwriting, frowned, flipped it open and hardly glanced at it before tossing it onto the table and giving his answer to the silent waiting attendant.

"My grandfather is not welcome here."

The man was gone in an instant without comment, whilst Corinna and Michael exchanged a glance, both sorry for the messenger who had to deliver that reply and both praying that Count Radberg would for once take notice of his grandson's wishes.

All hopes of that vanished the morning Corinna saw the liveried coach rattling down the road from the village, towards the estate across the valley. She ran home as fast as she could to report the sighting and when a breathless Frederick galloped up the lane to fetch them to help his mama fend off his lordship's demands, they were already on their way in the pony and trap. They found Sophie in the most indignant state any of them had seen her in, tapping her foot and pacing up and down the landing, waving her arms about, whilst Charlotte cringed nearby.

"The manners of the man! Barging his way in here. To be ordered out of the room, in my own home!" she exploded. Michael, Sophie, Frederick and Corinna entered together, to find Etienne sitting attending to papers, ignoring the statesman who stood in front of him. The Count turned, surprised at their entrance. He glared and tried to wave them away, but Etienne immediately bade them stay, reminding his grandfather that he had no jurisdiction in this house. The important man's antagonism was obvious. Etienne did not care. He sat scribbling a few notes on the papers in front of him.

"It appears that I do not receive the respect I am entitled

to" snarled Count von Hetsch-Radberg. But one moved, and he turned back to confront Etienne again.

"I heard you had been wounded. I have travelled all this way to make sure the reports are correct. I am pleased it is it is not serious," he said.

"I told you not to come," replied Etienne. "And I find your concern for my health a little hypocritical."

"I am not at all pleased with this latest escapade of yours," replied his grandfather. "I had hoped your obsession would lessen. Luckily you are astute enough to obey the Imperial Order."

"God's teeth! Damn your influence!" Etienne roared. His grandfather had never heard such words spoken to him in public, not from his equals, not even from the Emperor Franz Josef. He was hard pressed to control his immense temper.

"Be warned. I will have you dismissed from the Military!"

"Do your worst. I was tiring of my army career in any case. Why should I watch the competence of my men be wasted by the poor command of senior officers," Etienne snapped.

"You cannot remain in this provincial wilderness," stated Radberg calmly.

"This provincial wilderness, this place and my home here in particular, are exactly what suits me," came the forceful reply. By now Sophie had gone to her nephew's side, while concerned looks were being exchanged between the rest of them.

"That is enough, my lord. With respect I think you should leave. Etienne should rest," interrupted Michael sternly. The older man looked shocked at the impudence, but Michael had now advanced to stand face to face with him. If it needed all the male staff in the household to persuade him to leave, they would be summoned, her uncle promised.

"Sophie, Frederick will please fetch the staff to escort his lordship to his coach," said Michael.

They were both happy to do so, glad to be doing something useful. Meanwhile the remaining three facing his lordship felt relieved that they were out of the way, for at least any reference to the actual cause of the problem would not be disclosed to the rest of the family.

"Come back to Vienna," his grandfather asked.

"Why should I, when you refuse to help me achieve the one thing I have ever asked from you?" Etienne snapped harshly. The status of the court nobility is too important to you. Look how you disowned your own daughter and ignored Gerard and me, until cousin Felix died and you need a new heir. Are you capable of any genuine human feelings for other people?" He shook his head, declaring he had no intention of ever setting foot in any of his grandfather's residences again and the whole idea did not bother him in the least.

"Please leave, my Lord, you are not helping matters," Michael told Radberg again.

"I never took you for a sentimental fool, Etienne. Your devotion to your brother has exceeded expectation. Even when your young wife died, you proved yourself strong enough to carry on."

Corinna and Michael both gasped, horrified at these ill-chosen words. In the tense hush which followed Corinna saw a desperate look settle in Etienne's eyes, and a long slow breath was heard.

"Strong?" Etienne lowered his head to stare vacantly at the floor. "You really have no idea. I am nothing like you think. I wanted to die without Eva." His whole frame sagged at the memory.

"I think enough has been said. Sophie and Frederick will walk you out," said Michael. The aristocratic lord looked ruffled and displeased, a brief flicker of his eyebrows the only acknowledgement of his astonishment. Then, with the sounds of the staff gathering below, he nodded, apparently willing to concede that he was not wanted here. He turned and walked out of the room. His departure had little effect on Etienne, who now voiced his thoughts aloud in a breaking voice, heedless of his audience.

"I am only a man trying to get through life," he said. "I am still in my thirties, yet I am a war veteran and I feel like an old man. I have nursed the remains of my courageous men back from the disaster of Solferino. They will never be the same after one of the most terrible battles in history. When the smoke, panic and chaos, fire and screams ceased, we left behind forty thousand dead. You have no idea…"

His words faded. He had touched the deepest raw memory of that scene which now reflected on his strained pale face, and Corinna could not bear any more; it broke her heart. She had never seen this man so vulnerable, so desperate to make sense of the past, and so lost.

"Oh, Etienne." she whispered sympathetically, the struggling emotion in her voice an echo of his. She felt so inadequate as Michael took her elbow to guide her away, advising her that Etienne was best left alone, to deal with his melancholy in his own way. She was not sure, but Michael always knew best. Corinna and Michael left the building, the only witnesses to the depth of Etienne's private pain, both unwilling to dwell on the incident.

"Do not allow your sympathy for him to become something else," Michael uttered softly. Corinna stretched up and kissed him gently on the cheek. In truth she knew she would always be fond of Etienne, but she had passed that stage of complicating her life with irrational dreams.

These last few hours had drained her enough. She felt as if all the emotion had been sucked out of her. She just wanted to go back to the lodge, where she could heal herself and restore her strength and sanity. She wanted to be the Corinna she used to be, to be happy and not to have to worry over anything for a while. Surely that was not too much to ask?

CHAPTER NINE

The crisis with Count von Hetsch-Radberg over, life settled down to its normal routine, with Frederick often laughing to himself as he remembered the embarrassing departure their grandfather had had to contend with. The servants had formed a guard to the door, all armed in one way or another, with fire irons, pitchforks, roasting spits, even heavy ladles from the kitchen. It caused quite a stir in the household. Everyone remembered their part and would often refer to it with affection. And day by day Etienne was getting better, walking, then riding again, a sure sign he was recovering.

Corinna had just finished some baking in the kitchen when she heard a series of uneven steps outside, interspersed with a muffled disagreement. Drying her hands as the sounds came nearer, she was about to reach for the door handle when Etienne beat her to it. He pushed the door open wide with his foot, supporting a battered Frederick, who was leaning heavily on his shoulder.

"May we prevail upon your kindness?" said Etienne. "I am sorry to bother you, but I can't take him home in this state. Could we just clean him up and make a small repair to his coat?"

He helped Frederick into a chair, fingering a piece of cloth still loosely attached to the jacket before letting it fall back.

"It was his own fault for trying to show off. He should have known better," joked Etienne, giving Frederick a playful slap on the back and making him wince. Corinna exchanged a smile with the older Metzger and scolded Frederick for not having more sense. Frederick glared at them both. He was hurt, but despite his groaning he was receiving no sympathy, which made him sulk.

"Gods knows what has come over him lately," Etienne went on. "This overestimation of his horsemanship will not impress his mother, let alone Irene. Who would ever consider him a good prospect if he continues to act so foolishly? He could have broken his neck."

This latest remark made Frederick utter a mild, flustered defence before he realised his cousin was teasing. Corinna tended to her patient and Etienne settled himself to watch the proceedings, sitting on the edge of the table, with one foot slowly brushing the floor as naturally as if it had been a life-long habit. The content reflection continuing as he turned back to his cousin.

"To think I was glad to venture out with this idiot. Let us hope I do not suffer for it by having your mother deafening my ears for days because you hurt yourself, while you were with me."

Corinna could almost imagine Sophie's reaction to Frederick's condition. Etienne expressed his thanks and bundled Frederick back towards the horses, where poor Frederick sat uncomfortably on his circling steed, trying to stop it from galloping off, while Etienne seemed in no particular hurry to leave. Indeed Etienne deliberately turned his horse and bending low from the saddle, relayed a parting comment.

"I must return to Vienna – quite soon" he confided quietly.

"No! Please. You said you would not!" came her instant response.

"I must. I will talk to you privately before I go."

Corinna was not in the lodge, not in the grounds at all, yet he knew where she would be and set off into the woods, walking to her favourite spot by the little bridge over the stream. Sure enough she was there, but he saw her stiffen as she heard his approach. He cleared his throat, as was his habit before beginning anything disagreeable.

"I have to go to Vienna," he began. "Not because I was summoned, but for my own reasons. Believe me, Corinna, this time I will have an end to this."

"You declared that this valley, your estate and home, meant everything to you, and now you are prepared to spend so long away on an almost futile cause. You have already tried everything you could think of."

Etienne grunted, taking little notice of her words. She did not understand this sudden consuming righteous determination, nor the sudden euphoria which made him suddenly so sure of himself.

"No other futile errands out of the country?" she queried.

He shook his head, a wry glint in his eyes as he deliberately did not answer.

"You and Lietner are both eloquent at saying nothing," she mused. He shrugged nonchalantly, and they fell silent for a while.

"Why didn't you tell me about your encounter with Klaus and his father?" he asked a little later.

"How did you find out?"

"Your uncle felt I should be made aware of what happened.

I apologise for putting you in danger. I never thought he would try to abduct you in an attempt to influence matters. Did he hurt you?"

"No, not at all. It just frightened me," she admitted.

"Nevertheless, it should not have happened."

"It is over and done with. Forgotten." Corinna insisted.

"Not by me."

They fell quiet; they had both been honest with each other. And then he was gone.

The announcement of Etienne's return to Vienna surprised everyone, but the manner of his statement indicated he would not tolerate any inquisition into his decision. Sophie and Frederick were speechless and Charlotte was distraught at losing her dearest cousin for another period of duty. Corinna threw herself into tasks about the lodge, keeping deliberately busy. Nothing was too much trouble and when in the village on errands, she forced herself to chat to everyone she met. She smiled at each greeting and was merry at their banter and attentive to their conversation, although if anyone had asked her, she would have been unable to repeat any of the gossip she had just heard. She could not shake off the worry about what exactly Etienne would do in Vienna.

Frederick, of course was riding back and forth across the valley, filling both the lodge and his home with his happy babbling about Irene, interrupting everyone, his exceptional exuberance and infectious voice invading every quarter as everyone patiently put up with him. Even Michael could not hide a chuckle at this behaviour. It was years since he had witnessed anyone so madly head over heels in love, he remarked.

With Etienne away for months, Sophie decided to cheer the

place up with another soirée, a small affair which would include Irene amongst the guests, since she was Frederick's intended. Thus the Metzger house became a hive of activity as the preparations proceeded and Irene felt more than a little nervous, this being her first introduction to such a grand event.

Corinna remembered how she had felt at her first society function and deliberately arrived early to boost Irene's confidence. Irene had clutched Corinna's hand again and again as she thought of some fresh anxiety which might befall her tonight. All of them were dismissed as Corinna reassured her that all would be fine. She wanted Irene to feel special for this occasion and knew she could add some delicate finishing touches to improve her appearance. With a twist here and curl there, she decoratively arranged her hair into a more flattering style, then enhanced her dress with a few magic stitches. Irene was speechless as she looked at her reflection in the mirror. She paraded around the room to Corinna's many words of encouragement, approval and admiration. "Frederick will fall in love with you all over again," she enthused, and then impulsively she hugged Irene, before draping her own beautiful best shawl around Irene's shoulders to complete the picture.

Corinna slipped outside on the landing for a moment to herself, to soak in the genteel decoration all about her and listen to the sounds of the house she knew almost as well as the family who lived here. The event went well and Irene and Frederick shone, the benefit of being in love evident by their happy faces. Sophie was her usual congenial self and even Charlotte excelled herself by being nice to everyone without any effort.

The next day Corinna drove over in the pony and trap to collect her shawl. She found the house recovering from the previous night, the staff yawning their way about the building, their steps slow and uncertain. Charlotte and other guests had remained resting upstairs, the occasional tray of something edible being taken to their rooms rather than them having to brave the tiring journey to the dining room. Irene, although risen, lazily lay on the sofa, her eyes closed, trying to remember how she had managed to dance for so long, she murmured. Corinna smiled sympathetically, picked up her shawl and crept away.

Downstairs she saw Frederick, Sophie and a stranger talking by the front door. Alone in the hall and with the study door open in front of her, Corinna could not resist her chance for a long-overdue private look at Gerard's portrait. It had been ages since she been able to stand there gazing up at him with the same fondness as she felt when looking at the one of her mother back at the lodge. Sadly, unlike her mother's, which she could reach and touch, almost feeling the person she was through the canvas, this one was well out of reach. All she had was her imagination.

Tilting her head she smiled at Gerard, silently thanking him for what he had been to her mother and the happiness they had shared. Then, stepping back to bid him farewell for now, she saw that the lid of the bureau was slightly open. She knew that inside were Eva's letters, that little pack of letters tied with a faded ribbon. That he had not locked it seemed to indicate the regularity of his habit of reading them.

She stared at the opening and guiltily eased up the lid a little further, the slight squeak as it moved making her catch her breath. Yes, there they were in their precious haven, faded and worn by his frequent handling, a memory of his love and his devotion. It made her sad that there was no place for another in his heart.

The bulging contents of the desk were a testimony to his life, papers and documents crammed into various compartments, little boxes and items wrapped in tissue paper. They made her ponder wistfully about him a little more before shaking herself back to reality. This would not do; she must get back to the lodge.

But then amongst Eva's treasures she caught sight of the corner of a box beneath more letters tied together. The pattern on the box was a design she knew and she hesitated only for a second before flipping the letters to one side. The rustle of movement seemed so loud to her guilty progress.

It was a wooden carved box; one identical to her mother's. Her heart was beginning to pound nervously. Could it belong to Gerard? Surely yes. Matching boxes, what a wonderful romantic idea. How she wanted to touch it, to caress the magic it must hold; but she did not dare to break the spell it cast on her.

Then sudden approaching steps from the hall made her jump back instinctively and pull the lid downwards. She snatched her shawl up and walked away towards the window. Her hands were trembling. The knowledge of this box excited her; she needed to talk to her uncle, she had to find out more, but first she must make a graceful exit.

She pretended to stare out of the window as Sophie and Frederick entered and turned to smile at them. She fingered her cuffs nervously and then stopped herself, placing one hand firmly over the other.

"You seem to be the only ones to have surfaced this morning," she began merrily, "And to have received a visitor already is remarkable."

"It was merely a messenger from Etienne," Frederick replied dismissively. This was the obvious moment to depart, so Corinna gathered up her shawl from the chair and started for the door, offering the expected pleasantries about the previous evening.

"I do not know what he expects," complained Sophie.

"Is something wrong?" Corinna asked with a casual politeness, despite not being particularly interested. She wanted to get back to her uncle; she wanted to know if he knew the significance of that replica box being here. Would Uncle Michael know of its existence? Impatiently she concentrated on being her usual self, whilst trying to make sure no one noticed the odd way she was holding her hands.

"Etienne has invited Elizabeth Brecker and her family to stay here next month" said Sophie. "He will be escorting them on the whole journey."

Corinna stared at her in utter silence, puzzled and tilting her head slightly, a little unsure she had heard her correctly. She could not understand why after all this time Elizabeth was suddenly being feted once more.

"For any special reason?" she asked, not really expecting an answer.

"He says he is honouring a promise," Frederick replied, unconvincingly.

"How kind of him. I hope they enjoy their visit."

Corinna shrugged her shoulders philosophically, it did not really matter to her, she just wanted to escape and get back to her uncle. She had more important things on her mind at the moment. Etienne and his friendships were not, for once, part of her concern.

She ran to find her uncle the moment she was home, then grabbed his arm and dragged him inside. He was intrigued by her excited behaviour, wondering what on earth was behind it.

Corinna explained what she had seen and began her torrent of questions. What did he think, what did he know, she begged at his knee.

Michael smiled sympathetically and settled back to wistfully relate the little more he knew, which was not much. Yes, they had matching boxes, her mother had used hers as a jewellery box, so she could see it every day without her husband suspecting the delight it gave her. As for Gerard, he had no need to hide his box from anyone; it went with him where ever he went. He could look on it every day, whenever he wished and think of her. Corinna could easily imagine what the precious boxes had meant to both of them, and the thought of that made her feel tremendously content and happy. Satisfied, she sat quietly with her uncle for the rest of the evening, her head resting upon his shoulder and her arm tucked into his. Neither needed to talk any more, for both of them were comfortable silently mulling over their own thoughts together.

A few weeks later, the Metzger household burst into a flurry of hectic preparations once more, heralding the imminent arrival of Elizabeth and her parents. And when eventually the report of a shiny liveried coach arriving with his guests filtered through the valley, it left no impression on Corinna. Indeed their presence at the Metzger residence was of no interest. When several invitations were delivered requesting her to meet the new arrivals, Corinna saw no necessity to pay attention to him or his guests. Not that Corinna was the only one adverse to this visiting group; during their apparent sallies out, she learned that Charlotte was finding every clever excuse to avoid the sight of her cousin flaunting Elizabeth on his arm. For once Corinna felt in accord with Charlotte. She did not particularly wish to be included in their company either, and luckily she had every excuse she needed. When she was not helping in the preparation for the forthcoming village festival, she was looking after the younger children and keeping them entertained and out of the way.

On one of the rare afternoons she had to herself, she was perched in the upstairs window when she saw Etienne ride up the drive. At least he was on his own. Out of habit she went down to meet him, oblivious to the possibility that his visit would have any connection with his visiting guest. Indeed she had given such little thought to Elizabeth that Corinna had not even considered her to be the only reason for his journey.

"Corinna, damn you, you would try the patience of a saint. How many invitations do we have to send to get you to come to the house?" he snapped the instant he saw her. She told him very calmly, that she had no intention of witnessing the demonstration of his charming social graces on poor Elizabeth, and in fact she was quite astonished that Elizabeth should have any inclination to renew her acquaintance with him at all. After the indication in Vienna that she favoured another, she did not understand how he had persuaded her to travel all this way to become a house guest for a while, even if it was as part of honouring a promise made some time ago.

"Well now she is here, you might at least have the politeness to call on her," he declared, ignoring the arguments she had presented.

"Etienne! There is no need for me to fall in with your arrangements simply because you have tired of playing the host already. I refuse to pay polite conversation to a girl I met only once. Besides, she has Frederick, Irene and even Charlotte to amuse her, let alone the family members who came with her."

"If I told you the family came from Heidelberg, would that make any difference?"

She looked at him suspiciously, her eyes wide. "Why should it?" she replied cautiously.

"Why indeed?" he grinned.

Heidelberg - Max. He would not have gone back to Heidelberg, there was no sense in that! No, that twinge of hope leapt in her heart and then vanished. This man was only tormenting her to make her do what he wanted.

"You're wasting your time. I'm not coming."

"I'm surprised at your selfish attitude, Corinna."

Etienne paused, scrutinising her, somewhat annoyed that his words were having no effect on her. She had nothing else to say to him. Purposefully she went to the door, opened it and stood there refusing to look at him. He realised that he would achieve little by staying.

"Then I will have to bring her here," came his muttered parting remark.

Corinna grinned to herself as he rode off. She did not believe for one minute that he intended to bring her to the lodge.

When she heard the coach pull up below the next day, Corinna took little notice. A glance from the window merely confirmed that it was the coach from across the valley. Curled up with a book and not in a sociable mood, she returned to the pages. Martha could let him in if she liked; it wasn't going to make any difference to her intention to remain away from his guests.

She did not hear Etienne's stride through the hall or his voice blustering against her stubbornness, and assumed that the visitor had left, so when after a pause, the door burst opened and swiftly closed again, it startled her.

"Cor-IN-na!" yelled the excited voice.

Corinna froze like a statue. Her skin turned cold and a shiver went down her spine. She was sure she had stopped breathing. This was not true, this could not be! This person, this man standing there, was an hallucination. Yet he moved, smiled, a beam on its face from ear to ear…

It was Max. He swept across the room and lifted her off her feet, hugging her gleefully and spinning, whirling her around and around, laughing aloud. Corinna tried to stop him, eventually untangling herself and pushing him away. She desperately struggled to find any words.

"Max!" she gulped. She had to sit down. Her legs had gone weak, and all the whirling around had made her dizzy.

"Max, Max, Max! Why have you come here?" she pleaded, alarm in her voice.

"You would not come to the Metzger house. You ignored every invitation which was sent?"

The Metzger house! Etienne! No, No. Etienne had said he wanted to protect him, but to bring him to his own home? How was that keeping him safe? What about the other guests? Max could not hide there – or anywhere in Austria, was he mad? A hundred thoughts rushed through her head. If only he had sent a message somehow, warned her of his presence. How could he escape if Etienne had control of him again?

"Oh, Corinna. Don't look so worried, everything is all right. I am no longer a fugitive. Everything has been sorted out. I am safe to do what I want from now on. I am not in any danger. Really, it is true. It is so wonderful." There was overwhelming joy on his face.

"But how? How can you be safe? You haven't explained."

He could not stop himself. He picked her up again, hugged her tightly and then set her down to let her get her breath back.

Corinna had long learned not to believe in miracles, and she still did not believe in this one. "I presume Baron Metzger is responsible for you being here?" she asked him pityingly.

"Of course he is. It is all thanks to him that the military have given me a pardon."

"Why would they give you a pardon? Nothing has changed, you still deserted. Oh Max, how could you have been so foolish to risk believing…"

"Corinna. Stop worrying. Honestly, I have not walked into another trap. I had my own ambassador in Vienna recently, to find out if Herr Metzger remained genuine."

"You relied on someone else? In Vienna."

"Dearest, it was the only way. It had to be someone no one else knew. I had to be careful."

He was her exuberant brother once more, his old cheerful manner and uncontrolled happiness obliterating everything. He looked well and healthy, his face alight, his eyes dancing as he posed proudly in the best of clothes for her to admire. He obviously did not have a care in the world, but it was no good; she was still in shock. Her anxiety for him was a hard habit to break. She could not believe he was safe.

"Tell me exactly. How did Herr Metzger influence this outcome?"

"Oh, that can wait for later. Corinna, there is something much more important I want to tell you."

More important? Nothing was more important than this!

"No, no!" she screamed. But he ignored her protest.

"I met someone in Heidelberg. Her name is Ella. It is all thanks to her unconditional support and faith in me that I have a future. She has been brilliant in all this, I don't deserve her."

Corinna felt as if all the stuffing had been knocked out of

her; he trusted some pretty girl to that degree. She thought her head would burst. Max gabbled on so much that she lost track, she could not concentrate on the words. She could not absorb all this information.

"You'll be surprised. She's longing to meet you again. Let me bring her in. She's waiting in the coach." He had dashed out before she could refuse and returned dragging a female with him back into the room. A female Corinna recognised immediately. Ella was Elizabeth! She had been acting for Max and in league with Etienne. The pair of them had presented such a convincing act.

"How do you like my Ella?" he beamed, blushing slightly and holding tightly onto her hand as Elizabeth nervously smiled at her and bobbed a curtsey.

"Forgive the deception, I could not tell you in Vienna. I did not dare," Elizabeth whispered.

"Oh, Corinna. It was not her idea to deliberately mislead you!" Max laughed.

No, Corinna knew exactly whose idea it had been. She could see it quite clearly. Etienne's public display parading Elizabeth around Vienna and more recently, continuing the charade locally over these last few days, must have continued to amuse him, no doubt.

Max's hug made Elizabeth giggle. He kept his arm around her, the familiarity between them obviously nothing new. Corinna was lost for words. It was obvious they were besotted with each other, too relaxed in each other's company, too content for it to be a sudden infatuation.

"May I join you now?" came the voice from the hall.

"Of course, come in," said Max loudly.

Corinna scowled at his impertinence. Whose home did he

think this was, that he could give permission for all and sundry to saunter in as they wished? Especially since she knew the voice – Etienne. He too seemed to be under the impression that he could simply make himself at home there.

Etienne casually sauntered into the room to make himself comfortable in a chair facing them all. No longer the attentive host of recent days, he exuded a carefree charm, still smirking, his grin betraying that wicked mischief of old. In fact his self-satisfied attitude made her seethe. Why couldn't Etienne have just told her? She hated him for keeping this, of all things, a secret from her.

"Etienne Metzger! I have finally concluded that your main purpose in life is to deliberately mislead me at every opportunity, even on the smallest of matters. Although I fail to see the satisfaction you derive from making me feel a fool so often!" she declared, shaking her head wearily.

"I must admit, I cannot help myself. Besides, what could I have told you? Nothing was settled until recently. It would have been remiss of me to give you false hope."

"Herr Metzger has kept his word and everything has worked out perfectly," said Max, beaming and giving Ella another hug. "I would not come back to Austria without her."

Corinna watched them together, aware that Ella was the one he would look to in the future, the one he would think of first. This pretty girl had become foremost in his affections. Max had plans, and although Corinna smiled and murmured warm responses in the right places while Max bubbled on, she could not concentrate fully on what he was telling her.

She transferred her concentration to the devil who sat opposite. All she wanted to know was how Etienne had managed this.

"So how did you manage to secure the authorities' reprieve so suddenly?" she asked.

"We were lucky. Klaus made a mistake. He tried to be too clever, too greedy." Etienne shrugged. No, that was not good enough. It was too simple. Even if he had disgraced Klaus or made his usefulness redundant, how would that change anything?

Etienne could see by the expression on her face that she was far from satisfied, but eyed her defiantly, making it clear that any inquisition would have to wait. It would be in private and on his terms, not hers. This was not the place. True enough, Corinna read the meaning and disliked being put off, although she sensibly accepted that making a scene in front of this enthusiastic, happy couple would not be good for anyone.

Just then Uncle Michael returned, hurrying into the room to see who his visitors were. He was overwhelmed with Etienne's explanation of events and delighted to meet his nephew at last, immediately treating him with the same generous affection he had bestowed on Corinna. There were hugs and congratulations and a great fuss was made of his two new guests. Michael shook Etienne's hand enthusiastically, thanking him profusely.

Etienne tried to make light of his part in the saga, but Michael would not let him leave until he had revealed some of the story. Typically, he seemed prepared to tell Michael a little more than he would say to her, although as the pensive Corinna listened, the original simplified version had little detail added. Events had unfolded faster than any of them had been prepared for. Klaus Mahler had lost his usefulness to the state. Immunity for several reluctant informants had provided evidence against Klaus in court. The military authorities had accepted that Max had been forced into running away to prevent him becoming a witness to the other dealings Klaus was involved in. Max had been exonerated and cleared of desertion, and at last he was safe.

Everyone seemed pleased with his explanation, except for Corinna. For the moment Etienne could avoid her interrogation, but he need not think he had heard the last of this. Indeed her very silence, unnoticed by everyone else, registered her total distrust of his account. And when her eyes caught his, he merely returned an infuriating grin before he turned his attention elsewhere.

Eventually the excited banter subsided and the visitors left for the Metzger residence. Corinna made her farewells to Max and Ella, trying her best to be cheerful, hugging them each in turn and promising to see them soon. Her uncle repeated the display of affection, warmly promising to make frequent visits to see them, being eager to get to know Max as well as he did Corinna.

"I though you would have been ecstatic," Etienne whispered as he passed her to join them in the carriage.

"Not until I know what conniving ploy you used to achieve it," she responded.

"Always so cynical, Corinna. Why can't you just accept the fact that your beloved brother is safe and his reputation is restored?"

She smiled weakly. There had to be something else behind this turn of fortune. She had no peace of mind; she still felt anxious. Besides which, she was still far from convinced with Etienne's version of events.

Naturally enough, everyone was caught up amid the ongoing euphoria and making a fuss of Max, but Corinna could not quite adjust to this sudden development nor make sense of her feelings. She was pleased for Max, she really was, but she needed the old Max back, to share things with. Yet despite her visits to the Metzger house, she never had the chance to be with him in private, to sit with him, talk to him at length about anything, to remind him how they had each always been each other's closest friend. They had depended on, defended and cared for each other all their lives, and now she could not dispel the nervous fear that they had drifted apart, that the special affinity between them seemed to have been lost. It was obvious Max did not need her any more, despite all they had been through in the past, and she realised that they would never be so close again. She had been replaced as his soulmate and confidant. Max had someone else to take care of him. He clearly loved someone more than he did her, and it hurt. She felt angry, jealous and rejected, but she fought back her emotion.

"His head is in the clouds. You must forgive him. I am sure his depth of affection for you is still the same," Uncle Michael whispered.

The fact that her dear uncle had recognised the problem and tried to make her feel better was of little comfort. The disappointment was hard to shake off and she tried her best not to let her self-pity show. She knew it was illogical, but she could not help herself.

Max, Ella and her family were soon on their way back to Germany, his new life ahead of him. Even at this stage, Corinna could only go through the actions expected of her, the promises to write, the kisses and hugs, the wide smile on her face as they all waved goodbye.

She had lost her brother. Ever since his desertion she had

thought only of him, put him first in her life, and now she had this empty void inside which refused to ease. The contentment she should have felt over the situation refused to materialise; at times she felt detached, as if she was not here. Maybe it was because there were still matters she wanted clarified.

A few days later, while everyone else was taking refreshment on the terrace at the Metzger house, Corinna followed their host into the gardens. It was the perfect opportunity to confront Etienne.

"Are you ever going to explain?" she began.

"And how nice to see you today. Such a cordial greeting. Such gracious manners," he countered.

"It can't be that simple, Etienne. Just because Max was forced into running away to prevent him becoming a witness to the other dealings Klaus was involved in, that wouldn't be enough for the military to drop the charges."

"Why not? It sounds perfectly logical to me."

But Max had deserted; that was still a military offence. There was no changing that fact. It still did not ring completely true. There had to be something else behind this turn of fortune.

"What else? What lies have you fabricated?"

"You are never satisfied!"

How could she be? If it was based on a lie, it could become unravelled just as quickly.

"Klaus eventually went too far, even for his own father to condone," he said. "Once he became of no use to my grandfather, he ceased to protect him. So the Military were urged to reconsider Max's case."

Corinna simply shook her head, still unconvinced. The whole scenario had played out so far away from her, and it had all been beyond her control. She had failed to contribute one thing to make a difference. She felt worthless - that was half the trouble - but despite the logic of knowing she could not have achieved this outcome herself, she could not muster the overwhelming gratitude Etienne obviously deserved.

It left Corinna feeling at odds with everything around her; she felt deflated and tired of everything. She seemed to have no purpose, no ambition in mind; the intense emotional expenditure and concentrated activity now finally over, she felt empty. No one needed her any more, not really. Her only spark of enjoyment lay in looking forward to the village festival next week, where she could wear her precious regional costume and dance. That would surely cheer her up. She tilted her face to the sun and smiled.

The day of the festival had arrived, and Corinna gazed around the square wondering if Lietner, who had arrived for a visit with his friend, would be there in time to dance with her this afternoon. He was her favourite partner, being a fine dancer. She soon had her answer when Lietner detached himself from the rest of the Metzger party to push his way forward through the growing throng, waving as he came towards her.

"I missed all the excitement of your brother's return," he smiled kindly, as he joined her. She nodded, while refraining from further comment, tired of the whole matter.

"Who would have thought Etienne could manipulate his grandfather by such a simple deception," Lietner casually continued. Corinna's boredom with the subject immediately vanished, though she tried to hide it. It was obvious that Lietner assumed she knew more than she did. Well maybe she could get him to elaborate a little more detail.

"Deception – he is a master of that," she scoffed.

"He can't help himself. He enjoys the mental challenge of trying to outsmart people."

"He is deceitful and cunning to a fault," Corinna pouted.

"And he lies so beautifully as well, doesn't he?" Lietner laughed.

At that second the band struck up and Lietner gently hauled Corinna to her feet and swept her into the merry band of dancers without finishing the rest of his idle observation.

At the first interval, Corinna expected him to return, if only temporarily, to his hosts, but he made no such move, preferring to stretch himself lazily out on the ground beside her, as if it were the most natural thing in the world. There they sat quietly until she slowly became aware that he was watching her.

"Why are you looking at me like that? What is the matter?" she asked.

"Nothing at all. I was thinking – with Max's problem resolved, what do you intend to do with yourself? What do you want for yourself, Corinna?"

"I have no idea. Through everything, it was always Max. Max first, only Max."

"Poor Corinna, there is no hope for you," he said kindly.

"No, I don't suppose there is." She wrinkled her nose at him.

"If you want someone else to take care of, I am available," he joked half-heartedly.

"Oh Lietner, for someone who refuses to use his first name, you hardly encourage any girl to think of you romantically."

"Corinna, I would be happy with whatever name you gave me."

"Stop your nonsense. You are the last person who needs looking after, you have enough females taking care of you already!" she laughed.

"They are mostly family. Ah, well I tried." He wrinkled his nose back at her, and they both laughed. The musicians and the caller began again and without a second's hesitation they began to enjoy the dancing once more.

By the end of the afternoon, when the festival and the dancing were over, Lietner had returned to the rest of the Metzger party and Corinna was making her own way home. Although she had paid particular attention to her partner's conversation during the remaining hours, his pleasant company had not revealed any more about Etienne's 'simple deception'.

How could she force Etienne into telling her anything? And even if he did it could be another lie, she would never know. Corinna tugged her mind free of the awful thought and drove the pony and trap purposefully along the track towards the Metzger house. What she had not anticipated was that the Metzger coaches had arrived there before her and everyone was obviously already at home. With any luck they were all dining, which would allow her the opportunity to reach Etienne's private sitting room without being seen. There she would wait. She had to try to find out the real truth and avoid a public scene. Whatever the outcome, this was not the moment to turn back. Gathering up her skirts, she ran up the steps.

There was no one in the hall to receive or announce her, and she was relieved that no one knew she was here. Slipping inside his room, she paused; she found it empty and awfully quiet. She settled into one of the armchairs and let out a long sigh, wondering how long she would have to wait. It felt as if she had listened to the clock ticking for ages as she wriggled her toes impatiently, listening for Etienne's approach.

"I did wonder if I had said more than I should have done this afternoon," came Lietner's voice close to her ear, making her jump. She had not heard him come in. As she turned her head, he strode smartly past and threw himself into another of the armchairs, where he sat grinning at her.

"Well, this should be interesting," he said.

"I want to speak to Etienne alone."

"You might need my help."

CHAPTER TEN

Etienne entered his private sitting room, eagerly loosening his shirt neck and pulling off his dusty jacket in anticipation of throwing it carelessly aside and himself into a comfortable chair. When he saw Corinna and Lietner, the jacket remained in his hand. He he stood stock still on the threshold, looking from one to the other curiously, unable to understand.

"What? Why are you both in here?"

Corinna stood up, fully aware that his question was directed more at her than at Lietner.

"I want the truth. I am here to find out exactly how you arranged Max's pardon."

"I thought we had settled this."

"No, you just thought I would be satisfied by the briefest of explanations. Well I am not. How did you persuade Count von Hetsch-Radberg to help Max, after the Klaus factor was eliminated?"

"Who said he did?"

"I am not stupid. The military did not have to do anything unless someone in power put pressure on them."

"Gods, I can see your aunt's influence, questioning everything over and over again. Always straight to the point and speaking your mind, whenever we are in private. She trained you well."

Well enough not to be put off by this weak attempt to alter the direction of the conversation. Lietner had indicated a 'deception', so what had Etienne invented? Yet it had to be something tangible. His grandfather would not just accept his word about something. What had influenced him?

Her suspicions had been slow to form, but she was beginning to sense that his stubborn reluctance indicated that something bad was threatening.

"For goodness sake, Etienne. Just tell her. Tell her or I will!" Lietner snapped. "None of us can move on with our lives until you do. Corinna has her own future to consider, a life out there, one not burdened with niggling doubts. This whole affair needs to be explained finally and completely."

Etienne's mellow expression was quickly replaced by a scowl. His dark eyes narrowed, and he stared grimly at Lietner.

"I do not appreciate my best friend's interference in this," he said.

Corinna waited whilst Etienne battled with himself, considering Lietner's words, before he finally began to explain. He began with the rumours concerning the Mahler family. Henri Mahler was part of a Magyar Federation which wanted national independence. As the dominant race in Hungary, they had chafed against the Hapsburg rule for years. Austria had always struggled with nationalism because of its vast range of peoples, until the army had been used to impose an internal political unity. Klaus willingly passed on any information to assist their cause, but he was smart enough to also provide government agencies with rumours of other intelligence.

"I did begin to wonder how important Klaus was in the

grand scheme of things," Etienne commented. "I wondered what my grandfather and his associates would do if he permanently disappeared. Surely they would simply find someone else to serve as their informer. So what was to stop me arranging for him to vanish? The army had its own secret service; it could be done. I told his lordship that I would not mind personally killing Klaus and having his body disposed of. I am a soldier, and a crack shot."

Corinna's mouth dropped open. She gulped. Her impression of Etienne had changed dramatically.

"Don't worry, he hasn't," Lietner told her quickly.

"I did not have to." Etienne grinned. "Klaus made a mistake in his dealings for the Federation. He obtained delicate material without realising that the information he passed on was false."

"You engineered it."

"Well I was not getting anywhere with my other schemes," Etienne admitted.

"That still does not explain why your grandfather…"

"As you so shrewdly concluded, despite all this, even if Klaus was convicted for his other activities or even eliminated, that did not help Max."

"Instead he did something quite extraordinary," Lietner muttered.

Etienne continued, "I reminded my grandfather that his grand and precious name would always be instantly associated with the Metzger name after the public fuss he made when my mother, his daughter, married a minor impoverished baron. I informed him that he would soon find himself connected to a very different Baron Metzger. Since the title of baron from our father's side of the family had no actual intrinsic value, there was no law to prevent it being passed on to anyone, whether he was a blood relation or not, provided it was done legally."

"Please don't tell me – No, that is ridiculous!" Corinna took a sharp breath as she realised exactly what he was implying.

"I could kick myself. I should have thought of it earlier."

"But you should keep the title in the family. What about Frederick?" she challenged him.

"Frederick does not need a title any more than I do. He is happy as he is. No, I have the authority to dispose of it as I wish, and I have made it clear to Count Radberg that the title of Baron Metzger will be transferred to Max, with all its connections to the Radberg name. With my grandfather's own reputation to consider, it changed his whole attitude. He used his influence with the authorities and now Max has his full protection."

"What!"

"It was the only idea I had left to bargain with."

"You must admit it was creative," said Lietner.

"The necessary paperwork has already been drawn up, witnessed and recorded. It will become public knowledge in Vienna soon, not that it will affect many people's concept of the order of things. Another name in the lesser line of peerage, without lands or income attached, has little kudos."

His calmness indicated the confidence of his achievement. Corinna just looked at him.

"How much of this does Max know?" she asked eventually.

"All of it. He may not wish to use the title, that is up to him. I think not, personally, as he is quite happy to settle down with Elizabeth and live in Germany. The title will be enough to keep him safe and he is content with that – who wouldn't be?"

"It can't be that simple."

"I promise you it was. It is."

Corinna still found it all difficult to accept.

"He owes you so much. You have sacrificed so much."

"Corinna, I haven't sacrificed anything. I have what I need, Gerard's real legacy. I have his precious mementos close at hand and with them, my fondest memories of him. They are more important than a piece of paper and a spoken means of formal address."

"And what about your Grandfather's insistence that you will inherit his own grander title?"

"I am delighted to report that he no longer considers me a worthy candidate for that lofty position. I have disappointed him too much with my actions for him to forgive. I have abused his position and his own contacts to win the battle against him. It will be passed to another branch of the family, thank goodness. No, I don't need that noble title to complicate my life, there is too much skulduggery and intrigue in high places for my liking."

"But you enjoyed it so much!" Lietner smirked.

"For a short while, maybe I did. I had to deliberately voice my opinions too loudly to ensure that they reached every rare bastion of exulted rank and privilege. I had to stir matters up. I don't like to be beaten."

"Now there, you are exactly like your grandfather," his friend commented.

"It was only a means to an end."

Corinna found herself unable to join in the pleasant banter this conversation had turned into, because there were so many words spinning in her head as she tried to come to terms with everything.

Astonished by this latest discovery she returned to the lodge, where she hastily related everything to her sleepy relation, who became less and less sleepy with every sentence.

"What a relief, my dear. To finally know it all!" her uncle beamed, delighted with the news.

"I am stunned that he went to such extremes."

"As long as you remember, this was done to keep a promise to his brother. For Gerard. Nothing more, however it looks or turned out."

She nodded, she had long accepted that.

Corinna wandered off to her favourite spot in the woods, by the bridge over the stream. Yet she did not hear the mellow chirping of the birds or see the hypnotic dancing pattern of the sparkling water over the stones. It was still hard to believe that there were no more invisible shadows or dark secrets. The world felt a different place. The anxiety she had experienced for so long was gone. Life seemed ordinary and quite normal, except that it wasn't really, because she could not quite grasp what she was expected to do next or how to fill her days. Her mind was still so active, seeking something to concentrate on. She felt at a loss, until her own curiosity hit a spot.

She could not prevent her mind picturing the desk and the possible contents of Gerard's box.

A mere hour later, Corinna had found Etienne.

"May I see those letters my mother wrote to your brother? They must be amongst the effects you brought here."

"Why on earth would you wish to?" said Etienne, playing the innocent.

"Curiosity. To see my mother's words. To imagine her voice. To know her better."

The long-drawn-out breath, the depth of his sigh and the lowered eyes as he thought of the contents were an indication of his next words.

"It would not be wise. I promised your uncle I would not let you see them."

"Another promise."

"Yes."

"You have read them."

"Oh, Corinna! I have made many mistakes in your direction in the past, but this is not about to become one of them."

Then she remembered that exchange of sharp words between Etienne and Michael, concerning the letters between Theresa and Gerard. What letters did Etienne have? What other secrets did he keep? Was there more to Gerard's adamant demand on Etienne to help Max? She could only imagine one cause which might require such protection of their correspondence; to protect her from some indiscretion which might have occurred between them. Well, she was not some silly immature adolescent. She could handle the truth, whatever it was.

"Was there anything in their letters which might threaten anyone's reputation?" she had to ask, almost dreading the thought.

"No, there is not!" he snapped indignantly.

Thank goodness. She breathed again. Her fears were misplaced, her mother's honour remained intact.

"How could you have thought otherwise?"

"I could think of no other reason why you would refuse to let me read them. It is not as if I do not know what goes on in the rest of the world, despite my fairly sheltered existence."

"I have no doubt you are well informed. Your aunt, to her credit, has educated you about almost everything, but in this case your suspicions are misplaced."

"Then how can it hurt for me to read them?"

"No. Corinna, the contents are more than mere love letters."

"One day you will let me read them," she replied sweetly. Her eyes were wide, her smile broad, her manner so demure and innocent of guile. She left him in no doubt as to the total belief she felt in her parting words, before she walked down the hallway out of sight.

All she could think of was her mother's lovely face in those portraits brought to life by her uncle. How could any letters that merely expressed their devotion to each other be upsetting? The tender exchanges would merely enhance the depth of affection she felt for Theresa. Nothing could spoil the image she had of her mother.

Obviously she needed Michael's blessing. She needed to persuade him, yet every time she started to broach the subject he ignored it. Even if he understood her reasons, he simply refused to discuss it or change his mind. She was getting nowhere. Silently she wondered what he was afraid of, although afraid might be too strong a word, but she did not understand why the letters were to be kept from her.

It was exactly a week later that Etienne rode up the drive to the lodge. He was on his own and his expression and purpose were hard to judge. Corinna had seen him approaching and waited patiently on the front steps, prepared to direct him straight back the way he had come if necessary.

"Lietner has now joined your cause," he said. "I now have to endure his unnecessary cryptic innuendoes in my own home, whenever we are in private. Don't pretend you are surprised."

"I did not ask him to intervene on my behalf."

"Nevertheless, he has. I do not appreciate a combined attempt of the pair of you to undermine my decision."

If this visit was just to rebuke her for enlisting his friend's help, not that she had, she could not understand why he was wasting his day. He must have more important things to do.

At that point Michael appeared from the woodland, pulling a small handcart stacked with fresh-cut logs.

"We were discussing the letters again," Corinna told him, to prove she had not given up her cause. Michael's reaction surprised her. He scowled at Etienne.

"I warn you, Metzger!" he said sharply. "I expect you to heed my advice."

"And I have kept my word, so far." Etienne hissed back, looking over Michael's shoulder at Corinna. Michael in turn glanced back to her before facing his visitor again. Then mumbled an apology for assuming the worst, expressed his regret and shook the hand offered to him. Corinna realised that this affable conciliation did not help her cause.

"Will you reconsider, uncle?" she asked.

"No." Michael's reply was too quick.

"Etienne?"

"No," Etienne added reluctantly, looking to Michael for guidance, but her uncle gave no indication of relenting.

"I wish to read them all, the good and the bad. May I?" she asked quietly, her eyes pleading. Etienne stood like a statue, his face blank and controlled, his gaze fixed over her head towards the distance.

"I must abide by your uncle's decision," he said finally.

Corinna knew this moment was important. it was no good shouting or stamping her feet. Throwing a tantrum was not her style, and besides it would get her nowhere. A softer approach was needed. She raised her head to the breeze, shook back her hair over her shoulder, a light in her face, brightness in her eyes. There was an air of complete calmness about her.

"Normally a child develops a life-long bond with its mother as it grows," she said. "I did not have that opportunity. I only know what she was like from other people. How can you deny me the chance to learn from her own hand, to gain an understanding of all she was and all she endured? What would she want?"

Michael shuddered; did he hear Theresa in Corinna's words? What would she want, his dearest sister? She would want her children happy. Max was more than happy, Corinna - not exactly. How would any of this help her? He had his doubts. Oh Theresa! He felt exhausted by the moment. The longer he looked at Corinna standing there, so like her mother, the better he knew that there was no arguing left in him.

The journey to the Metzger house was completed soon after, with Etienne on horseback leading the way, while the pony and trap containing Corinna and her uncle rattled and jolted behind. None of them spoke. On arrival, tight-lipped, Etienne escorted them through the hall and into the study, where he closed the door behind them. He sat Corinna down at the desk, went to the bureau, took out a wooden box and placed it on the desk in front of her. The design of the box she knew by heart. It was identical to hers.

"There they are. Letters which I confess I wish I had not read, the contents of which were only meant for those who wrote them. How Gerard wished he had persuaded Theresa to leave her husband, to save them both from the misery they suffered afterwards. The fears of a sick woman. Their lives, all committed to record in these papers. The truth is there in black and white," he whispered, his voice cracking and thick in his throat.

"Thank you," she said softly, looking only at the wooden box. Then promising that Corinna would not be disturbed and that she had all the time she wanted, Etienne ushered the reluctant Michael from the room to wait with him on the terrace.

Corinna nervously stretched forward to touch the surface of the box, running her fingertips along the pattern until she reached and turned the catch. Inside the letters had so tightly filled the box that they burst out onto the table as she lifted the lid, causing her to instinctively snatch back her hands. She paused. Did she have the right? She had adored her mother without question, worshipped her. Would the discovery of her human frailties and faults change the way she felt? Would it make a difference? Should she have been so stubborn in wanting this?

Apprehensively she opened the page nearest to her and pressed the crease flat. It was part of a letter, and she studied it word by word, reading it and then reading it again, to make sure she had understood. It expressed her mother's deep regret that she had no part of Gerard to love and watch grow. She had her memories, the brooch he had given her and the wooden carved box to remember him by. The matching boxes they had bought for one another. The words were no surprise; they merely confirmed what Corinna had always known. A wonderful sense of peace settled upon her.

Corinna read the letter once more. It was wonderful to see her mother's words, her beautiful writing flowing eloquently line after line. She was content with the image it brought to her imagination as she imagined her sitting writing it. Corinna smiling happily, wondering which of the pieces of jewellery was the brooch from Gerard. She would have to ask her uncle later; he was bound to know.

Slowly she began to open the other letters. She was forced to stop several times as the words became blurred before her eyes. She read of the doomed romance and her mother's state of mind during those last years. She read of her desperate turmoil, torn between guilt and happiness at the beginning, the slightest excuse to seek relief for her husband by making visits there, the recklessness of her freedom, the fearful doubt of returning home. She rode out too long, came back exhausted and flushed. She was gay and excited, and in love for the first time in her life. It was a secret love to which she had no right, one which she could not hide, ignore or control. The utter bliss of their hours together was all she lived for, simply to be there to see him and touch him were enough to fill her heart and obliterate the rest of the world. The memory of this love gave Theresa an inner strength, even after they had been forced apart. Their smuggled letters were her every breath, a confirmation of their unending devotion.

Corinna paused, her mind wandering briefly. She remembered witnessing the effect of Eva's letters on Etienne, his private memories and the obvious depth of his past devotion. Now she had another example, that of her mother and Gerard, to serve her and demonstrate the true strength of feeling these people shared.

It forced her to acknowledge that her sentiments towards Etienne were nothing like those between her mother and Gerard. She had been right in what she had told Lietner recently; she had only thought she loved Etienne because she had not known what love really meant. Besides, how could she believe in a love which had been so utterly unobtainable?

Corinna remembered her uncle's affectionate comments about the two of them. He had said, "There was no denying the absolute certainty of belonging they felt towards each other, some rare precious and undeniable quality, filled and touched their lives. You had to see the serenity those two found together, to understand." Yet here among these pages were painful revelations, sad events, the untold tragic truth of a husband who bullied and tormented his wife. It was clear that both Max and she had been unwanted and unloved by their father, whilst their dear mother had cherished them the more, while she could, to compensate for his rejection.

How it hurt to read her mother's words, to imagine her at the mercy of her harsh father, to comprehend all she had endured. Her poor mother! That was the hurt, not for herself, not the hurt of not being told, that she understood fully. Yes, this was what her uncle and Etienne had wanted to keep from her. By trying to protect her, they had merely delayed the revelation of her father's despicable character.

Her head ached with so much to absorb. All this time, she sighed, Michael had sheltered her from this sad state of affairs. How he must have dreaded her questions, yet he had answered them as best he could with a cheerful face to disguise the same hollow, cold emptiness she now felt. Whilst Etienne had also shared this, how she marvelled at his control during their many arguments. Even when provoked and trading insults, he had never made a slip.

Corinna sat back in the chair for a while. The house seemed to be resting and quiet, as if in sympathy with her emotions. The sunlight filtered through the windows and the world outside existed only to those outside the room. A timeless vacuum had settled around her. Taking a deep breath, she forced herself to resume her task. The sentiments of those private letters were expressed so vividly, their affection, their intense need for each other. She slumped forward, crumpling one particular letter in her hand, her mother's last. For this was the hardest to read, and it tore at the very depth of Corinna's heart, brought a lump to her throat and tears trickled slow and silently down her face.

My dearest,

I have returned to my bed. I am exhausted and very weak and do not think I have many days left to me. Yet I must write to you. I have to thank you for the wonderful happiness you have given me during our time together. How I have treasured all the beautiful hours and days we shared. Your tender kindness and understanding through the years have made my life so special and so delightful.

I have kept each little gift from you safe in my treasured box and even now I am looking at the pretty brooch you gave me for my birthday. It is still my favourite.

Please remember that you are my first and only true love. I had waited a lifetime to find you and you gave me everything, you have been my very soul and salvation during our happy joyous days. And even in these last hours you are close to me, for I can feel you holding my hand and giving me comfort. As I close my eyes, I cannot express the blessed peace the picture of your face gives me. You are smiling. The touch of your lips will burst my heart.

Please do not be sad for me, Gerard, do not let your grief obliterate the memory of our fondest feelings for each other. Breathe in that clear country air, look at the sun and the blue sky and enjoy it as if I were with you.

Live for me, my darling. Live through all the seasons and years ahead, live them for me.

Corinna trembled with emotion, staring at the blurred page. How clearly Theresa expressed her love, how much Corinna felt for them both and how much she wished it had ended differently. How unfair life could be!

She sat quietly gazing at the poignant letters for a long while, tenderly fingering the precious pages, before eventually she folded each one carefully, laid them in the box and closed the lid.

All her curiosity had been satisfied, and she knew she would never read the letters again. She did not need to. They belonged to and were meant only for those who had written them. There was no changing history. The past was gone, and must be put aside.

She walked slowly out into the bright afternoon, to where Michael fretted and pounded the terrace anxiously waiting for her. She was smiling and perfectly composed, although her eyes were a little red from the tears she had shed, tears which she would have hated him to see. She fell into his arms.

There was nothing left to ask, except to enquire which amongst her meagre collection of jewellery had been the brooch Gerard had given her mother. Michael patted her hand and sadly told her it was not there.

Not there! Corinna let out an involuntary gasp.

"It was gold and enamel. It was beautiful," her uncle told her.

That dear little brooch she had given to Max when he had fled for his life – that precious gift she had looked at for so many years, without knowing its true sentimental value. She felt suddenly overwhelmed by its loss as emotion hit her again.

"Come Corinna, there, there. Stop crying."

"But it must have meant so much to her!"

"Enough. Let it go." He tipped her chin up, kissed her lightly on the forehead and brushed her tears from her face. Her dear uncle meant the world to her and leaning against him, she could feel his heart beating, the rise and fall of his chest as he breathed.

He had given so much of himself, been so wise and understanding. He had been her strength and support through all her moods and changes of fortune.

Neither of them noticed Etienne's departure; they were both too immersed in comforting each other as they strolled from the terraces to wander through the soft shadowed colonnade of climbing plants, past the regimented lawns and around the small fountain to an arbour shrouded in white wisteria. There, in the tranquil atmosphere which hung about the place, they eventually talked, quietly and at length, as slowly Uncle Michael managed to help her put everything into perspective.

Etienne and Lietner had sat on the terrace for hours. The quiet, lazy afternoon had put them both into another world of their own, each lost in thought. Lietner stared blankly into the sky before eventually walking to the steps, where he leaned on the balustrade, his shoulders sagging. He looked back at his best friend.

"I am going home. Tomorrow."

"So soon? I thought you were staying longer."

"I am not going to accept that post at the Ministry. I need a change."

Etienne lifted an eyebrow sceptically towards his friend.

"A change! Are you mad, that is a well-paid position? Why give it up? What will you do?"

"I have absolutely no idea. I don't really care."

Etienne was still staring at him. He did not believe what he was hearing. Where had this tone of disillusionment suddenly come from? There had been no warning of Lietner's intentions.

"You can't mean it."

"You are the only one who is content, content with your life, with the whole situation. You returned to all your old rural pursuits without any difficulty. You are happy to live with a memory, you are happy to love the pure memory of Eva. Somehow it is enough to satisfy your very existence, while the rest of us poor mortals still struggle for some happiness."

Yes, Etienne was content, more content with every day that passed, for everything had settled into place. And Eva, yes he had that too. Her touch, her breath, her whisper in his ear and the smell of her soft hair. How easier these days it was to be transported back. But that was not the point. What was wrong with Lietner? What had caused this change? His mind raced over their time together, everything they had done, trying to find a reason. Over and over he analysed. Then he grinned.

"You are in love with Corinna!"

Lietner did not deny it; he sat stone-faced.

"Oh, Varro."

"Don't call me that name. You know I hate it."

"Lietner, my friend, she is so unpredictable, and much more complex than either of us expected. Look at the way she tried to outsmart us."

"I seem to remember it was mainly you she was trying to outsmart, not me."

"I am merely saying she could be much more woman than you might imagine."

"You being the expert in all matters female!" snapped Lietner.

"Usually!"

"You think it is a foolish prospect?"

"No! I didn't mean to imply anything of the sort. I am sorry. She is unique. You must tell her how you feel."

"Why?"

"Because I believe you could share quite an extraordinary life together."

Later in the week Corinna went to thank Etienne, in particular for allowing her access to the precious letters belonging to his brother. She needed to thank him again; he deserved that much. They sat sharing refreshment on the terrace, both in a mellow mood. They were finally at ease with each other, both comfortable and at peace with the past. Somewhere the transition between irritation and comfortable acceptance had taken place and they had finally become friends.

"Who would have thought we would ever have become so well acquainted," she reflected.

"Or have antagonised each other so much. Goodness Corinna, there were moments when, if you had been a man, I could easily have throttled you!"

"And times when, if I had been a man, I would have shot you," she retaliated.

He winced. "Mmm. And I sense you might have been a better shot than the man who did."

"Most definitely."

They both laughed.

"I used to wish that we had met under different circumstances. That we could have been more to each other. That you might have loved me," she said softly into the quietness between them. It sounded improbably simple, a whisper, a precious secret shared.

"Loved you or made love to you?" he mused, as if they were discussing nothing more important than the weather.

"Either would have done!" she laughed.

"Why, I am shocked at you, Corinna, expressing such ideas," he muttered – not that he was really shocked at all.

"Etienne, don't pretend your other females haven't voiced similar expectations."

"And if they had, I am certainly not repeating their opinions to you."

Corinna smiled to herself, pleased that he was still gentleman enough to spare her blushes.

"Anyway, how could I compete with those others ladies you prefer," she teased.

"Ladies! Lord, Corinna, Some of them were not ladies!"

"Maybe, but I suspect they all still loyally and desperately love you."

"Love, passion, a kiss, a moment, a mistake."

She didn't expect him to admit to his skill with women, although it was a fact that women were susceptible to him, content to enjoy any brief period they could share with him and not complain. By reputation he revelled in and enjoyed their company, and his flirtations merely demonstrated his normal response to a pretty woman. And to think she had even considered becoming another of his conquests!

"You kissed me once, I remember. Not that it was much of a kiss," Corinna sighed wistfully. Etienne leaned forward to look her directly in the eyes, his eyes twinkling. Then he quickly stood up and pulled her to her feet, so they stood face to face.

"Even a kiss can be a lie, a seductive pleasure, a simple temptation," he said.

She caught her breath and stared at him. His dark eyes were soft and kind, reflecting something of her own. They held her spellbound there as his hand stretched out to lightly brush her cheek, tracing its contours to linger about her mouth. Slowly, so slowly his mouth came to hers and they kissed. So simple a kiss, not hard or over long, yet it was the most beautiful kiss she had ever known – not that she had experienced many. She felt a shudder tingling right down to her toes.

"To expect more of me would be foolish," he whispered. Then, just as gently, he stood away, and Corinna knew this precious moment between them was gone. She watched him turn away. Her lip trembled slightly, even though she was perfectly resigned to the fact that here was a man who refused to allow himself to truly love anyone else. Etienne was perfectly content in his devotion to Eva, and everything else was pretence.

"It was wicked of you to do that, Etienne," she told him.

"I know" he confessed, without a sign of regret.

What a blessing that he had never taken her in his arms or kissed her like this long before and somewhere else. She had been saved from falling totally under his spell and having her heart broken completely, like all the others. She was truly fond of him in a different way. Her romantic dreams about him had gone and somehow today his flirting did not matter, because in the end she found it really meant nothing to her; it was simply his habit. She wanted more from a relationship than he would ever offer.

He had returned to his chair, collapsing back into the soft upholstery.

"Tell me Corinna, did you enjoy that?" he yawned, settling deeper into the chair, his eyes almost closed.

"Too much, as well you know. And please spare me any more attempts to prove your theories."

He raised an eyebrow and smiled forgivingly. "To be honest, those beautiful dark eyes of yours deserve to be appreciated by a better person than myself," he said.

Corinna stared at him, sceptical of this apparent compliment and suspecting that it was merely another way of making fun of her. She did not need him to practise his seductive tones in her ears. He really was incorrigible.

"Indeed there is a better person, one who is even more than fond of you than I am," he went on.

"Don't tease me about such things. It is not kind."

"I am not teasing."

"There is no need for you to interest yourself in what admirers I may or not have. Please stop it."

"I believe you suit each other."

How on earth had he managed to twist the topic of conversation around? She had no intention of discussing her romantic intentions - not that she had any - with him of all people, and she refused to embarrass herself by taking any notice or making any comment on the matter.

"I have no intention of pursuing this topic. If you are going to continue with your fanciful ideas, I had better take my leave."

"You cannot ignore the matter for ever. Travel is much overrated and I doubt Lietner will stay away long."

His words stopped her in her tracks, and her mouth dropped open in surprise. There was little doubt as to what he meant. How dare he suggest such a thing? This was ridiculous. His imagination was quite extraordinary! She did not believe him. How could he be so cruel? Would he ever resist the pleasure and satisfaction he found in teasing her? It was not fair to joke about his best friend like that. Yet the longer she looked at his unflinching kindly expression, the more she began to wonder if he was speaking the truth. The whole idea proved quite unexpected and a little unnerving.

Her heart beating like a hammer, she hurried away, urgently seeking the quiet of her favourite spot by the bridge to compose herself. She needed to be alone, she needed – she did not know what she needed. Her thoughts were full of Lietner and his past involvement in her life. She found she could remember his every word and gesture, his kind expressions; his merry smile, the toss of that thick flecked hair and his comforting voice. She had not noticed how easily they had grown close. How could she have been so blind? Lietner, dear Lietner! To find that he felt more for her than expected, was wonderful.

"How very extraordinary," she said aloud.

Much later, still in some sort of daze, she eventually wandered on towards the village, hoping that the usual dancing and music arranged for today would distract her mind from this new sensation for a while.

She sat on a low stone wall which surrounded part of the village square, amid the other groups of people, trying to concentrate on the spectacle in front of her. There she sat tapping her feet in time with the music. She did not notice the man who arrived not long after herself or see him as he strolled, apparently without purpose, amongst the locals, stopping at intervals to watch the musicians and enjoy the afternoon.

Yet he did have a purpose. Slowly he made his way to join her. Intuitively, she became aware that there was someone behind her, and she knew exactly who it was. His very nearness thrilled her, making her spine tingle and making her catch her breath. A shudder of pleasurable anticipation of his touch filled her.

Lietner continued to stand there. Then he bent very low over her shoulder to whisper close to her ear.

"Dance with me."

Corinna smiled to herself, gently placed her hand in his and stood up. She knew that their future together held much more than this dance.